PREDATORS

Previously published Worldwide Mystery title by
FREDERICK RAMSAY

IMPULSE

PREDATORS

FREDERICK RAMSAY

W⊕RLDWIDE®

TORONTO • NEW YORK • LONDON
AMSTERDAM • PARIS • SYDNEY • HAMBURG
STOCKHOLM • ATHENS • TOKYO • MILAN
MADRID • WARSAW • BUDAPEST • AUCKLAND

To His Excellency Festus Mogae,
President of Botswana, 1998-2008.

Recycling programs
for this product may
not exist in your area.

Predators

A Worldwide Mystery/February 2016

First published by Poisoned Pen Press

ISBN-13: 978-0-373-26980-8

Copyright © 2009 by Frederick Ramsay

Printed in U.S.A.

Acknowledgments

I must express my very great appreciation to the people of Botswana for their kindness and willingness to share their country and their lives. And special thanks to their former president, His Excellency Festus Mogae, to whom this book is dedicated, for the gracious hospitality extended to my wife and to me, for his humor, and for sharing with us his unstinting love for Botswana and its people. Also, I would be remiss if I did not thank my son, who sits in the center of things in Botswana, for his suggestions, corrections and insights in the construction of this tale. And thanks also to my daughter-in-law, Sekgabo, and my grandchildren, Kopi, Ati and Alex, proud citizens of Botswana, for their encouragement and patience in vetting this book to assure the old man did not stray too far from the truth of things.

Another round of thanks goes to the gang at Poisoned Pen Press, who allow me to spin these yarns and stories pretty much to my heart's content. Thanks to Barbara, my editor and chief critic, who keeps me more or less in line, and Robert, who allows the ink to flow to paper and thence to books like this.

Finally to the people who edit and review, my wife, Susan, Glenda Sibley, and those whose names I cannot, or perhaps should not, name, who willingly tell me if the notion I am purveying at the time has any merit. I hope they will forgive me for sometimes not taking their advice.

FOREWORD

WHEN THE AUTHOR of this book approached me for an endorsement, how could I say no? My favorite crime fiction writer had set his latest novel in my favorite place—the magical Chobe region of Botswana. But Botswana detective fans be warned: this book is no traditionally built tea party. While a certain amount of mating occurs, neither is it another rushed comedy of manners about white mischief in the wilderness. It is a far deadlier tale of dark souls in a sunny place; a stage full of intrigue and betrayal, where jaded ambition collides with murderous intent. Yet among its cast of seemingly amoral characters, there is also a subtle moral center waiting to be discovered. In addition, *Predators* is also an insightful study of animal behavior in one of world's last great Arcadias, the unique environment of northern Botswana. Here, in a place where elephants outnumber people by a ratio of eight to one and hippos are a leading cause of homicide, the lion still reigns as the king of the forest. As with any great African adventure, not all of the lions in this volume are quadruped. The pride includes a ruthless tycoon and mysterious Russian, as well as restless cubs and an out-of-place cougar. In the end what more could any one wish for as company on an airplane, a camping trip or a lazy Sunday afternoon?

Dr. Jeff Ramsay
Communications Coordinator
Government of Botswana
Gaborone, Botswana

ONE

THE LION BLINKED and shifted its weight to one side, hoping the dull pain that deprived him of sleep would abate. It didn't.

A pregnant moon painted thin clouds silver as they scudded across a star-splashed sky. This extraordinary beauty, which would cause visitors to catch their breath in wonder, was lost on the lion. The wind shifted. The scent of the nomad, the young male in search of a pride, drifted to him. He blinked and yawned. Tomorrow, at first light, the interloper, who had spent the previous afternoon bellowing challenges at him, would come in, the future of the pride at stake.

The cub lying next to him stretched and yawned, imitating his father. In two years, if he lived that long, his plaintive squeak would become an earsplitting roar. But he might not get that chance. His prospects hung precariously on the strength and ferocity of the old male next to him and that, in turn, teetered dangerously on the cusp.

The guides who led game drives from the hotels in Kasane had named him Sekoa, the Setswana word for invalid, because of his apparent illness. How the other beasts referred to him, if at all, is not known. He shifted his weight again. The pain increased. He let out a ferocious roar; a roar heard as far away as six kilometers and which caused the eyes of the hundreds of species within hearing, to pop open in panic. Males from distant prides answered. The nomad padded away into the bush. It would be only a temporary retreat. In the morning, at daybreak, he would shuffle back, head lowered, shoulders hunched, and determined.

The females had had no success hunting that night but would try again at daybreak. Desperate times call for desperate measures. They lay with their cubs and two older adolescent males within a few meters of Sekoa. Normally they would be separated by several meters, perhaps more, but not this night. Perhaps they sensed his failing health, perhaps not. He ruled an unlucky pride. Disease and inbreeding had reduced its numbers. Probably the reason he'd managed it so long.

The old male had no way of knowing that his body was slowly and inexorably being destroyed by bovine tuberculosis exacerbated by FIV/AIDS, the leonine variant of human immunodeficiency virus, HIV/AIDS, that he shared with those bipedal creatures that alternately feared and admired him. Normally, it would be a benign presence, but his reduced immune system had left him vulnerable to the tuberculosis that daily ravaged his lungs. It was a disease he might otherwise have been able to resist or at least endure. The combination meant that his remaining time as the alpha male of his pride might be numbered in hours, his life in days, perhaps, if he were lucky, weeks.

The only certainty in his existence was that on the morrow, soon or late, he would have to face this young pretender. If, by some chance, he succeeded in driving him off, there would be another after him, and then another. Holding his territory and place had defined his existence since he'd taken the pride from an older lion four years previously. The image of those lurking, waiting males caused him to growl—a low rumble.

If he failed, if he lost the pride, his cubs would be killed to bring the adult females back into estrus. He knew that. He'd done the same when he took over this pride. One of the females, as if her thoughts resonated with his, gathered her cubs closer to her, and licked them with her tongue, an organ rough enough on its surface to scrape raw meat from a bone but soft enough to smooth her cub's fur. The cub batted at her and tried to attack her massive paw. The female swatted it, an act of love.

In the moonlight, Sekoa, the four females, the cubs, and the adolescent males appeared a uniform gray. At daybreak, they would become tawny brown, and on parts of Sekoa's otherwise darker mane, almost orange. But these colors would not register on their functionally colorblind eyes. Day or night, their world was uniform in coloration, bright or dim, but predominantly gray.

His night vision, on the other hand, was near perfect. He swiveled his massive head right and then left. That fact and the moonlight allowed him to assess his surroundings. He could make out a slight rise at his front, leading toward the heaviest growth in the bush. His rival would charge from that direction, using the grade to propel him down and into the grassy patch in front of the sleeping pride. If Sekoa were to stand there, the attacker's momentum would surely knock him off his feet and leave him open to teeth and claws. He would have to find a better place to engage this usurper.

Another sharp stab of pain blocked this intuitive rumination. If he didn't sleep, he'd never have the strength to fight. If he did drift off, he might not wake. He shifted once more and growled in pain and frustration.

Fifteen kilometers to the east, in a small cluster of rondevals outside Kazungula, the village elders pondered the fate of Lovermore Ndlovu. He had crossed the line. He had acquired a bad reputation. The other young men from the village worked hard at whatever they could turn their hand to. For some it meant gathering firewood, which they would sell on the roadside. Travelers journeying to and from Francistown or Nata would stop sometimes, but most of the sales were local. Or they could work in one of the safari lodges on the Chobe River, work that paid well but was hard to get and not steady. A few of the older girls and boys danced in costume for the hotel guests. Sometimes a tourist from America would tip them as well. The majority of the young men and women made the long walk to school willingly. Education would bring them advancement and open doors. But always, their thoughts and eyes turned south to the capital, to Gaborone. There they could find good jobs, earn much pula. Each year, a few from the village escaped to the city and came back wearing new clothes and with spending money in their pockets. The cities, Gaborone, Maun, Palapye, were the goal—for all but Lovermore.

He'd slipped across the border from Zimbabwe along with the growing exodus of persecuted Kalanga tribesmen and economically strapped citizens. But Lovermore did not come to Botswana because of persecution or penury. There were certain authorities in Harare who had a keen interest in him, which, in turn, spurred his decision to immigrate and join his cousins among the Ndebele-speaking Kalangans clustered close to the Chobe River, near Kazungula. There he knew he could fit in. And, of course, everyone spoke English with some level of proficiency. He'd met Sami Mokole by chance on the road leading from the ferry across the river into Zambia. They struck up a friendship. Later he moved in with his new "cousin." Lovermore paid for his share of the food with cigarettes he stole from the Chinaman's shop. When Sami left to join his family at their cattle post, Lovermore had to find a new means of support.

It came to him late one afternoon when he stumbled upon a car jack by the side of the road. Some careless traveler, probably a tourist, must have changed a tire and left it by mistake. A jack like that, he thought, could come in handy. After some thinking on the matter, he'd put it to use that night. Tires can be expensive, especially up in the north, away from the cities. The jack, and moonless nights, put him in the used tire and wheel business. A risky business, as the car parks in Kasane were very public, but he had become used to risk-taking in Harare. He borrowed his cousin's roadside shed and painted a new sign—Ndlovu Spares 'n' Wheels. He thought to call his business *Bosigogare Tyres*—Midnight Tires, but decided it might beg the question and he didn't need that. *No mathata*.

There were many flat tires produced by the numerous potholes on the sixty kilometers of road between Nata and Kasane. Finding buyers turned out to be simple enough. Always shrewd, he made a point of repainting the wheels lest some previous owner appear and cause trouble. He had a spray can in hand and had managed to start on the first of his latest acquisitions when the old men appeared.

Theft, they declared, was not acceptable. Not for anyone and certainly not for a guest from Zimbabwe. Theft reflected badly on the village. These thefts, they said, must end. They confiscated his jack and the wheels and were taking him to the police when they decided a session in the *kgotla* following customary law would be in order first. Punishment, in the form of a sound beating, should precede a turning over to the police, they decided. That sort of justice had been taken from them with Independence—a fact they accepted but with which they disagreed strongly. They dragged him toward the *kgotla*. Lovermore did not fear the thrashing. He had been through that many times. But the thought of police, who would surely deport him, threw him into a panic. He bolted away, zigzagging through the alleys of Kazungula and into the bush across the Kasane road.

Lovermore's bad attitude, the behavior that inevitably got him into trouble, stemmed from a disinclination to listen and learn from those wiser and more experienced than he. The bush, as every young person on either side of the border learned at an early age, was life-giver, and life-taker. It was to be shared. By day, it cautiously belonged to people; at night it absolutely belonged to the animals. Lovermore had missed that last part. His dash into the bush to evade the old men lasted about three hundred meters. It was there he met an immature, still maneless, but very hungry lion recently driven off as it came into sexual maturity by his pride's alpha male.

Lovermore never had a chance.

TWO

DAWN. THE SUN oozed over the horizon, splashing brilliant gold and orange light across the savannah. Nocturnal animals drifted into their lairs. The area's lone leopard crept into its tree, its lurk. She surveyed the ground near her, then closed her eyes for sleep—intermittent sleep. She would open them again throughout the day, swing her head around to be sure, and sleep again. Herds of wildebeest, gazelle, impala, and zebra began to graze northward toward the Chobe River and its promise of water. There, hippopotami and crocodiles shifted their relative positions. The reptiles moved toward shore to bask and wait for an unwary drinker, a potential meal, and the hippos went to deeper water. Birds began their morning cacophony. Sekoa stretched very carefully, conscious of his growing weakness. He would have to stand and defend his range, his pride, and his life, or, wisdom being the better part of valor, he could simply skulk away. In any case, he would have to face this young upstart. He stood. The effort made him roar. The disease that ate at him from within had not yet affected his outward appearance. The roar and his stance caused the nomad to hesitate. Sekoa picked his way around the females, sniffing and acknowledging their presence. They stared stoically into the distance. Their fate, and the fate of their youngest off-spring, hung precariously in the balance.

The young lion paced back and forth ten meters away, gauging the old one's strength. Eventually hormones overcame uncertainty. He charged. Sekoa stood firm. He had enough strength and bulk to repel one onslaught. But he could not counterattack. The young lion realizing that, paused and then trotted forward, jaws open and victory in his eyes.

MICHAEL LAY WIDE-EYED and awake, seeing nothing. His breathing rattled in his sunken chest. Sweat glistened on his face and soaked his pillow. His mother gazed at his emaciated body. Her heart ached. If only...if only he'd gone to the clinic sooner, if only she'd paid closer attention...she should have known. She'd watched her husband fade away from the long illness, *phamo kate,* the disease that has a short name. Until recently, one did not say AIDS. To have done so would have been too direct, too absolute. It had taken her husband, and now it would claim her son as well. Too late to hope for the treatments, the ARV treatments, treatments that had restored Mma Serote's man.

She swallowed the sob that caught in her throat. The clinic doctors had been very angry at her for waiting so long to report Michael. "You should have known," they'd said. "You saw your man die with this."

But she did not know. Michael had hidden it from her. Every day, until the last, he had gone to work at Naledi Super Motor Repairs and Panel Beaters. Mr. Naledi had taken Michael into mechanics training lately. With the influx of so many late-model used Japanese automobiles now, there was not much call for good panel beaters anymore. Each evening he came home to work on the old Toyota HiLux, which stood on cement blocks in the court.

"Soon," he'd promised, "I will make it go again, a HiLux cannot be destroyed." He'd added with a grin, "A HiLux is Botswana's Model T." She did not understand what that meant. Something to do with America, she guessed.

"If I can fix it," he'd said, "you will not have to take a *combie* to work. You will drive your own *bakkie*. We only needed a little more…" He didn't finish the sentence but she knew—a little more luck.

Should she have known? Maybe it was because she didn't want to know. Perhaps someone had bewitched her. This same Mma Serote had consulted the diviner. "Who can be so sure about those white doctors," she'd said. She had anointed her man with a potion she bought from the diviner. Mma Serote said maybe Mma Michael had angered someone and they had gone to a *moloi*, a witch. She shuddered at the possibility.

"Perhaps," Mma Serote had said, "you are not appreciating the customs, are not respecting the ancestors."

Everyone knew Mma Michael had modern notions.

No! She shook her head. She did consider herself a modern woman and had put those old beliefs behind her, but…why so much bad luck? Another shake of her head. No, Michael had the disease and she did not know it in time. That was all there was to say about the matter.

People called her Sanderson. Her full name was Mpoo Kgopa Sanderson. The naming came from her uncles, one of whom, when seeing the saucy look in her three-day-old eyes, thought *kgopa*, which means snail, would keep her humble. It didn't. The people of her village called her Mma Michael, but elsewhere, at work, she was just Sanderson, the game ranger.

She left the room to find her daughter. Where was

that girl? It was time to make porridge and dress for work. Mpitle should be ready to go to school. Sanderson washed up in the tub just inside the door and sponged her uniform. She would have to see to washing it soon. Perhaps if all went well, she could take it to Ms. Maholo. Ms. Maholo owned a washing apparatus. She would ask her if she could use it.

She worried about her daughter. That boy, that David Mmusi, he was too pretty, too insistent. He might not take the precautions, even though the President himself said everyone should, even though condoms were sold everywhere, at the pharmacy, at the checkout counter at the market, everywhere. Should she ask if he'd been tested? No, that would be overstepping. But, he might be one of those who wished to believe *phamo kate* came from the spirits, or from witches, or the wind. Many in her village still did. Rra Kaleke said the education brought it on. Before the government started sending just anybody to school, there was no disease. He was very old with *wulu*, white hair, and was thought to be very wise, but in this she believed him wrong. She would speak with Mpitle. She had lost too much already: her cousins, a husband, and soon a son. No more.

She would put a condom in Mpitle's backpack.

She could not lose another child.

THREE

FROM HIS WINDOW, Bobby Griswold stared vacantly across Lake Shore Drive at the lake. Automobiles, red brake lights winking, their exhausts billowing white in the chilled air, crept bumper-to-bumper working their way north in the late afternoon rush hour. At his back, to the west, a sharp-edged winter sun glittered in a cold, gray sky. In Lake Michigan, low waves lapped along its shore and splashed against concrete abutments. Ice had already formed on some of them. The autumnal equinox had come and gone, and winter hovered just over the border in Canada, waiting to pounce on Chicago with its annual icy fury.

"Dead? What do you mean, you want your stepfather dead? What're you planning to do, shoot him?" Brenda, his wife of a few months, slouched on the sofa sipping a diet Coke.

"I'm just saying…"

"You're just saying…what, Bobby? I know Leo is no treat, but he's your stepdad…why would you want him dead?"

"Leo is so *not* my stepfather. He married my mother. She died. Now he's married to Lucille and I'm out."

"You said he adopted you after your mom died."

"Yeah, well dream on. At her funeral he comes up to me and he goes, 'That's it, kid, you're on your own.'"

So, that's the deal on the adoption thing. We're in for nada, zilch."

"Look, you don't know. He gave you a job, didn't he, and you still have your mother's stock in the company, right?"

Bobby turned and walked to the wall and flipped on the recessed lighting. He paused to inspect the Mondrian original on the wall. He hated that painting, just a bunch of colored squares and lines. He'd wanted to buy a Stephen Holland painting of Brett Favre, Super Bowl XXXI. But Brenda had taken an art appreciation course at night and had overruled him.

"Don't you?" she repeated.

"The job is bogus, Brenda, I sit at a desk in accounting and count paper clips. Some days I go to lunch and don't come back and it's, like, nobody even notices."

"Jeeze, Bobby, are you bragging or complaining?"

"You don't understand, Brenda. I mean, I should be a vice president or something, you know. Now, if Leo goes through with the IPO, if he takes the company public, I'm toast. I work there because he says so. He exercises all his stock options, collects all that cash and retires, and who'll want me then?"

Leo Painter manipulated their lives like a marionette master. Once, Brenda thought, he cared for them in his own peculiar way, but now he seemed to enjoy watching them fail; well, watching Bobby fail. Somewhere between Leo's second wife, Bobby's mother, and wife number three—that would be Lucille—he had suffered the latest in his series of cardiac accidents and had turned from being distant but tolerable to personal and nasty.

"Maybe he'll have another heart attack in Africa and you'll get your wish," she said, "but I don't see how that works for you. You should want him alive. You should be in there making nice to him, so even if he does sell or whatever, you'll have something."

Brenda studied her husband as he wandered aimlessly around their apartment. He had been an only child who'd been coddled by an overprotective mother, so that he'd achieved manhood without a clue about what it meant to be a responsible adult. She'd found his boyishness attractive in the beginning, that and his money—especially the money—and their life together had been an endless party. Then his mother died, and all that came to a dead stop. No allowance, no free rein. Leo gave him a job as much to get him out of his hair as a sign of paternal felicity. Bobby was a man-boy. She wondered if he would ever grow up.

"He hates me, Brenda." His voice had taken on the whining quality she'd come to detest. "He'll just laugh me out the door. And listen, if he goes, you can kiss your Michigan Avenue boutiques goodbye, too. Never mind me and not having a job; how about you? Can you get a job? What are you good at, Babe, besides maxing out our VISA card? Are you ready to go back to pole dancing? Besides, Lucille would get it all anyway."

She nodded. She'd thought of that, and the idea that the money could really dry up, however remote or incomprehensible, scared her. She'd been poor before and knew what she would face. She did not like it. The idea of even relative poverty coalesced and condensed into something akin to a black hole in her mind. Fall into that and…no way was she going back to dancing as Brenda Starr—"yeah, like in the funny papers," she'd told her friends, though few of them had ever heard of the comic strip, its intrepid gal reporter and her eye-patched mystery man, much less read it.

She'd danced as near to naked as the Chicago vice squad allowed. Every night, except Mondays when she had a night off, she performed for a legion of grubby, groping, intoxicated strangers. All that ended, though, when she'd managed to snare Robert Scott Griswold, presumptive heir to the Earth Global fortune, and acquired this soft berth on the Near North Side. Brenda no longer worked for a living; she shopped.

There'd been talk at first, of course, and she had that private detective Leo hired to handle, and the other things, but she'd done it. No, whatever this new wrinkle was, there had to be a way out. Brenda Starski was not going back to that life if she could help it.

"You still didn't answer me. What about your stock?"

"I sold it to Travis Parizzi."

"You did what?"

"Hey, the way you go through money, what was I supposed to do?"

Brenda groaned. "You're an idiot." Bobby, she realized, had the brains of a guppy.

"Hey, I have an option to buy it back at 10 percent over the sale price. It's mine, sort of, like collateral on a loan, so it's safe and all. He gets to use the stock for stuff, and we get money."

"You mean, if you can raise the scratch to actually buy it back. How long is that option good for? Why did he want your stock, anyway?"

"He said he wanted to secure a voting position if the time came, or something. The option's good for, like, a year…" Bobby didn't sound so sure.

Brenda sighed. Of course he could buy it back, only

he wouldn't. If he ever got the money together, he'd find some other way to spend it.

"That is so totally lame, Bobby. How much is left?" Bobby shrugged and shook his head. Not much, she guessed. Well, at least now she knew where the Maserati and the trip to Europe had come from.

"Maybe something could happen to both of them, Leo and Lucille, I mean…you know, like an accident or something. Isn't Africa, like, dangerous to drive in and stuff?"

Brenda's knowledge of the Dark Continent derived almost entirely from movies and the cartoons she'd watched as a child. Black men with bones in their noses and brandishing spears, jumping up and down and dancing—the Watusi, something like that. And there were elephants and tigers, too. Was that right? Her friend Desiree said there were no tigers in Africa. She couldn't remember where Desiree said they came from, but that couldn't be right. Her father had taken her to the circus as a child and the big cat tamer had lions and tigers. Of course they must come from the same place. Bobby wheeled around the coffee table and grabbed a handful of trail mix from a bowl in its center and stuffed it into his mouth.

"Lucille and Leo are hardly speaking to each other. She's probably as ticked about the public offering as me. The board forced it on him, I don't know why, but he's hot to go with it, anyway. Her pre-nup assumed all of Leo's net worth was in a privately held company. If he takes it public, he can bury 85 percent of it in paper with no assessable value, and then dump her. Maybe she'll kill him. That would solve all our problems."

"You think?" Brenda frowned in concentration. "How?"

"It's complicated," he said.

"Tell me anyway. I'm not as stupid as some people think." Brenda's education had been limited to eight grades of formal schooling before she'd run away from a sexually abusive stepfather. It had taken three attempts to leave before her parents gave up trying to find her. As part of her newly found freedom, she'd majored in personal survival. In her twenty-one years of making it on her own she'd learned to stay ahead of the curve. A return to exotic dancing was definitely not on her radar screen. Her husband flopped down on the sofa next to her and put his head in her lap.

"I don't know, Brenda. There's a will I guess, and then if the IPO goes through, whatever holding anybody has is either converted to preferred stock or maybe can be turned into common, but the percentage you hold is, like, diluted by the stock held by the new buyers. It's something like that. I don't know. He told me, but I couldn't get it straight."

"Who?"

"Travis Parizzi, I just told you."

"Maybe you're going to inherit. He can't last forever. What's in his will?"

"No clue. I'm pretty sure I'm not."

"Because...?"

"*Because* he said I'm on my own at the funeral and all."

"If Lucille did it and got caught, wouldn't she go to jail, and then you'd get a whole lot of money, right?"

"For Christ sake, Brenda, how many times I gotta tell you? We're out of it. Besides Lucille isn't about to do anything. She's more likely to file for divorce before the papers are signed. You know, like a quickie divorce in Las Vegas or some place, and cash out before the money gets lost in one of Leo's shell games. We have to do something, Brenda, and soon."

"Do? Do what, Bobby. You want me to ask Frankie to get us a hit man? How's that going to work?"

He nuzzled her belly and took her hand. She sighed. That was his answer to all his troubles. What is it with men anyway? You have a problem; you work on it. Bobby never faced a problem in his life. They call women ditzes. Like, they should meet Bobby Griswold. His idea of how to solve a problem was to blot it out with booze and sex and let someone else figure it out. Since his mom died, that job had fallen to her. She looked at his boyish face and sighed again. She disliked doing what he wanted but, hey, where else was she going to get a gig like this?

FOUR

LEO PAINTER STARED at the same slate gray lake. His view, however, was considerably better than that from the Griswolds' Oak Street Beach apartment. His office was high in the Willis Tower. He liked it better when it was the Sears Tower. Sears said Chicago. Who in the hell was Willis anyway? On a clear day, Leo could see across the lake all the way to the Michigan shore or south to the Indiana dunes. The view was spectacular. For what he paid for the space, it ought to be.

Travis Parizzi sat on the edge of an expensive leather chair, briefcase open in his lap. He shuffled the papers it contained and sorted them into the order he wished to deal with them. Travis had learned years ago that Leo liked his sessions with his COO to be quick, to the point, and no nonsense. Travis looked up, waiting for Leo's signal to begin. This morning, it seemed, Leo was in no hurry. Finally he turned from the window.

"We're set for Africa?" he asked.

"Yes, I think so. Has Mrs. Painter made up her mind if she's going?" There had been a debate about Leo's wife being included in the trip. Somehow she'd discovered the company would be going public and had thrown a hissy-fit. She'd threatened to dump Leo on the spot. He promised to renegotiate her pre-nup, but Travis doubted it would happen. Ethical behavior and fairness were never part of Leo's makeup as far as Travis could determine. If they were, Leo would still be running errands for Harry Reilly, his first wife's father. But his shrewd sense of mining, a growing emphasis on their newly developing oil business, and his inability to feel guilty about anything had culminated in the ouster of the old man, a quick divorce from the daughter, and transformation of tiny Reilly Petroleum to Earth Global, now the third largest oil, gas, and mining company in the country. Its real-estate department alone rivaled Donald Trump's. Or at least Leo believed so. Travis had his doubts.

"No, she decided to take a pass on this one. She's going to fly to Des Moines and visit her sister."

Leo Painter was not political, just eager to have a voice in the regulatory process and access to public lands, if and when it seemed they might become available for exploitation. So, he made generous political contributions to both parties and at every level. He'd learned early on that state legislators often had as much influence in the areas in which he held an interest as their better known federal counterparts, and their patronage was considerably cheaper to acquire. Charities, on the other hand, had less to do with altruism than with providing access to people and events that could prove useful in the future. Travis admired Leo who, he decided, was Hamiltonian in his belief that money, power, and prestige drove people and nations to achieve greatness. Had he known him better, he might have been surprised at how off the mark he was in this estimation.

The State Department, at the request of the President, asked Leo to travel to Botswana to consult on the extraction of methane and any other natural resources that lay beneath Botswana's soil. It wasn't that Botswana had a shortage of willing companies eager to exploit its

resources, but the State Department desired a more substantial hegemony in the area. Leo had agreed, less out
of a spirit of expanding capitalism in Africa than to forward his ambition to assume an interest, a controlling
interest preferably, in a nickel mine recently acquired by
the Germans. He thought if he spread around some cash,
twisted a few arms, and applied the right sort of hard-
to-come-by information judiciously, he might be able to
convince certain people to see it his way.

But that wasn't the big prize. Securing or, worst case,
obtaining an exclusive U.S. license for ActiVox could
net the company billions and effectively put all of his
competition out of business. A dozen other mining con-
glomerates had lost out in the bidding war for the process
previously but would be back eager to secure a license
as well. Travis knew about Leo's intentions even though
he'd not been told directly. A COO had a need to know,
even if his boss didn't care to share.

Leo finally sat and turned to him. "Tell me who finally agreed to go."

He was not cooperating with Travis' agenda this
morning, and Travis had to remove a sheet of paper
from the bottom of the stack. "You, me, Rose Hayward
from the PR department, Henry Farrah, your stepson
and his wife—"

"He's not my stepson. He is an idiot. I give him a
job and he won't take direction. Half the time he leaves
at noon. He thinks no one notices. If it weren't for my
promise to his late mother, he'd be on the street with his
paltry trust fund."

Leo had managed three wives and probably myriad
lovers. The drill, however, meant Travis feigned igno-
rance of any and all, true or false—Reilly's daughter,

Margaret Griswold, who had died and left Leo a widower and with the responsibility for a putative stepson and Lucille. They were all anyone dared acknowledge. Travis wondered sometimes about Leo Painter and what about him so intimidated his employees. But then, he guessed he already knew.

He completed the list, which included core staffers from the engineering and research department. The party had to be kept to twelve to match the company's Gulfstream V seating configuration.

Leo turned toward the window again. "You're going to have to drop one of the engineers. I need a place for a man named Greshenko, Yuri Greshenko." Travis lifted an eyebrow. "He's…ah, let's just say he's a consultant. I contracted for his services last week." Travis lifted the other eyebrow. Leo spun around and gestured dismissively. "I didn't tell you about him sooner because a certain amount of, shall we say, discretion is required here."

Travis didn't like this. Whenever Leo said he needed discretion, things usually moved into areas that ultimately required the combined skills of the company's legal department and possibly another handful of private operatives to straighten out.

"If Mrs. Painter isn't going, we should be okay."

"I'd leave the two kids behind if I could," Leo continued, "but, as I said, I promised Griswold's late mother I'd look after him. She couldn't see the weasel she'd raised. She once said…do you believe this…'he's a lot like you.' He's as much like me as Paris Hilton is like Mother Teresa."

In some ways, Travis thought, but wouldn't articulate, she'd been right. Bobby Griswold presented just as self-centered, arrogant, and lacking in conscience as, he thought, Leo. Unlike Leo, however, he had not acquired any of his stepfather's ruthlessness or drive. Had he, he might be in a position to head the company, if and when Leo died. Travis had witnessed Leo's will the previous February and that possibility existed, at least as an option if shrewdly executed. Travis could make that happen if he wanted to. It stood second on his list as Plan B. Plan A centered on his own elevation to the presidency—a plan that would be monkey-wrenched if the company went public too soon. Time. He needed time. And that, after Leo's three major cardiac arrests and a quadruple by-pass, seemed increasingly uncertain.

Travis didn't press about this new advisor, Greshenko. He guessed Leo was up to something that he did not want to know about but, in his need to stay alive in the sea of sharks in which he swam, he'd better find out. He tapped his papers back into a neat stack and stowed them in his briefcase. "There are papers to be signed to move the IPO forward. Are you sure you want them dated after you return from Botswana? If something happened to you—"

"Like what?"

"Not to put too fine a point on it, but your heart, Leo. It's not too reliable, and if you should…well, it could lead to certain complications."

Leo laughed.

As it currently stood, Travis' only hope for the future did not rest exclusively with the event that Leo would die or retire soon, leaving him a clear shot at the board of directors, most of whom he had carefully cultivated over the last decade. Travis had an alternative that he could put into effect, but not now. Later. With Bobby Griswold's shares, the right combination of Board members, and other interested parties, he…well. If Earth Global were to function in the absence of Leo Painter, it would be with Travis at the helm.

"One last thing…"

"What?"

"Your will, is it in order?" Travis asked as a formality. "Henry tells me you haven't done anything since the last one after—"

"Margaret died? After the company goes public, I will see about a new one that covers all the changes. For now, let it be. Hell, if I die, I won't be around to care, will I?"

"It's a stretch, I know, but, you realize that might put Bobby…"

"Then it's in everybody's best interest to keep me alive. Everybody's," he repeated, and smiled. Like a wolf eyeing an injured deer.

Travis' expression did not alter. Not quite, boss man, he thought. He finished his briefing and snapped his case shut. Leo returned to the window. "It's a good thing we're heading out. It looks like a bitch of a winter is on the way."

"Yes, sir. We leave Friday at six AM, from Signature Flight Support, that's at Midway—"

"I know, I know. Just tell it to the driver. Oh, and make sure Rose calls everyone to confirm the time and have her send a car for the boy and the bimbo. They're liable to oversleep."

FIVE

Mr. Pako, her supervisor, did not like Sanderson. It was nothing personal; he just felt that being a game ranger was not a suitable job for a woman. This opinion he shared with the local police superintendent, Inspector Mwambe. Even though the police force had employed women constables for several years, the police superintendent rankled under this government decision. If the *dikgosi,* if the chiefs, were still in charge...well that wasn't true anymore either. There was that Kgosi Mosadi, that woman chief...well.

When queried as to what jobs these two important persons considered appropriate for women, they had no answer. Out in the north, acceptance of change lagged behind the south. Gaborone had many women in big jobs, even on the High Court and in the National Assembly. Mr. Pako and his friend despaired at the direction their country seemed to be headed. If it were up to them, this Sanderson would be tending goats.

Mr. Pako shuffled papers at his desk. Sanderson stood still, waiting for him to speak. He looked up at her. What to do? The request from the village subchief for an investigation into the disappearance of a young boy topped the pile of papers on his desk. Why had they waited so long?

It would be a futile task. No good could come from it. He would send Sanderson. He authorized the use of the old Land Rover and sent her away. Good riddance. The phone rang. He straightened his uniform, slicked back the scant hair on his nearly bald head, and answered. The district superintendent had a position to fill. Did Mr. Pako have a reason not to accept a transfer? He thought a moment. No he did not.

SANDERSON MET WITH the subchief and then with the men in the village from which the boy disappeared.

"Why did so much time go by before this reporting?" she asked.

"That boy was a bad boy," he said. "When he ran, we waited for him to return. What kind of a foolish person will run into the bush at night? Surely the Kalanga taught him sense in Zimbabwe. We believed he went to the road and on to Kasane, so we went to our houses to sleep. In the morning, things were busy with the cattle being herded to the *kraal* for transport to the abattoir and then there were other things..." His voice trailed off.

Sanderson understood "other things"...she had passed the bottle store and bar hut on her way in.

"He is a bad boy," the old man repeated. "We thought, well, he has gone to another village to be bad. He will not return here. Then Rre Amanzie sees the vultures and we are then thinking, maybe this boy has not gone to another village after all."

"Which way did he run?"

The old man pointed up the hill, toward the bush. Sanderson walked back to the Rover and unsheathed the rifle. It was not likely that she would have trouble in the daylight, but she wouldn't take that chance. She loaded it, got behind the wheel and drove off the road and slowly into the bush.

She found the scant remains of Lovermore Ndlovu four

hundred meters in. He had been dragged some distance, it seemed. After studying the broken bones and bits of clothing she guessed a big cat had taken him. After it had finished, other animals had cleaned up. She inspected the ground. Too many sets of spoor to reveal much. She noted the larger set, those of the cat, and squatted in the dust to examine them more closely. An old leopard might have done it. But she'd heard no reports of a leopard this close to the town. Although leopards hunt at night and would not be averse to taking down a man if they happened on one like this, they were shy and rarely ventured this close to civilization. Too much time had elapsed to be sure of anything. She put her finger in the paw depression. Time had blurred its edges and even size. Still it looked more like a lion, probably an immature rogue or nomad. The owner of those paws was not heavy enough to be full grown and probably too heavy to be a leopard. There were always young lions about this time of year, raiding *kraals* and stealing cattle. So, a lion, not a leopard. But she couldn't be positive.

She stood and glanced once again at what was left of that bad boy. All that remained belonged to the insects. She put on rubber gloves. Collecting body parts would not be pleasant nor would she be expected to do a complete job. Bits and pieces would be scattered over a half hectare. She returned to the village half an hour later and deposited the plastic bag with the headman who would try to contact the Zimbabwe officials.

"Missus," the old subchief said, "these wheels must be returned to their rightful owners. You must take them to the police."

She inspected the wheels; saw where the bad boy had started to repaint the rims. She loaded them into the back of the Rover. When she returned to Kasane, she attempted to deposit them at the police station. Inspector Mwambe gave her a hard look and told her to take them away, that he had no time for her and did not need more paper work. She asked what she should do with them.

"Do whatever you like, woman," he said and lowered his eyes back to the shiny, very empty surface of his desk as he dismissed her with an impatient wave.

Mr. Pako had no suggestions for her either when she called him.

"Throw them away. I do not wish to have a conversation with you about it."

BLOODY AND BEATEN, Sekoa staggered into the bush and settled in the shade of an acacia tree. He had not walked away, as wisdom would have suggested, but stayed through a second attack and then he turned and walked. He had not been badly injured in this his last battle. In the past, his bouts with other lions had frequently ended in severe wounds, the scars of which still marked his face and shoulders. And he had managed to impose on his conqueror a few wounds as well. In the distance he heard the roaring and yelping as his replacement assumed sovereignty over the pride and decimated the youngest cubs—the older males raced away into the grassland where they would live or die by their wits. Soon this new alpha male would mate with the females and receive, as his dowry, the disease that, more than his strength, had won him his victory.

Sekoa had not hunted in years. That duty usually belonged to the females. He instinctively knew he could not run down any fleet-footed animal and did not have strength enough to pull down slower, larger ones. His only hope was to feed on the carrion left by others, to steal the kill of smaller predators, to hunt down the sick, the lame, and those like him who were dying. And then there were the hated hyenas who, if they sensed his weakness, would track him, waiting for the moment when he collapsed. The eternal animosity between the two species would be played out once more. He huffed and swished his tail at the plague of flies that had come to torment him.

He would go to the water. Eventually all animals had to go to the water. There would be game there for the taking. He might survive another day.

SANDERSON DETOURED TO her house before parking the Land Rover. She needed to deposit Lovermore Ndlovu's purloined wheels in her court. She had no idea if they would work on the HiLux. She was not mechanical and assumed that all automobile wheels were pretty much the same. Perhaps larger or smaller but the significance of the number of lug nuts for each had never registered. Four, five—who knew?

Michael slept fitfully under his mosquito netting. It had become necessary to fit this gossamer cone of protection over him as he, in his weakened state, could barely brush the flies and mosquitoes away. She tiptoed into the room and looked in on him, half hoping he would wake so she could tell him her good news, tell him of their change in luck. After a minute she left. The vehicle must be returned to its proper place. Mr. Pako must be assured of her presence on duty.

SIX

HENRY FARRAH TOOK the call even though he couldn't imagine what Bobby Griswold's wife wanted from him.

She told him.

"What you're asking for is confidential lawyer-client information," he protested. "Now wait a minute, Brenda…" He clenched his jaw, his face turned a bright, first-day-at-the-beach red. "Okay, okay, I hear you, but this has got to stop. Remember, you may embarrass me, but, if I have to, I can destroy you. What happened at that club is history and don't forget, I didn't interfere with you and Robert when I could have, so we should be even."

He held the phone away from his ear and sighed. "No need to use that kind of language. Very well, but I can only give you a rough outline—only what concerns your husband. That will have to do for now. Is that clear? Good." He ran his fingers through his still thick hair. It had once been red but with the years had turned muddy, the red fading into gray.

"This is the last will Mr. Painter executed as far as I know. Since I am his attorney, you may assume it is definitive. There is a 25 percent share in the company's stock that is held in trust by Leo until Robert turns thirty-three. What?…I don't know. Leo must have been genuinely fond of Robert's mother, Brenda. That fondness doesn't extend to Robert, by the way. Anyway, if Leo dies before Robert turns thirty-three, he inherits it immediately."

Farrah wasn't sure how much of what he related would register with the woman whom he'd first encountered in the Golden Cage night club. Just another gold-digger who, he believed, would milk whatever assets Griswold had and then dump him.

"The what?" Farrah's expression switched from condescension to alarm. "How did you hear about the public offering? It's supposed to be a secret...Bobby told you? I, we, the company, that is, could get into big trouble with the SEC if they find out...Okay, but don't say anything to anyone else, you hear? I mean it. If it comes out, the wrong people know the sale could be canceled."

A new problem to aggravate his ulcer. He reached into a desk drawer and retrieved a package of antacids, shelled one out and placed it on his tongue.

"No, if the offering goes through, Bobby's stock converts to preferred stock. Since he is not top management, it confers no stock options to him."

This conversation had drifted into areas the woman could not possibly grasp, he thought, and wished he had never begun.

"What?...Well, it means that combined with his mother's share he received at her death he'd have a very nice income stream. Preferred stock is paid dividends before common stock. That's pretty much it."

Farrah listened as Brenda summarized her understanding of what he'd said. To his surprise, she had it right. When she'd finished, he acknowledged it as correct and hung up. With the news about the possibility of the IPO leak, he had a full day ahead. It had used up all his favors, and then some, to convince the board to force an IPO on Leo. This leak could ruin everything. The SEC needed to be queried—discreetly. He had contacts there.

And the firms he'd contacted needed to be warned that there might be other parties in play when the offering was announced, if it made it that far.

WHILE HENRY FARRAH fenced with Brenda Griswold and fed his ulcer antacids, Travis also placed a phone call. He'd used Dalton Inquiries frequently in the past. His continued climb in the corporate world required that he know as much as possible about his rivals, subordinates, and employer. Andrew Dalton supplied that information for a price. A high price, in fact, but one Travis paid without question. Dalton's data was always reliable.

"Andy, I have an assignment for you and I need a report by Thursday."

"That's not much time, Mr. Parizzi."

"I know, I'll pay—"

"Of course you will. What is it you need?"

"Everything you can find out about a man named Yuri Greshenko. It's important."

"Hell, Mr. Parizzi. I don't need to wait until Thursday, I can give that to you right now. The word on the street is Yuri Greshenko is Russian Mafia."

"Russian Mafia? I didn't know Chicago had—"

"They're not big here, not yet, anyway. Greshenko is what you might call their advance man."

"Russian Mafia. Jesus, what is Leo thinking?"

"Your boss is dealing with this guy?'

"I don't know. I guess he must be."

"I'll send some stuff over to you today. A word to the wise, Mr. Parizzi: give Greshenko a very wide berth. He could be poison."

"I'll be careful. Send the ActiVox file over as well."

The board had discussed ActiVox when the revolutionary process had been announced. They had authorized Leo to bid on it when the Australians had indicated a willingness to sell. The chemical leaching process could restore played-out mines, particularly nickel, to profitable production again. To their consternation they were quickly outbid by a Canadian group who, in turn, before Earth Global had a chance to counter, sold it, at an enormous profit, reportedly in the billions of dollars, to a Russian syndicate. Travis knew from Leo's personal secretary, to whom he paid substantial bonuses, that Leo had not given up on ActiVox. Earth Global had options on several played-out mines and controlled vast holdings where they continued mining. They were barely profitable and Travis intended to see them shut down so the company could pour its resources into sectors with a better return on investment.

But who was Greshenko? More appropriately what was Greshenko, besides a Mafioso? What were Russians who dealt in that business called anyway? Was he the Russian connection Leo needed to close the ActiVox deal? He needed to know more about him. Timing, it all came down to timing.

BRENDA STARED UNSEEING at Lake Michigan through skeletal tree branches. The sky had turned darker, grayer. It would snow soon. Bobby had gone out, God only knew where, and she had some serious thinking to do. If Farrah had told her the truth, there would be some huge changes if and when the IPO thing went through. On the other hand, if Leo's heart were to crap out, this time for good, her—well, Bobby's—options were considerably brighter than she'd imagined. She could raise the money to redeem Bobby's shares from that slime-ball

Travis Parizzi. Frankie at the Golden Cage could arrange for the funds, if she explained it to him right. She'd have to pay a pretty high vigorish to the sharks, probably, but it would be worth it. Anyone wanting a major stake in Earth Global would jump at a chance to buy them out— for really big bucks. But that would have to be before the IPO, or with Leo dead.

"Income stream," Farrah had said. Crapola. That might appeal to the congenitally lazy Bobby, but not to her. Leo was a tough old bastard, though. He was just contrary enough to live another ten years. And Farrah said if the wrong people…or was it the right people? If they found out the IPO had been leaked, it might be canceled. She needed to think about that, too.

LEO PAINTER SETTLED behind his desk and steepled his hands. He considered lighting a cigar. Smoking was strictly forbidden in the offices, and by his doctors, but Leo ignored those dicta as he did most others. RHIP, he would say whenever someone called him on it, rank has its privileges. He rolled the cigar, one smuggled in from Cuba, between thumb and forefinger next to his ear. Perfecto. He decided to wait. It would taste better after lunch with his second martini.

Telling Bobby Griswold about the IPO had been a stroke of genius. When Farrah found out, and he was sure the idiot boy would let it slip eventually, it would give Farrah a double duck fit. The greedy bastard would then have to square it with his new friends, his "partners," the guys who wanted to take over the company, and then, who knew what the SEC would do if they found even the hint of possible insider trading? Farrah should have taken the early retirement offer, the proverbial "golden parachute," when he had the chance, but apparently he couldn't resist the thought of a big payoff. Now, he could end up with nothing. Served him right, the disloyal son of a bitch.

Leo swiveled around to contemplate an angry Lake Michigan again. Clouds piled in from the north. Waves crashed against the seawall, where some of the spume began to freeze. What, he wondered, should he do about Travis Parizzi? If only the guy would learn patience. Leo liked Travis; well, not liked, exactly, Leo didn't dare to like anyone, but he recognized talent when he saw it, and Travis had it. He had what it took to step in as his successor. The company needed an insider to finish the projects currently on the table. Travis could do it. A new management team, AMG Partners, Freeport McMoran, the group that bought out Phelps-Dodge or, whoever else might be in play, would take too long to settle in, and the process would engender too much infighting. The moment would be lost. Continuity was the answer. And then there was the real estate division, soon to be a spinoff if everything went as he hoped. It needed capital, though. Leo wondered if he'd be better off sharing his plans with Travis.

Perhaps, he thought, in Africa they'd have a chance to talk.

SEVEN

KGABO MODISE WAVED his hand at the second-hand smoke drifting in his window. It was summer in Gaborone, the windows open, and on the whole he'd much rather be somewhere else having a cool drink and admiring the young girls bustling about their business. Instead, he re-read the thick file in front of him. There were two parts: a cursory and not very helpful summary from Interpol and several older, more detailed documents from the predecessor agencies of the Directorate of Intelligence and Security, the DIS. Yuri Greshenko had had his fingers in many pies in his day.

Modise thought all those old *apparatchiks* were gone and forgotten, whiling away the time in their dachas with pensions or shaking down the new generations of capitalists in the mother country. But now this one turns up like a counterfeit thebe to disturb his day. Back when Botswana was in its infancy and all the major players were attempting to establish hegemony on the continent, Greshenko and people like him were busy. They were part of the back channel creating the uneasy triumvirate of the DeBeers, Russia, and Botswana cartel, which would exert control over most of the world's kimberlitic diamonds. Efforts to break the cartel by the CIA, Zaire, Australia, and some other players, had occupied Modise's predecessors for years.

So, what was this aging Russian operative up to now?

And how did he fit in with Earth Global? His acquaintance with Botlhokwa worried his boss. The government was eager for Earth Global to come and invest but was understandably chary of Yuri Greshenko. His past was problematic.

WHEN SANDERSON ARRIVED back at the station, Mr. Pako, puffed with the newfound importance his imminent promotion gave him, called her into his office.

He stared at her rudely. He often did that. Sanderson thought he was a dirty old man. He had once asked her for sexual favors. She had fended him off by reminding him of her late husband and that he had died of AIDS and perhaps she too…She did not need to finish the thought. Mr. Pako quickly changed the subject, but he was never polite to her again.

"I have been on the line with the headman in Kazungula and he wishes that this lion which has taken that boy from Zimbabwe be found and shot. In this, the managers of the lodges agree. It is bad for business if the guests have to worry about a killer lion. You must see to this."

He assumed she would not be able to comply, as he believed, along with Police Superintendent Mwambe, that a woman could not operate a firearm, much less shoot down a four-hundred-kilo lion. He looked extremely smug when he gave her this order.

In truth, Sanderson agreed with him. She did know how to load and fire the rifle. And in years past, had had some success hitting targets with similar pieces. Her late husband, before he took to visiting that woman in the village who had infected him, had shared this skill and many other happy times with her. But shooting targets under the watchful eye of the police and hunting a lion were very different things.

She asked if tranquilizing the animal and relocating it would not be a better idea. He scowled at her in a way that clearly indicated he considered any suggestion that contradicted his orders a great affront. He brushed the notion of tranquilizing away with his hand.

"No, it must be killed. It has tasted human blood. It will be a man-eater from now on. It must be removed."

Mr. Pako authorized the use of the old Land Rover, but only during the day. She must return it every evening, he said. She also received a note to draw ammunition. How she was to track this lion, which had tasted human blood, and kill it he did not make clear. Mr. Pako's desire to see her fail and perhaps be mauled by that lion in the bargain was eminently clear.

She would not give him that pleasure. How she would complete this duty, however, seemed less certain. She would ask in the village. The old men would know. They had once hunted *ditau*, the lions, in their youth, and the older men without firearms but with spears. They would know what to do. However, she could not be sure they would share that knowledge with a woman, with her. Perhaps, she thought, she could recruit them to do the hunting. That would make it all right. They would like to do that. Hunting the *ditau* had been taken from them years before. How could a boy grow up to manhood, they asked, if he cannot hunt the lions?

Becoming a game ranger had been her ambition since she was very small. It had not been easy to pass the tests and wait for an opening. But she had done it and all the Pakos in the world were not going to take it away from her. She nodded her acquiescence. Mr. Pako smiled, confident of her inevitable failure, and then, with a superior smirk, told her he had been transferred to Maun. It was, he declared, a promotion. He would leave at the end of the week. Much to his amazement, she congratulated him profusely.

Her luck had changed.

BY LATE AFTERNOON, Sekoa had traveled five more kilometers and needed a place to rest. The river seemed a long ways away. To his right he heard the rustle of feathers. He crouched and managed to flush a guinea fowl from its nest. He couldn't bring down the bird, and the hatchlings darted away from him. He chased them for a few yards and then stopped, exhausted. A pack of hyenas trotted out of the bush and stopped a few meters away. With lunatic eyes, they contemplated their traditional enemy, measuring his strength. A rush of adrenaline enabled him to stand, tall and whole. He opened his jaws wide, yawned, let out a low growl, and feinted toward them, claws extended. The hyenas backed away, hesitated. A small herd of Thompson's Gazelles minced across an open area behind them. The hyenas, long incorrectly thought to be mere scavengers, wheeled and gave chase, disappearing in a cloud of dust. The lion trotted after them. If they missed, but crippled one, he might eat again. Perhaps, if they parted and fed separately, he could intimidate one of them into giving up the kill. If his pride were with him, he could do that. But he had no females anymore.

He trotted on. He could smell fear. A small, very young impala, a "lion snack," they would say of it at the Safari Lodge, bolted into his path. It did not expect a lion to be hunting so close to hyenas and, with panicked eyes rolled back at its pursuers, bounded directly at him. He swatted it down with one paw and clamped his jaws on the poor beast's neck. Sekoa would eat. It amounted to no more than a few mouthfuls, but he would live another day.

EIGHT

THE GULFSTREAM V POWERED smoothly to a gentle landing in Gaborone. "Wheels down at 15:43," the pilot announced. "Your car is waiting for you outside the terminal, Mr. Painter. As soon as you clear customs, it can take you to your hotel. The tower states there is a greeting party that will meet you at the door."

Leo Painter released his seatbelt buckle even though the plane continued to taxi. He signaled for Yuri Greshenko to join him. Greshenko hesitated, looked at the flight attendant who shrugged her shoulders. Apparently she had grown accustomed to Leo's perversity. Greshenko shook his head and slid into the aisle and made his way forward. He lowered his bulky frame into the seat opposite Leo. In his day, Greshenko could have played outside linebacker for the Chicago Bears. If Leo were forty years younger and forty pounds lighter, he might have played in the middle on the same team. Leo handed him a fat envelope.

"As soon as you clear customs, contact your people and then get up to Kasane and look around. I want to be sure this deal will fly. There's a guy up there named something like Ray Bolly-hock-wa. Check in with him, but I don't want to use him unless it's absolutely necessary."

"It's pronounced rah...Rra Botlhokwa." Greshenko rolled his R's with practiced precision. "In English it means Mr. Important, or something like you would say in America, Big Shot or Mr. Big."

"Interesting. I hired you because a mutual friend said you knew things about this country. Apparently that was an understatement. How did you know that, the Mr. Big Shot thing?"

"Years ago when I was younger, you understand, we, the USSR we were then, had certain interests in Africa, this country in particular. We knew it had mineral wealth, particularly diamonds. It would be a major player in the diamond world with us and DeBeers. The kimberlitic diamonds here and in Siberia would form a cartel that...well you can see how that would play out. Diamonds would be many, is that the word? They would be plentiful and controlling the price and distribution important, yes? And we were interested in their nickel and copper mines, of course. Also there were political considerations that... well, anyway, I served here as commercial attaché. I knew Botlhokwa then."

"Commercial attaché? As in...you were a spy? KGB?"

Greshenko shrugged. "There are attachés and there are attachés, you understand. I was sent to southern Africa as part of the interests we had here. I spent some time in Zambia, Johannesburg, Mozambique...around. Botswana found her diamonds after Independence." He shrugged again and smiled. "In Botswana, all rights of ownership of minerals are vested in the state, irrespective of the district or region in which they are found. Any individuals or companies wishing to obtain a prospecting license must apply to the Minister of Minerals, Energy, and Water Resources. That gives the minister the responsibility for natural resource regulation and management. And, so they also managed to keep the minerals for themselves. We were all shut out." Greshenko frowned.

"Wait a minute, you know this guy Rah Whatever, Mr. Big?"

"Knew, Mr. Painter. I knew him when, as you say, he was a player. A very interesting man, Botlhokwa, one of the few recipients of the Bechuanaland Protectorate Scholarships to Oxford. Would have been a classmate, you could say, of presidents, leaders, both in Botswana and surrounding countries. He turned his back on government and went into business. I don't know what he went into after that. But I will find out. The last I heard of him he'd moved into some shady areas. But he has hotels and casinos here and there. He should be happy to see us, if he wants to recapture his respectability."

"Well, that's your bailiwick, I think. Back to the Russians. Your people are active here, it seems. You bought ActiVox, and it's being used here, in Botswana. So you won after all."

"Not won—prevailed, I think would be a better description. And that process is on the back burner, as you Americans would say. Because of the global economic meltdown, the sale of the raw materials in Botswana has dropped precipitously, leaving the economy a little shaky. The mines in particular are in financial trouble and have struggled to pay their employees. The country needs help from institutions like the African Development Bank."

"A good time to invest, or not?"

Greshenko shrugged as if he had closed the book on that part of his history. "You're the minerals expert, it's your call, Mr. Painter. Capitalism is not quite my line of country." He tilted his head at Travis Parizzi. Leo glanced in Travis' direction and shook his head.

"Travis? No, he doesn't know. I'll fill him in when the right moment comes. In the meantime...well, I don't need to tell you, discretion, Greshenko. This may be a developing country with more goats than flush toilets, but they're as shrewd as snakes—"

"And innocent as doves?" Greshenko finished for him. Leo's eyebrows shot up. He had been raised by fundamentalist Christian grandparents. The only residue of that rigorous and often painful upbringing was his ability to quote occasional bits of scripture. That Greshenko recognized and could complete the passage from Matthew on top of the Botswana connection came as complete surprise.

"Jury is out on the dove bit. Word in Washington is the pols here, unlike those in my beloved Chicago, are incorruptible. We'll have to see about that, but in the interim, be careful. We don't want to be seen as the wolves."

Russians never ceased to amaze him. He guessed he did not have Greshenko's story, not all of it at any rate, and possibly never would. He wished he were younger. What he, what Earth Global could have done in that vast country with men like Greshenko! Hell, the man even had a better grasp of English than 90 percent of the dolts who worked for him.

The plane lurched to a halt. A minute later, the pilot had the door open and steps down. Leo Painter and his party descended onto the taxiway to be greeted by two officials who steered him and his party through customs and on to their hotel. They set the time for the appointments with the minister of Mineral, Energy, and Water Resources, BEDIA, and a handful of other functionaries. The purported purpose of Leo's visit had begun. In the confusion of off-loading baggage and passengers,

Yuri Greshenko slipped through customs to a waiting
SUV. He did not notice the official-looking car at the
curb behind him.

Kgabo Modise had been waiting. He'd watched the
sleek corporate jet touch down and disgorge its passengers. His eyes, however, were focused entirely on the
man whose picture was clipped to the folder on the seat
beside him.

No one noticed Greshenko's departure except Modise,
who started his car and followed a discreet distance.

NINE

HENRY FARRAH WAS not part of the official meeting-and-greeting taking place in the hotel's ballroom. As a matter of fact, he didn't even know why Leo had brought him along. But knowing Leo as he did, he knew there would be a reason forthcoming and he would find out soon enough. He wandered into the hotel bar and, turning his back on the three or four other patrons perched on stools near him, began punching numbers on his cell phone. There would be a seven-hour difference between New York and Gaborone, eight to Chicago. He needed to know if the SEC had tumbled to the leak; he needed to know what his partners knew or were prepared to do if it had. He was in as close to a state of panic as ever in his life.

As in a European pub, his order for whiskey translated to Scotch. Henry didn't like Scotch. His ulcer positively rebelled at Scotch. He signaled to the bar tender.

"Sir, something wrong with your drink?"

"Take it away and bring me a beer."

"Certainly. What brand would you like?"

"I don't care...a local beer, then."

The bartender retreated, returned, and placed a can of Saint Louis beer and a glass on a napkin in front of Henry.

"I asked for a local beer."

"Yes, sir. This is local beer."

"Saint Louis is local? What's the name of the others? San Francisco, Duluth? Old Milwaukee is taken, I'm afraid."

The barman only looked at him and nodded agreeably.

He signaled for the bartender to pour the beer and turned his attention back to his phone.

The call to his contact in New York was inconclusive. The man in the SEC either did not know, was not in the loop, or had decided to dummy up. Farrah cursed and pulled out his notebook. It had been a present from his wife two Christmases ago. Just before she'd left him and moved in with her tennis instructor. That hadn't lasted. Cougars can't hold on to their prey very long, it seems. She'd asked him to take her back. He'd refused and now she lived with his daughter in tight-lipped silence in Winnetka.

He jotted a few notes in his pocket memo—he'd never been able to master the Blackberry he'd been issued. He had his secretary keep it up to date in case Leo ever asked. His secretary hadn't traveled with him so he reverted to his pocket notebook. Besides, the notes he was keeping at the moment would not be the sort of information he'd want in the Blackberry anyway. He didn't know the extent to which that device could be accessed remotely, but he'd become convinced that Leo had somehow managed it in order to spy on his employees. Why else would he have issued such an expensive perquisite? What finally appeared in Henry's Blackberry files were the innocuous details about items everyone knew.

He clicked off and drummed his fingers on the polished bar. A second call confirmed the first. Either the SEC knew nothing, knew but saw no cause for concern, or his contacts weren't as tight with the commission as he'd been led to believe. Henry scowled and dialed Chicago.

The investor consortium he'd assembled and in which he'd been promised a substantial equity share based on his insider position were understandably skittish. They hadn't heard anything and were less than pleased to hear there might be a leak. Since his future depended entirely on the IPO going through, they said, he'd better put a lid on the rumor immediately. Easier said than done. Perhaps he should have another talk with Brenda Griswold. He wrinkled up his nose at the thought. Like so many of his social class, he held people like Brenda in disdain—being a predator in the market place was somehow classier than being one on the streets.

It required ten rings before his secretary answered. She gibbered something about a Christmas party, giggled, but had nothing to report. When reminded that it was only nine in the morning in Chicago and only the eighth of December, which meant Christmas was still seventeen days away, she hiccupped, made an effort to acquire a serious and sober tone, and agreed it did seem a bit early to celebrate. She'd have a word with the girls.

"I asked you to pull the IPO file and fax it to me on the plane. You didn't. I need it. Fax it to me at the hotel."

She seemed to struggle with her pronunciation but did manage to ask for the fax number.

"How the hell would I know? Look in the itinerary on my desk and find it. I want that file ASAP."

Henry slapped his phone shut with a curse uttered loudly enough to attract the attention of several guests. He slid off the stool and stormed out of the bar, his beer untouched and his bill unpaid.

FROM HIS VANTAGE point in a booth to the rear, and unseen by Farrah, Travis Parrizi watched as he pulled out his notebook and scribbled furiously for a minute. He wondered what had become of Henry's Blackberry. Everyone in the company had been issued one, Henry included. All notes and correspondence that related to Earth Global were to be entered in the devices. Apparently these notes were personal, or they were some other kind of business—business Farrah did not want anyone to know about. Farrah made a second, a third, and a fourth call. His expression seemed to grow darker after each. Then he'd left in a hurry. Interesting. The barkeep started to say something and held up a bar tab. Farrah ignored him and kept walking.

Travis sidled over to the bar and signaled to the barman.

"Here, let me have that. I'm with his party." He took the bill, scanned it, and signed. The bartender smiled a thank you and held out Henry's notebook.

"Would..." he peered at the signature line on the tab, "Would Mr. Parizzi be kind enough to return this book to that gentleman?"

"Certainly," he said and pocketed the pad and its miniature gold pen. And he would return it—eventually—after he'd read it, made a few calls of his own, and weighed the consequences of several new options available to him.

TEN

BRENDA NEEDED TO talk to someone. Bobby should have been her first choice but that wasn't going to work. Even if she could explain what she had in mind, and even if he understood—a stretch at best—the idiot boy would not go along, she was sure about that. It was funny. He watched cage fighting, gloried in the violence offered by his collection of video games, but when it came to the real world and tough choices, he turned into a bunny rabbit. Brenda smiled at the thought. Bunny, that was good. The only thing Bobby did with any skill was... well, like a bunny. Well, at least there was that. A girl needs something and he did help her out there. She'd just have to handle the rest. The question before the house now was, who should she confide in?

Travis Parizzi rounded the corner. He had a notebook in his hand and was so absorbed in it, he nearly ran her down.

"Oh, sorry. I nearly knocked you down, Mrs. Griswold."

"Hey, could have been worse. You could have knocked me up."

Travis slipped the notebook in his pocket and evidently decided to let the remark pass.

"Yes. Well, sorry."

Brenda thought it was a hoot talking off-color to guys like Travis Parizzi. Freaking stuffed shirts. They loved it when you did it at the club or in bed with the lights out, but out in the polite world it, like, made them crazy. There was nothing like dropping the "F bomb" into an otherwise polite conversation to get things rolling. Well, you could take the girl out of the strip club, but you'd never get the strip club out of the girl.

"We need to talk, Parizzi."

"About what?"

"The stock you screwed Bobby out of. I want to exercise his option to buy it back."

"I'm not sure what you mean. What stock, what option?"

"Don't bother trying that tap dance on me, hotshot. Bobby sold his stock to you. Spare me the razzle dazzle about you don't know. He said he had an option to buy it back inside a year. The year ain't up and I want it."

Travis looked at her for a nearly a full minute without speaking, apparently trying to figure out where this could go.

"You want to buy. As the guy in the movie said, show me the money."

"Now? I don't have it right now, but I have it on tap."

"On tap? What, like it's a keg of beer? Look, Mrs. Griswold, you want to redeem stock that your husband sold me for a considerable amount of money, more, I might add, than it would be worth on the open market, and you want me to surrender it on your say-so? Not going to happen. By the way, I didn't have to screw it out of him. He was only too happy to sell."

"Look, I can get a letter of credit faxed to me tomorrow. When I do, I want you to, like, sign back Bobby's shares. Got it?"

"A faxed LOC. You're kidding, right? Look, you want

the stock, you can get it, but with cash. I want cash, and that means you can only redeem it after we get back to Chicago and…" He paused and studied the woman in front of him, "And, after other things."

"Other things? What other things?"

"It's business. You wouldn't understand."

Brenda had survived as long as she had and succeeded where others might have failed because she could read people. Her handler back in Chicago at the club before she left to become Mrs. Robert Griswold said she'd missed her calling. She should have been a professional poker player.

"You're working a scam, aren't you?"

"Scam? What do you mean?"

"You need that stock. You need it and you need time, and probably some other help, more options, I'll bet, than you have your hands on right now, to pull off something."

"What? Pull what off? What other stock?"

Brenda realized she'd hit pay dirt. Travis was up to something, and she'd bet her hottest red thong Leo didn't know anything about it. "If I take the stock out of your hands, the deal goes south. Am I close?" Travis turned to leave. "Maybe I should talk to Leo. What do you think?" For a split second, Travis looked stricken. It was enough. "You want to buy me a drink and talk some business? Or do I have a chat with the boss man?" Brenda raised her eyebrows and smiled.

"In an hour, in the bar." He growled, turned on his heel, and stalked away.

Brenda pumped her arm and whispered "Yes!"

MICHAEL SEEMED STRONGER that evening. Perhaps the medicine was working, after all. Hope springs like new flowers in the desert after a rain. False or real, hope enabled Sanderson to endure.

"You are better, then?"

"I am feeling better, yes. Show me these tires you have achieved."

"Can you walk?"

"For the HiLux, I can dance." Michael shuffled his feet, lost his balance and staggered, and caught himself on the door jamb.

"You are not ready, Michael. You must rest."

"No, I am fine, you see. I must see these wheels."

It took a long time for him to walk outside to the court. He sat on its low wall to catch his breath. Sanderson pointed to the late Lovermore Ndlovu's stolen property. Michael smiled, a weak smile, but a smile nonetheless. It was the first time he'd done so for months, it seemed.

"You were lucky. These will fit the truck. See, the number of mounting holes in the wheels is correct and we have the lug nuts." Sanderson was not sure what lug nuts were, but she beamed. She couldn't be sure what pleased her more, the acquisition of these wonderful wheels or seeing Michael up, smiling, and maybe a little better.

Michael stood and wrapped his hands around one of the wheels. He couldn't lift it. He tried again and then collapsed on the wall, his face distraught.

"I cannot do this thing, Mma."

"I will do it, but you must tell me how."

Michael instructed her how to mount the wheels on the truck's axles and tighten the down the nuts.

"Now we must ask Mr. Naledi for the loaning of a jack. We must lift this machine off of these blocks."

"A jack?" Sanderson rummaged in the pile of equipment stacked at the side of the house. "Like this one?"

She held up the other prize from her trip to Kazungula—
Lovermore's jack.

"Yes, like that. Is it another present from the police
superintendent? He is a very generous man."

"With other people's property, yes."

Several of the young men of the village had gathered
to watch and offered to do the removal of the blocks for
Mma Michael. It took longer than it might have, had
Michael been able to do it alone. There was a great deal
of competition among the boys for leadership, and then
there were disagreements as to which wheel and which
side should be lowered first. In the end the HiLux stood
on its own four wheels, dented, rusted in spots and still
missing a few parts, but in Sanderson's eyes the most
beautiful machine in the country.

"We must ask if Mr. Naledi has a fender we can beat
into shape for the right front, and then we must paint it,"
Michael said. Sanderson shook her head and tried to hide
the tears streaming down her face.

"I would like a red *bakkie*," she said.

"You should paint it that color, then." Michael slumped
forward.

"Back to bed with you."

With the help of two of the boys she managed to get
her son back to bed. Michael smiled once more.

"Tomorrow I will finish the engine and we will charge
up the battery again and you shall drive your beautiful
machine." Michael closed his eyes and lay very still—
too still. Sanderson's heart was in her throat. Then she
saw him draw a breath. He slept. Death had not yet come.
There was still hope.

ELEVEN

SEKOA REACHED THE shore of the Chobe at dusk. He approached the river's edge cautiously. Crocodiles lurked beneath its surface and while he had never witnessed one attack a lion, he had seen a nearly grown zebra pulled in. He studied the water's surface and satisfied there was no danger, crouched and began lapping. His tongue, like that of all of the *Felidae*, was not particularly adept at drinking and it took him some time to finish. When he was done he rose up from his crouch and tested the air. In the past he'd relied on his eyesight to search out prey and relied less on his sense of smell. A movement to his left brought him to full alert.

One of the members of the pack of hyenas that had dogged him earlier sidled from the bush and stared at him, its tongue lolling. The lion growled and took a step toward the hyena, who scuttled away back in the direction he'd come. The lion watched him leave. He was downwind, and now he caught the scent of the rest of the pack. They were trailing him. Waiting for him to die; perhaps they might even hurry that process along.

He followed the shoreline, trotting eastward, away from the park and toward a set of vaguely familiar odors. He recognized some of them. He'd caught them before when the large stinking beast with no legs came forward and sat near the pride. It never attacked and they'd become used to it. It made a curious growling noise and when it did so, it emitted a strong smell and made other noises like birds but there were no birds on it like on the buffalo, just dangly things that smelled like what was in his nostrils now—definitely an animal smell. Possibly human, although he could never separate it from the large legless beast. He knew he needed to shake the hyenas off his trail and they, as most of the beasts in the park, always shied away from that beast and its appendages. If he could get close to it or them, perhaps they would leave him to die in peace.

A giraffe and its mate stood motionless, watching him from afar, ready to employ their hooves if he were to change direction and come at them. Those hooves could be deadly. He never hunted healthy giraffe. Impala and kudu scattered from his path as he trotted along the river bank. He ignored them. He would have liked to pull one down but he knew he had neither the endurance for the chase nor the strength to actually drag it to the ground. His earlier lucky kill had provided enough sustenance to last for a few days. In the old days, when the pride would hunt, he could eat fifteen or sixteen kilos and sleep for a week. But that was no longer the case. He would have to steal a smaller predator's food or find carrion.

BOBBY GRISWOLD PACED the hotel room. He didn't know what had become of Brenda and he worried. Not about her safety, but about whom she might have met and what she might be doing. Before they'd married she'd confessed the affairs she'd had. He'd accepted them. After all, he wasn't exactly a saint, and in her line of work, he couldn't have expected anything else. Hadn't he been one of them, at least at first? But he still had jealous moments when he thought of the men in her past, the ones she met at parties, and the ones he imagined her meeting but he wasn't aware of. He couldn't trust her alone and out of his sight. More than once this constant surveillance and suspicion had brought him to the edge. What if she had hooked up with some guy?

He had doubts, not for the first time, about his decision to marry and in fact often wondered how it had happened. He couldn't remember thinking about it but, well, Brenda had a way of getting what she wanted. He heard the key in the lock and hastily found a chair, sat, and opened the paper.

"Hi." Brenda tossed her bag on the bed and strolled to the bathroom. He didn't like that. Why did she need a bathroom right after she came in the door?

"Where've you been?"

"Around, you know shopping and all. What else have I to do with my time? I mean, I thought we were coming to Africa and to see wild animals and things, not mope around a hotel all day. This could be downtown Cleveland, for crying out loud."

"You left me an hour ago. So, what did you buy?"

"I didn't see anything. The stuff in the gift shop is, like, real tacky. Like I said, this could be Cleveland."

"We're supposed to go to some river where there are the animals and things, the day after tomorrow. Leo is going to send the engineers and most of the others back home and we're flying out to a resort or something."

"Resort? You're kidding, right? What kind of resort are you going to find in the middle of Africa? Geez, Bobby, use your head. It's gonna be tents and MREs."

"No, no, look at the brochure on the table. It's where we're going."

Brenda scanned the pages. "You're sure this is the

place? Do they have a spa? I don't see one in this thing? I could use a massage."

"Come over here and I'll give you a massage."

"Can't do it, Babe, I have to meet somebody." She slipped out of her jeans and into a short skirt and blouse. The neckline made Bobby frown.

"You'd be better off if you wore a bra with that blouse. Who're you meeting?" Bobby's jealousy antennae were up.

"Nobody. It's, like, business. Don't look at me that way, Bobby. It really is business."

"The only business you know is—"

"Don't even say it. You are going to have to learn to trust me. It might as well be now. I say it's business with a capital B, and that's what it is."

Brenda applied lipstick, gave her hair a pat, and left. Bobby waited until he felt certain she'd reached the elevators and rose to follow her. He'd find out soon enough what kind of business she was up to.

TWELVE

LEO FOUND HENRY FARRAH in the lobby turning out his pockets. He watched as his lawyer checked and rechecked them. He inspected the floor close to where he'd been sitting, and then he seemed to have an epiphany, stood upright, and headed for the hotel bar. Leo followed. As Farrah disappeared around the door jamb at the bar entrance, the double set of elevator doors opened. Brenda exited from the first, Travis Parizzi from the second. The corridor to the bar suddenly seemed crowded. Neither saw Leo, who slowed his pace and edged to the wall out of their line of sight. The two followed Henry into the bar. Leo continued his walk and nearly ran into Bobby Griswold who bolted from the stairwell.

"You headed for the bar as well, Robert?"

"What? No…ah, yes. Maybe. Should I be?"

"Everyone else is. Henry, your wife, Travis, and I'm thinking I might join them. Then again, perhaps I should let the children plot and scheme for a while before I embarrass them with my presence. What do you think?"

"Um, I don't know, sir. Whatever."

"Articulate and decisive as always. Are you waiting for me to die, too?"

"Sir?"

"Never mind. Walk with me, Robert. We need to have a word."

WHEN TRAVIS AND Brenda entered the bar, Farrah and the barman seemed to be having an argument. The barman pointed in their direction and said something to Henry.

"What's that old bag of—?"

"Oh, oh, he wants his notebook back." Travis waved to Henry.

"Henry, I've been looking all over for you. I have your notebook. Here," he reached into his pocket and produced the book and its pen. "You left it here earlier. The bartender asked me to return it."

Henry squinted at Travis. Finally, he held out his hand and took the book.

"You forgot to pay your bar tab, too. You owe me sixty pula and fifty thebe, whatever that works out to in dollars."

Henry pocketed the book, reached into another pocket and withdrew a one hundred pula note. "Here, keep the change." He pivoted and rushed out of the room.

"Thank you, Henry. I'll have a drink in your honor." He turned to Brenda. "He bought a scotch and a beer and didn't drink either one. Left them on the bar."

"What was in the book?" Brenda steered them to a booth away from the door where they couldn't be seen from the corridor.

"How would I know?"

"I saw you reading it, so don't give any of your—"

"Okay, I looked. I couldn't tell for sure, but I think he has been a naughty boy."

"Meaning?"

"I could put something really big on permanent hold if I wanted to. You wouldn't understand."

"Does it have something to do with the public offering?"

"How'd you know about that?"

"There's lots of stuff I know, mister. Just because I ain't been to Yale or someplace like you did, doesn't mean I'm a complete ditz."

"I didn't attend Yale, either. Okay, you called for this meeting. What is it you want from me? I've already laid down the rules for redeeming your husband's stock. You will do me a favor if you will let this all ride for another two weeks at least."

"I'm okay with that for now. I want you to level with me. What are you up to that needs Bobby's stock in play?"

Travis weighed his options. He could feed Brenda Griswold a line of complicated nonsense and hope to fool her, he could give it to her straight, or he could shoot for something somewhere in the middle. The fact she'd tumbled on to anything at all persuaded him that nonsense wouldn't sell and might possibly antagonize her to the point she'd precipitate a move that would be rash, or stupid, or both. Before he decided which way to go, Brenda started to guess. She laced her thesis with more Anglo-Saxon epithets and figures of speech than he'd heard since his days in the army, and he'd heard plenty. And that didn't include the straight up profanity. His mother, had she been there to hear it, would have described her discourse as "earthy." Somehow, a business deal as Brenda described it sounded wholly different than when the same deal was presented in a board room with PowerPoint and spreadsheets.

And her guesses were very nearly correct. He looked at her with new respect. Potty mouth or not, this woman had a functioning brain in there with all that organic fertilizer. Clean her up and she'd really be something. Educate her and she'd be dangerous.

He had to interrupt her in midstream.

"You're close. Do me a favor. Cut out the locker-room language and listen."

"I didn't spend much time in locker rooms, pal, at least not since the year I was a junior cheerleader and had some things on with the football team, but that was a long time ago. I learned this way of talking from CEOs, COOs, and other hot shots like you, with alphabets after their names that came to the club and figured they could let go with the girls. You never came to the club, did you?"

"No, never had the pleasure. Unlike the guys who can't or won't go home, I live a very full…That's all neither here nor there, though, is it? The truth is, I can do this without Robert's stock. It will take a little longer and cost more, but I can still do it."

"What if Leo finds out you're trying to move in on him?"

"He won't unless you tell him, and I'm betting you won't."

"Why?"

"Because your stock holdings give you zilch unless Leo drops dead. With that crappy heart of his, that could happen, of course, but if you throw in with me…" he left the rest hanging.

Brenda frowned. "I think we need to take this conversation somewhere private. We can't go to my room. Bobby's there and if he gets involved he'll only screw it up."

"My room?"

"Sure, why not?"

"You're not afraid of being alone in my hotel room?"

"I been in plenty of hotel rooms with more guys than

I care to count, and I can take care of myself, believe
me. If you can show me how this can work so me and
Bobby get a bigger payday, I may surprise you with some
moves of my own."

They left the bar and took the elevator.

LEO TOOK BOBBY'S elbow and steered him out to the lawn
to the pool area.

"What did you want to talk to me about?" Bobby's
tone was just short of surly.

"Boy, I promised your mother I would look after you.
That job is getting harder and harder. I gave you a job
that a high-school kid could do, and the head of Accounting says you're a slacker with a capital S. You take
three-hour lunches, sometimes don't return. You are over
your allotted vacation time. And if you weren't under
my protection, you would have been fired months ago."

"Yeah, well, since when did you start caring?"

"My God, you are a tiresome boy."

"I'm not a boy. Why does everybody treat me like
a kid?"

"Because you act like a teenager who's had too much
money and not enough responsibility, which in fact is the
case, only you are not a teenager anymore, and you have
no excuses. I'm tired of putting up with you, to be honest. I might like to see if you can live off the dividends
from your stock and that little trust fund you have. I'm
done with you."

"What?" Bobby turned away. Leo saw the panic in
Bobby's eyes.

"You just realized that you wouldn't last a week on
what you draw down from that. Am I right?"

"You're firing me?"

"The minute we get back."

"But…"

"But what?"

"I need a loan."

"A loan? You're kidding. I just fired you and you ask me for a loan? I have to hand it to you kid, you got balls."

"I need it. I'll pay you back."

"How? You don't have a job after next month. You don't have even the minimum skills to land employment at one third what I pay you now, and even if you did, that skank you married will have you broke inside a week." Bobby seemed close to hyperventilating. "What is it? You look like you just soiled yourself."

"I don't have any stock and my trust fund doesn't even pay the rent."

"What do you mean you don't have any stock? Of course you do."

"I had to sell it to Travis Parizzi."

Leo studied the boy-man in front of him, guessed he told the truth, and took his elbow again. "My room, now. You need to tell me everything."

Brenda and Travis, their backs to the corridor, were entering Travis' room when the elevator doors slid open and Leo Painter and Robert Griswold stepped out.

THIRTEEN

THE SUN HAD set hours earlier, and torches and a few dim electric bulbs lighted the area. With the help of the neighborhood boys, Michael had finally finished the repairs on the Toyota HiLux, and now the villagers gathered around the vehicle, waiting. It had taken him hours to do what he could have done in minutes before. He reached in the cab and turned the key in the ignition. It took some doing, but the motor finally coughed to life. The HiLux's engine roared and produced a huge plume of gray exhaust. Michael sat down in a chair in the court yard, grinned, and made an attempt to wave.

"You cannot destroy a HiLux," he said, his voice weak but clear.

The men from the village cheered even as the smoke from the exhaust pipe spread across the ground and drove them back. A beaming Sanderson climbed into the cab and positioned herself behind the truck's cracked steering wheel.

"Drive it," A man shouted. She smiled and put the pickup, her *bakkie*, in gear and let out the clutch. The vehicle lurched forward and steadied. She drove it in a wide circle past the houses and huts that constituted her small village. The headlights wobbled and blinked off and on, but the truck moved. The younger men and women cheered, but some of the older men stood back in the shadows and looked on disapprovingly. It was not the place for a woman to be driving about in such a machine, they seemed to be saying. She pulled up in front of her house, set the brake, but left the motor running. Michael said they needed to be charging the battery.

"We will paint it next," she declared. "I will go to the store and buy a great can of red paint and we will make this a beautiful truck, you will see."

The men, and a few women, walked around the truck, banging on the side panels, squinting at the interior, kicking the tires, and muttering their approval. Mma Michael and her poor son had performed a miracle for certain.

Sanderson sat down next to him and patted his knee.

"I will need your help on this next thing I must do."

"To paint?"

"No, no, I will need you to talk to those old men and the others who know hunting. I must find a bad lion and kill it. It is a thing I do not know how to do. They will listen to you. They will do it for you. I am not so sure they will become hunters for me."

"Mma, you are old-fashioned. They will listen to you."

"It is not I who am old-fashioned. These men are from the days before. They are not ready to listen to this woman. If you ask, they might."

"And they might not."

"Yes, that is so, but if I am the one to ask and I fail the first time, there will be no second. But if you ask, there will always be a chance."

"Mma, this is not necessary. They must hear you. It is the way, now."

"Do this favor for me, Michael. I cannot be taking a risk. If they do not go hunting with me, I am lost. Mr.

Pako is sure I will fail and will report it. I might lose my employment. You must do this for me, please."

Michael nodded and signaled to Rra Kaleke, the oldest and therefore the man held in highest esteem in the village, to come over. The old man approached and saluted them.

"*Dumela, Mma,* Michael, *o tsogile jang?*"

"*Ke teng, Rra Kaleke, tanki.*"

"You wish to speak to me, then?"

"My mother begs you to do a thing for her."

"What sort of a thing?"

"Her boss, Mr. Pako, requires her to hunt a lion and to kill him."

"This Pako, he asks this of a woman?"

"Yes. He is sure she cannot do it, and it will be hard for her if she fails. As you can see, she must not lose her employment."

"That Pako is a foolish man. Hunting *ditau* is not a suitable occupation for women. I am admiring you, Sanderson, but this is a very bad thing for you to be doing."

"Thank you, Rra Kaleke. You are correct, but it is so. I know you and the other men of the village know of hunting lions. I wish you to ask them if they will help in this."

The old man scratched his head. "We have not been permitted to hunt *ditau* for many years. Young people today, they do not know how. We hunted them before. My father used his army issue Enfield to kill a lion, and his father, my *rremogolo,* killed a lion with a *lerumo,* with his spear, you understand? We have hunted the lion for many generations. It is not a thing to take lightly. This Pako must be very stupid. Hunting lions must be done by the man who knows how to do it. It is very dangerous."

He closed his eyes and Sanderson thought he must be traveling back in years to when he was young and alive, before Independence, before the new way of doing things, back when he might have led a party of English hunters into the bush.

"We will meet in the *kgotla* and talk of this, Mma Michael. *Sala sentle."* He nodded, turned, and shoulders back, strode away.

THE MEN OF the village gathered in the *kgotla* later. They sat on an assortment of chairs, some wood, several plastic in a variety of garish colors, and upended crates, Michael sat at their center, Sanderson at the extreme end of the semicircle. A late arrival required her to give up her chair and so she sat on the ground, legs extended.

As he was the oldest, Rra Kaleke assumed the leadership of the group.

"We are being asked by Mma Michael to hunt a rogue lion. This lion has killed a man, and the government wants it removed. She has sensibly asked us to help in this hunt. I ask you, now, Missus, where is this lion doing his killing?"

Sanderson pointed east. "The boy ran into the bush at night near Kazungula."

"When did this take place, and why would he do such a foolish thing?" a tall man with a scraggly beard asked.

"This boy ran into the lion over a week ago. He wished to avoid punishment by the men of his village. They caught him stealing."

Sanderson did not mention that the items the boy stole were now mounted on the truck they'd admired earlier that evening.

"Kazungula is on the other side of Kasane and away

from the park. He will be a Zimbabwe lion, I think." The man said. The others murmured in agreement.

Mr. Naledi, Michael's boss, turned to the assembly. "You are better at hunting than I. You have tracked the lion in your youth. I have not. I speak with respect to you, therefore, but does it not seem that by this time that lion is back in Zimbabwe. Have there been any more reports of him? Are there goats missing, cattle, and other sightings since this event?"

Sanderson shook her head.

"Mr. Naledi says the truth. There is game in Zimbabwe, *dipitse ya naga* and *dikolobe*." The men grunted their agreement. There would, indeed, be zebra and warthogs over the border, impala, too. Game a lion could track and kill.

"Perhaps," a third man said, "but if this lion has been run off by the old man of the pride, he might not be so happy to go back to Zimbabwe so soon."

"You are right there, but if he did or did not, Mma Michael is still burdened with the task of finding him and sending him to his ancestors. We must at least look at the place where the death happened and see," Mr. Kaleke said.

"I can take you there." Sanderson said. The men seemed to hesitate. "Mr. Naledi will drive the truck."

Mr. Kaleke shook his head in approval. "Tomorrow we shall visit the place where the lion killed the man, and then we will see."

The men nodded their heads and disappeared into the night to their homes. One by one the torches guttered out leaving the sky brilliant with stars and a three-quarter moon.

Sanderson was pleased.

FOURTEEN

"SHE WENT INTO his room. She said she had some business to attend to but that's Travis' room. Why did she do that?"

"Pipe down and follow me." Leo steered Bobby down the corridor to his suite.

"I need to go see what she's doing."

"Don't be stupid, son. You know what she's doing. I told you about her before you let your hormones dictate to your brain and went ahead and married her anyway." Leo shoved Bobby toward the couch.

"But—"

"Shut up and listen to me. That woman is nothing but trouble."

"She's okay. It's just…I need to see—"

"Tell me she hasn't spent every dime you've got and some you don't. You stay with that slut and you are doomed. Now, tell me about the stock that Travis Parizzi bought."

"I told you, I sold it to him. I have an option to buy it back, though." Leo stared at the boy and waited. "I can have it back inside a year."

"What's he charging you to take it back?"

"He said there were fees and things. I don't know, transfer fees and stuff. He said I could buy it back for what he paid for it plus ten percent."

"That's a nice return on investment in a year, especially since I bet he squeezed you on the price and he knows you'll never find the funds to do it. Not with that whore you're married to raiding the cookie jar all the time."

"Brenda's not a whore."

"No? Then what's she doing now in Travis' room, playing canasta?"

Bobby slumped down in the sofa and hung his head. His hands dangled between his knees. "I don't know."

Leo lighted a cigar and paced the room. Something was up and he needed to know what. He'd scoped out Farrah's scheme early on and believed he had it under control, tumbled to it early, by God, the dumb suck. But Travis cutting in behind his back, he had not seen that coming.

"What'd he say to you when he asked about the stock?"

"What?"

"I said, what did he say to you then? Did he mention what he wanted it for?"

"Something about a vote. He wasn't very clear. Hell, I don't know. I had debts and at least one loan shark on my case. I needed the money, so I sold it."

"He said a vote. You're sure of that?"

"Yeah, I'm sure, like, there's a meeting coming up soon or something. Maybe it had to do with the IPO."

"And you thought you'd let him play with your stock for a year and then you'd buy it back."

"Well—"

"Shut up and let me think."

"I need to find out what Brenda is doing."

"Sit still. You want to know what she's doing? Put

your ear to the wall. They're next door. But don't you leave this room. I'm not done with you."

Bobby seemed to consider putting an ear to the wall, rose, and then sat down again with a groan. Leo studied the young man on the sofa and scowled. He didn't like Bobby very much. He thought him a fool for marrying the tramp from the night club and an even bigger fool for letting himself fall into the kind of debt he acquired. His promise to the boy's mother notwithstanding, his first impulse was to toss him to the wolves. But as he had learned from one moussed, moronic, motivational speaker, that every failure carries within it the seeds of an equal or greater benefit. Bobby Griswold could be useful at the moment. He would help him.

"Listen to me, boy. Here's what you need to do."

TRAVIS PARIZZI AND Brenda Griswold were within fifteen feet of Leo and Bobby. Had they been aware of that fact, they might have been more discreet. But they were caught up in their own conniving and sublimely unaware of their potential for destruction. Brenda might have discounted the danger, but Travis had been around Leo Painter long enough to recognize it, had he known.

Travis decided the woman could be trusted with what he planned. He did not fool himself about her fundamental dishonesty. She would sell him out in a New York minute, but he also knew she would be driven by self-interest and would work with him as long as the rewards outweighed the consequences.

"It's like this," he said, "Leo is losing his grip. Somehow, he's got it in his head that licensing ActiVox will save the company's copper and nickel division. A down economy doesn't even register on him. 'Cheap nickel

and copper,' he says. 'We capture the market by selling low. Low enough to stay in business until things get
back to normal.'"

"What's that to me?"

"Between us, with the stock I bought from Bobby, we
control enough stock to move him out. I take over the
company, make some restructuring moves, and we jump
into the black. Minerals are dead. Alternate forms of energy are in. This country we're visiting has gas reserves.
We need to be talking to the minister about drilling, not
mining copper and nickel."

"I still ain't heard anything that makes me moist, pal."

"Stay with me, here. I can do this without you, by the
way. You won't have the money in time to buy me out,
and the deal is with Bobby, not you, anyway."

"He'll do what I tell him."

"Yeah? Well, even if you don't get him to go along,
there are other places I can go to get the votes I need."

"Bullshit, Parizzi. You must think I believe in the
Easter Bunny, too."

Travis sighed and wondered if it was even worth the
effort to recruit this woman. But the truth of the matter, it
would be infinitely easier to pull the thing off with Griswold's stock than without it. And there was the problem
of timing. He plunged ahead.

"Do you know Leo's story—how he took over the company?" Travis didn't wait for an answer. "He married Harry
Reilly's daughter to get a job, made a career, then forced
Reilly out and dumped his daughter. He has spent the last
decade trying to buy up the Reilly family holdings. That
old man's dead, and the rest of the family would shoot
Leo on sight if they had the chance. About 10 percent of
the outstanding shares are in their hands, by the way. Leo

has used shadow companies and straw men to get those shares but so far has failed. Did you know that one of the Reilly grandsons works for Leo? His name is Bart Polanski and he's in Engineering. He's staying in this hotel. He will vote the Reilly stock for me if I need it. I have other options out there as well. They all have a cost, but I can exercise them. I will level with you, Brenda. It's easier with Bobby's stock, but even without it, it's doable."

Brenda sat and waited for Travis to get to the part where she could cash out. He stared blinking and then went on, "I'm guessing you want the stock to sell to either someone wanting in before the IPO, or after that, which could produce a big payday for you. Half a payday, if you decided to dump Robert or he decides to dump you."

"Not going to happen, Travis. That kid is, like, a Brenda addict. I can do things for him that makes his brain turn to yogurt, so forget that."

"Still, it's a one-gun bullet. You sell and boom it's over. No more cash cow. I happen to know Bobby's debt profile. It'll all be gone in a week. Dump or not to dump, you end up with zip. Are you with me so far?"

"Like, what do you want from me?"

"First, you need to leave the boy. He's never going to make it for you. He has a trust fund that you go through in a month. He is basically unemployable at any level beyond flipping burgers at some fast food joint. Leo has kept him on as a charity. When I take over, he's toast. And I will take over."

"Not so fast. You know what's in Leo's will?"

"I do. Do you?"

"Yep. When Leo dies, we get a bundle."

"After the public offering, it will be preferred stock

and an income for you. Do you really want to live on dividends? What happens in a down economy when there are no dividends? I'm telling you this now, and nobody else knows this yet, I've seen the books. There are no dividends this year. If the IPO goes through there will be none for the foreseeable future."

"But Farrah said—"

"Henry Farrah is a lawyer. He doesn't know squat about business. That's why Leo is about to bust his balls when we get home."

"But the public offering, the IPO, what about that?"

"It's a maybe. I can't always read Leo, but I think he has something up his sleeve. That's why we need to move fast when we get back to Chicago."

"And the will?"

"There are wills, and there are wills. Do you really think Leo will let the old one he drew up two years ago stand? There is another will, you can count on it."

"What's it say?"

"I don't know. I don't know for sure if there is one, but Leo is sneaky. Don't count on that buzzard sending anything good your way."

Brenda turned the information over in her mind, seemed to make a decision.

"Let's talk about you and me." She leaned back on one elbow on the bed and smiled.

FIFTEEN

HE WAS UPWIND so that the hyenas' scent did not carry to him, but Sekoa sensed them. Every nerve in his diseased body jangled and urged him to move onward. They were tracking him, an easy task for them given his deteriorating physical state. He kept padding along the river until he encountered a fence. He could be cornered there. The hyenas would not attack him as long as he could turn and move. But if he were to stop or be backed up…He shifted his weight from right to left. On his left, the river shimmered and rippled in the moonlight. His instincts told him to stay clear of the water. The crocodiles might be dormant in the dark, and they might not. Knowledge of their habits did not register in the instinctual portion of his brain. On the other hand, swimming he did only *in extremis*. He turned to his right and headed away from the water, following the fence line south. The scent of humans began to fade as he turned his back on the town. The hyenas seemed to be gaining.

After ten minutes of jogging his tuberculosis caught up with him and, gasping for breath, he stopped. Ears up, listening, he faced back the way he'd come. The hyenas had reached the fence and were moving up from the water toward him. He moved forward a few meters and spotted a gap in the fence, probably made by elephants on one of their sojourns into Kasane to forage for fermented morula fruit. He slipped through and back-

tracked toward the river until he met the pack of hyenas
bearing uphill toward him, but on the other side of the
fence. He stopped and faced them, daring them to come
for him. They stared back at him through the steel mesh.
One after another three of the pack charged the fence
and bounced off. One chewed at the links in frustration.
The lion rose and moved further downhill and away from
the gap. The enraged hyenas followed him yipping and
yowling. After a few dozen meters he turned and continued east toward the human smell. He caught the scent
of goats as well. Goats were food.

The hyenas raced along the fence line, half of them
south and the other half north, back toward the river.
Unless some easy prey diverted them, they would find
the gap soon enough and follow. He hoped the proximity of humans would eventually cause them to turn back.

Had Sekoa a sense of irony he might have appreciated the circumstances that sent him to seek protection
from the very beings that, although he and his kind fascinated them, would kill him in a heart beat had they
known he was loose in what passed for their territory.
He trotted on.

LEO HAD BEEN pacing for nearly an hour, asking questions
Bobby couldn't answer and puffing on a seemingly endless series of cigars. Bobby supposed they were expensive. He wouldn't know. He didn't smoke, except for the
occasional joint, and though smoke usually didn't bother
him, by the time Leo fired up another cigar, it began to
take its toll on his respiratory system.

"I gotta go." Bobby stood and headed for the door.

"Stay put. I may need you."

"Can I at least open a window? You're killing me with that cigar fog."

Leo gestured toward a set of French doors and continued pacing. Bobby considered listening at the wall. The hotel may have been one of Gaborone's best, but sound still carried through it.

"Okay, here's what we're going to do."

"We?"

"Just listen. I told your mother I'd take care of you and even though my instincts are to make good on my intention to fire you, I think we can help each other."

Bobby looked hopefully at the man in front of him while straining his ears to make out any sounds from the room next door.

"How?"

"First, you dump that wife of yours."

"Dump Brenda? I can't do that."

"Yes, you can and now is the best time to do it."

"But…"

"Will you stop saying *can't* for once and listen. If you weren't such an idiot, you'd be worth some real money by now, and that little gold-digger would be divorcing you instead. Now, if you divorced she'd get at least half of what you have. But idiotically you stumbled into the perfect set-up. You don't have a dime. Your debts exceed your assets and, as of today, you don't even have a job. She might be awarded some alimony, but with no income and no prospects, she'll be happy to settle for some cash."

Bobby started to say something, but Leo shushed him.

"Then, she might hold out for the stock that you sold to Travis, but since you won't own it anymore, there's not much she can do about that either."

"She said something about knowing what's in your will. She could go for that."

Leo smiled. "She must have been talking to Farrah. That's even better. Wills can always be changed, if you catch my drift." Bobby did not catch his drift or, indeed, much of anything else Leo was saying.

"But just in case she thinks about working the option deal with Travis and collecting, we'll have to take that away from her, too."

"I don't know about an option deal. You mean she'd ask for half of whatever I could sell the...I don't get it. How?" Bobby was warming up to the idea of being free from Brenda, but the thought of being penniless and unemployed still scared him.

"In a minute. You own or rent that condo of yours?"

"Rent, but I don't see..."

"You don't have to. Don't try to think your way through this, Robert. Leave the details to me. What's in the condo? Any valuables?"

"Her jewelry and some art crap she bought."

"She'd get the jewelry in any event." Leo pondered a moment. "Unless we can arrange for a burglary. I'll have to think about that. We'd have to split the proceeds fifty-fifty. I'm not sure it's worth it."

"Split what with who?"

"Never mind. Now, if she goes for the stock, you won't have an option to share with her because I'm going to redeem that stock from Travis before she knows what hit her. Well, actually, you are going to redeem it, but with my money. You will assign it to me first and, for your services, I pay you one hundred thousand dollars. See, you have a deal. So, if she comes sniffing around your financials all she'll find is what's left of the hundred grand. You with me so far?"

"I think so, but—"

"Good. Now, as for the grounds. I guess that's easy enough. She's next door boffing Travis, as far as we know. Sue for mental cruelty, adultery, and fiscal irresponsibility. I'll get you an expensive lawyer, and he'll make her go away cheap and be thankful."

"But we don't know that she's…you know…with Parizzi."

"I'm your witness. If we say she was, she was. We'll say we were suspicious and went out on that balcony and peeked in and caught them *in flagrante delicto,* as the shysters would say, and it's a done deal."

"There's an adjoining balcony?"

"Out those French doors, yes."

Bobby rushed to the doors and worked at the latch.

"Too much noise. You don't want them to know. Here this way." Leo eased the latch, and the two stepped out on the balcony. Eight feet away a matching set of French doors gave in to Parizzi's room. The curtains were not completely drawn, and they peered in.

"You satisfied now?" Leo whispered.

"I'll kill her."

"Shhh, come back inside. We need to put some things on paper."

Once inside Leo's suite Bobby repeated his threat.

"Killing is a really bad idea, son. In the first place, I don't think you have the guts to do it. And even if you did, Botswana is a capital-punishment country and its courts would not be reluctant to hang you, particularly if it deems the crime to have been premeditated. So, unless you can line up a really good hit man, you'd better stick to the divorce court."

"I don't know, I..."

"Just do as I say. Once this is over, I'll find a job for you that you can actually do, and if you work at it instead of slacking, it could even lead to something better. Now, go back to your room and act like nothing happened."

Leo sounded sincere. He always did when he was about to slice and dice, but Bobby didn't know that and smiled his thanks instead.

The part of his brain that had to do with self-restraint was coated with Teflon, and "acting like nothing happened" did not stick.

SIXTEEN

WHEN BRENDA SLIPPED into the room at three A.M., Bobby was sprawled, mouth agape, dozing in the chair by the window. He'd intended to stay awake and confront her when she returned, but as agitated and angry as he'd become, the two double scotches Leo insisted he drink canceled out all of those good intentions. She was undressed and headed for the bed when he awoke.

"Where've you been?"

She stretched and yawned. "I just went to the bathroom. I didn't want to wake you. Sorry."

"You didn't just get up to go. I've been sitting here all night waiting for you. You've been with Travis."

"For a little while, yeah. I'm working on getting the stock back. Frankie at the club set it up so we can get it back. You need that, Bobby. Trust me, I have a deal. You should be thanking me, not hassling me about where I've been."

"That won't wash, Brenda. I…" Leo's admonition to act as if nothing happened caught him up and Bobby shifted his ground. "And you're paying for them, how?"

He rose and stepped close to her. He was not the brightest dude in the world, he knew, but he could tell when somebody has had sex, especially if it wasn't with him.

Brenda hesitated, apparently weighing in her mind what he might or might not know. Finally she took the

approach that had always worked for her in the past.
She went on the offensive. That would be offensive as
a descriptor. "I told you, Frankie set it up. Look, you
dumb bastard—" Brenda didn't finish her sentence because Bobby slapped her. Slapped her hard. She stood,
slack-jawed and unbelieving. Her cheek began to burn.
It wasn't that she'd never been slapped before. Beginning with her alcoholic mother, then her stepfather, and
a handful of men she'd had dealings with in her former
life, she'd had her share of physical abuse, but never before from Bobby. This was something new and poten-
tially dangerous.

Bobby slipped over the edge. "You've been doing
more than talking with Travis."

"No, I…look, Bobby, I've set it up so we can work
a deal where we can get out from under Leo's thumb,
make some real money. Travis will put it together for us."

"For us or for you? Sure he will. Forget it. I'm not
working with that guy. You can have him if you want
him, but not me. I don't need him, so I'm out, you got
it?" He decided not to mention divorce until Leo had
everything nailed down.

"Not you? You are, like so not getting it. He can make
it happen. You can't do squat and—"

Bobby smacked her again. "You slut, you must think
I'm really stupid."

"Stupid isn't the half of it," Brenda screamed and
launched into a tirade so intense and scorching it might
have peeled the wallpaper off the wall, had there been
any. During the course of her diatribe she managed to
include most of the commonly exercised profanities, ob-
scenities—some that seemed to be the exclusive usage
of exotic dancers—and at one point managed to use the

word associated with sexual intercourse as an adjective, noun, and verb all in the same five-word sentence. Had Bobby majored in English in his brief stint in college, he might have appreciated the skill it took to put together this nonstop bit of invective. As he hadn't, and because he had no other place to go with his anger and sense of betrayal, he picked her up, threw her face down on the bed, and acted out at least one of her characterizations of him.

Bobby had played football and lacrosse in school. He still retained some strength and agility in spite of his dissolute lifestyle, and Brenda could only struggle helplessly and scream at him. He shoved her face into the pillows and finished what he started.

A porter, who happened to be cruising the corridor, heard the commotion and started to knock on their door to be sure no one was in trouble, but when he heard what he took to be moans and bedroom activity, he smiled and moved on. That was the room with the hot American tourist, after all.

Travis, one floor up and two rooms over, tossed and turned in his bed oblivious to the commotion he'd manufactured and instead wondered what he'd gotten himself into. Brenda Griswold might not be the best ally for the undertaking he had in mind, and he surely did not want her hanging around after it was over, but he needed to hold on to that stock, and he guessed she would be the price he'd have to pay. At least for the short run.

LEO PAINTER COULDN'T SLEEP. Travis' apparent duplicity hurt. Yet, he didn't know whether to be angry at him or admire his chutzpah. Leo guessed if their positions were reversed, he might be doing the same. Not might, most

assuredly he would. He smiled and checked his watch.
An eight-hour time difference separated Gaborone and
Chicago. It would be a little after six in the morning.
Probably too early to call Baker, the snoop.

He lighted a cigar, puffed twice and stubbed it out. He'd
been smoking all night, and his mouth felt like old burlap.
Even with a good Cuban, taste paled after a while, and
your tongue went to sleep. His doctor had warned him,
"You want to die, Leo, keep on drinking, smoking, and
juggling all those corporate balls." Well, that last part
would be over soon if Greshenko did his job.

He stood and paced some more. He still hadn't heard
from Greshenko. It had been three days, and they were
due to fly to Kasane in twenty-four hours. He pulled out
his map of the Chobe River National Park and the area
nearby from the pile of papers on the desk. There was
an airport and commuter service in and out of Kasane.
More important, its landing strip could handle corporate jet traffic. Perfect. He'd need to build a first-rate
FBO on the field to handle the private planes he figured
would be arriving. He'd have to talk to someone in Jet
Aviation or Signature Flight Support about leasing and
managing it when he did.

He ran his finger across the map following the course
of the Chobe River. There were four main lodges on the
river and several smaller ones. If push came to shove,
he might have to settle for one of the lesser ones, but he
hoped not. The Chobe Game Lodge was probably out of
the running, too, as it sat deep in the park and had limited access. What he wanted was an easy in and out with
a view. The Safari Lodge was near Sedudu Island. That
would work best. He'd discounted the Okavango Delta
for the project. It had more in the way of tourist attrac-

tions and better animals, but was hard to get in and out of and more or less seasonal. Maybe later.

He checked his watch again. Still too early to call. The Bears had made the playoffs. He wondered how they'd fared. Football interested him only slightly. Just enough to hold a VIP box at Soldier Field, which he used to lubricate politicians and potential business associates who could do him favors, provide him with contracts, or introduce him to the people who could. But his real interest was baseball. He followed the Cubs and suffered though the years of disappointments that only true Cubs fans knew. The same sort of VIP arrangement did not work at Wrigley. You had to be a fan. Most pols were into instant gratification.

Watching the Cubs required patience.

SEVENTEEN

DAWN. SEKOA, HIS ravaged lungs gasping for air, approached a small clearing at the edge of the forest. The multiple scents of humans overpowered all others. He paused. This was not an area he would have ever willingly entered in the past. In front of him, a small pile of dirt barely covered buried trash. Farther on, the remains of a fire pit made a black smear on the ground. The ground seemed trampled, and what little grass there was grew in scattered clumps around the edge. He no longer sensed the presence of the menace that had trotted along his trail most of the previous day. Either his nemesis, the pack of hyenas, had not found the break in the fence or, wisely, they had refused to venture this close to humans. Except for elephants, Sekoa feared nothing, and on occasion not even one of them, but humans were a puzzle. He wouldn't have ventured this close, either, except in desperation. He turned toward the river a few meters away. He would drink and then find a resting place and perhaps sleep. His need for the latter made him stumble at the water's edge and that, in turn, attracted the attention of a large crocodile. Much as it might be tempted, it would not attack. At this early hour it needed time to bask in the sun to bring its metabolic rate up to a level sufficient to tangle with prey as large as this.

He found a bower back from the water and collapsed. In the past he would have dozed and awakened peri-

odically to take in any shift in his immediate environment. But so complete was his exhaustion, he would
sleep through the comings and goings of area wildlife,
including the few humans using the facilities in a building no more than fifty meters to the east. His tawny coat
nearly matched the bush seared by the seasonal drought.
To any but the most experienced eye, he was all but in-
visible. He slept.

Leo Painter rose every morning at four-thirty. He would
gulp down the array of pills the cardiologist at Rush
Medical Center prescribed and be at his desk an hour
later. Leo had little use for the doctor whom he referred
to as "the fat quack," but he knew from painful experience that if he skipped them he could expect a bad day
and possibly a trip to the ER. He usually substituted
some pastry and two cups of strong coffee at his desk
for breakfast. He expected his employees to keep the
same hours—at least those who shared offices on the
same floor with him.

    Henry Farrah considered himself a night person.
When he retired, he planned never to get up before nine
in the morning and to dress no earlier than ten. So he
presented himself to Leo at six the next morning bleary-
eyed and annoyed. Leo gestured toward the pot of coffee and tray of pastries on the side table. The odor of
stale cigar smoke nearly made him retch. Henry filled a
cup, wolfed down a croissant, and sipped at his coffee.
He found a chair as far from the ashtray as possible. He
wished Botswana was as diligent in reducing the health
consequences of smoking as it was in its attempt to rid
the country of AIDS and alcoholism.

    "Henry, I need some paperwork done and right away."

Farrah started to protest but Leo waved him to silence. "There should be a business center somewhere in this hotel, and if there isn't, there'll be one in town somewhere."

Henry sighed. It was typical of Leo to impose on and inconvenience his underlings. Henry had a planned visit to Debswana, the diamond sorting center, this morning and had even arranged for a taxi and a tour. That would have to be canceled.

"What sort of paperwork, Leo?"

"I need a bill of sale sort of thing, a transfer of title, maybe, that shows the ownership of Griswold's shares in the company have been assigned to me. It has to be iron-clad, Henry. You understand? I can't have any outside lawyer coming in and finding a way to fiddle with the effect. When you're done, sign it as a witness."

"I can't sign as a witness to something I didn't see."

"Sign it anyway. When I get Griswold up here later you can come back and watch, but I want the thing in place pronto."

"How many shares are we talking about?" Henry knew but asked anyway. Something was up, and he wanted Leo to keep talking. He had a big stake in the events of the next few weeks, and it wouldn't do to be caught on the short end of the information stick.

Leo frowned and pursed his lips. "Write it so it covers any and all. You know what his share total is supposed to be, but he may have acquired more or dumped some since then. So, make it inclusive, Henry."

Farrah nodded and rose. It should be a simple enough matter to frame up a document. Back in the office he'd ask one of junior members to pull some boilerplate off the hard drive and fix it up. Hell, a paralegal could do it. If he got on it right away, he might still make his tour.

"I want a second copy, but leave out the names. When you get that done, check back here. I should have Griswold up and more or less awake by then, if that doxy of his hasn't reduced him to jelly."

Henry opened the door. His mind had already begun to frame the wording for Leo's document.

"One more thing. I'll be calling the States in a few minutes and may have another thing for you to do."

Another thing? Since Henry had thrown in with the consortium of wheeler-dealers in Chicago, he'd become paranoid, perhaps clinically so. Leo, he knew, could never be trusted to tell him the truth except when it served his purpose better than a lie, and Henry doubted very much he'd get much information if he asked. Nevertheless, he tried.

"Another thing? Will this have something to do with the IPO?"

"No."

Henry realized there would be no more information forthcoming and left the room. His next act would to be to call Chicago to find out if they knew if there'd been any new developments. His ulcer started talking to him again.

"WEASEL," LEO MUTTERED to the door as it closed on Farrah. "You'd sell your grandmother to find out what I'm up to. Not going to happen, Bub."

He reached for his Blackberry and speed-dialed Sheridan Baker, his personal snoop and errand boy. What kind of a man has two last names, or two first names, either? Henry James, Nick Charles, Forrest Tucker, Michael Steven Gregory. Weird.

"Yes, Mr. Painter." The wonder of technology, caller ID. "I have the information you requested. But I'm afraid you're not going to like it.'

"Let me be the judge of that, Baker. What have you got?"

"Very well, I found your son. He wasn't at the address you gave me, though, and he doesn't work at the ad agency anymore, either."

"What? Why?"

"They had to let him go. He missed too many days. Called in sick."

"He's sick?"

"Yeah. Listen Mr. Painter, I'm not sure you want the rest of this. Why don't you just let this go? Send the kid some money and drop it."

"Send money? He won't take it from me. He won't let me help him in any way. That's why I sent you out to find him."

"I think he might now. I talked to his significant other, private-like. You can send it to him and he'll see that it gets to Junior."

"He's living with someone. What's she like?"

"You didn't hear me right, Mr. Painter. It's a he, not a she."

"What? Not a woman. I thought you used that idiotic expression to describe the person he's in a relationship with."

"Yes, sir, I did. And you heard the rest correctly, too. You didn't know, you couldn't have known. Your son is gay, Mr. Painter."

Leo dropped into the chair next to the table. The phone seemed to weigh twenty pounds.

"The sickness that cost him his job…?" Leo waited for Baker to answer for what seemed an eternity.

"AIDS, Mr. Painter. I'm sorry. Yeah, he's got it pretty bad. He's getting treatments at a local hospital, and they aren't cheap. The…guy he's living with, his name is Edwin Cavanaugh, Eddie, he's called, and he said they're about out of resources to keep up the treatments."

"You want me to give money to some stranger who… hell, he probably gave the disease to my boy. I'll kill him."

"As near as I can tell…Medical records are hard to get hold of, even harder to read, but it looks like Cavanaugh is AIDS-free, sir. And there's the other thing."

"There's more? What else can there be?"

"Your son is married."

"Married? I thought you said he was gay. How can he be married if he's gay?"

"He's in California, Mr. Painter. He's married to Cavanaugh. Cavanaugh has spousal rights and will inherit if Leo Junior dies. He has Junior's power of attorney as well. You can give him the money. He'll be sure to see your son is taken care of."

Leo held the phone away from his ear and stared at his reflection in the mirror over the dresser. He didn't recognize the haggard gray visage. He took a breath and returned the phone to its functioning position.

"I'll have to call you back. Jesus."

Leo reached into his jacket pocket, withdrew a silver engraved pill box and popped a nitro under his tongue.

EIGHTEEN

BRENDA WOKE SLOWLY and stretched her body full-length, arms extended over her head, toes to finger tips. On any other morning she would luxuriate in that stretch, muscles tight, body humming. But then she remembered last night. She sat bolt upright and looked to her left. No Bobby, empty bed on his side. Where? The room was in shambles, her clothes were scattered across the floor where she'd dropped them when she'd tried to sneak in last night—no, in the morning. Her nightie dangled over the bed post, its straps in tatters. And she was sore. She never got sore down there, hadn't since she was a kid. That bastard Bobby. The assault, that's how she thought of it, and she knew all about assaults—oh yeah. The assault had been rough and lasted for an hour or more. She'd endured it because she had to, because she'd been raised to, because she didn't have any other choices, not yet. But that would change, and soon. She pounded her fists on the mattress and cursed men in general and Robert Scott Griswold in particular. That's how men worked out their frustrations, beat up on women.

She took a breath and collected her wits. The residue of stale drinks and sex assailed her. She needed a plan. As soon as she worked the deal with Travis and they'd cashed in, she'd file for divorce and clean Bobby out. She'd see to it he got nothing. She'd take her share and his, too. And alimony…oh yeah, he would pay big time for what he did to her. She shook her head. Her blond hair whipped her face. She needed a shower. She slipped out of bed and stumbled to the bathroom and stood under the hot water until she finally felt clean. She stepped out and toweled off and slipped on her robe.

The worst part of what had to go down in the next couple of weeks? She'd have to be nice to Bobby, the creep, at least until the deal was done. He wasn't going to be asked to join Mensa anytime soon, the dumb ox, but he could be sneaky, and last night he showed he could be rough, too. He'd have to be kept calm and flexible. That's the word, like plastic man or something. Bend but don't break. Hell, she'd been doing that, like, all her life.

Bobby hinted that something new had been added to the mix, something to do with Leo. If Leo was in the game, look out. She'd need to find out what that was all about. She could do it. She knew how. She'd get him to feeling guilty about last night, remind him he owed her from before when he'd had the accident, and then she'd seduce him and when he was turned to mush…oh yeah, she'd find out.

She made a mental list: 1) Call Travis and tell him to cool it for a while. Maybe they could get some time together up in Kasane. Bobby would probably get drunk up there. He always had at least one fall-down most weeks. 2) Call Frankie at the club and see if he would wire the money to her so she could pay off Travis right away. That would lock it up pretty good. It would cost, but what the hell. And 3) She needed a massage and a spa treatment.

She called the front desk to set up the spa date first.

SANDERSON MET WITH the village men at the *kgotla* as the sun cleared the trees in the east. Pako had authorized the use of the old Land Rover. He didn't waste her time with admonitions about the care and safety of the vehicle, as he would have done in the past. Apparently, his mind focused on his new assignment, probably. She pulled up at the edge of the low wall that defined the *kgotla* and walked toward the group of men. They were carrying weapons of some sort. One had an old Enfield rifle, contraband, and she should have to report it, but she wouldn't, not just yet, anyway. The rest had spears or heavy clubs.

"I do not think that you will need those weapons today," she said. The men shuffled their feet.

Rra Kaleke, as the eldest and, therefore, presumed wisest and their leader, stepped forward. "You cannot be so sure, Mma. That lion, if that is what we are seeking, may be close by. If he was successful once in that area, he may think he will be again. And if it is the leopard, well, he will be there, too."

Sanderson realized there was no point in arguing with them. Carrying a weapon made a statement about manhood. She just hoped the rifle stayed out of sight.

She climbed back into the Land Rover, the men climbed into the bed of the Toyota pick-up and, with her in the lead, they bounced out of the village common area and onto the road to Kazungula. It was a fifteen-minute drive. Sanderson had not thought through how she would approach the hunt. There would have to be one. Mr. Pako would not let it rest until there was. The big hotel lodges in Kasane insisted on it. A predatory big cat that had tasted human flesh posed a threat to their guests; even though it was unlikely that a lion, even a maneater, would venture that close to the town, an attack had occurred, a man had been killed, and something must be done. Pako said there were procedures to

follow. She had never heard of them, but then there had
not been a lion incident in the area in her memory, so
that could be the reason.

She slowed when the two vehicles reached the spot in
the road where Lovermore Ndlovu had dashed into the
bush. She signaled the truck to follow her, and she turned
in and followed the tracks she'd made the previous week
through the grass to the spot where the body had lain.
The truck pulled up behind her and the men piled out.

Rra Kaleke led them to the spot that Sanderson
pointed out.

"This is a very old track." He squatted and studied
the ground. "See, this spoor is almost covered with all of
the other animals who have come to share in this meal.
Not so many as in the park, no, but some. I don't see any
dipheri." The men peered over his shoulder and agreed.
There were no hyena tracks.

"They will not come so close to the people, I think."
He studied the tracks some more. "It is a young lion,"
The others nodded again.

The men walked slowly away from the spot search-
ing for more tracks. "Here," one called. "Here is where
he slept his meal away." The men crowded around the
place where the tough grass had been flattened.

Rra Kaleke turned to Sanderson. "I am thinking this
bad lion returned to Zimbabwe, Missus. See these paw
prints? They are headed east toward the road and the
border is just over there." He waved in the general direction of the border hut where the flags of Botswana
and Zimbabwe fluttered above the crossing site. "Even
if we wanted to, we cannot follow him over there. The
Zimbabwe people will have to shoot your lion."

Sanderson was crestfallen. Pako would not accept

that, she was sure. He wanted her to fail and he wanted that failure to be public. He would not accept this reasonable explanation.

Kaleke seemed to read her thoughts. "If you want, Mma, we can go find another lion and kill him for you. That should make the men at the tourist hotels and your Mr. Pako happy. This lion will not be coming this way again soon, you know. There are *dipitse ya naga* over there. If this *tau* keeps clear of the old fellah who chased him away, he will not come back to this place."

An abundance of zebras, as Kaleke said, was problematic. But he had it right. The lion would not try to cross the busy highway into Kasane again. He would stay across the border. She could not accept their offer to kill a random lion just to please or confound her boss. She would have to figure out a different story to placate Pako until he left for his new post. What his replacement would want was another thing entirely.

"No, we cannot kill another lion, Rra, but, if you will do another thing for me, I will be very grateful. Will you hunt this lion for a few days as if the spoor led in the opposite direction?" The men looked at her quizzically. "It is important that the lodge owners feel something is being done and the situation is under control."

"We would like to help you, Mma Michael, but to do that is a waste of our time," Naledi said.

"But you will be hunting legally. Who knows what you might stumble on while you look for the *tau*?"

"Ah, you think we may have to remove some beasts from this area that could be considered a problem? You think by reducing the possible food supply, this bad lion will have to show himself, if, of course he is still here?"

"You never know, with lions," she said.

The men smiled. They had not hunted in many years. Fresh meat would be a blessing.

"We will help you out in this undertaking for a week, Missus," Kaleke said. "That should keep that Pako satisfied." The others nodded in agreement.

NINETEEN

"HE'S NOT HERE." Brenda sounded angry. Had the boy actually done something? No, not likely. She added that she didn't know where he was and didn't care, either. Of course not.

Leo hung up, put on his jacket, and headed out the door. He patted his jacket pocket where he'd secured Farrah's documents, neatly folded into thirds. Bobby would be in the restaurant or the bar, more than likely. He'd find him soon enough. But first he had to go to Barclay's Bank and retrieve the check, spelled *cheque*, as the message from the desk had it, from the wire transfer he'd arranged with Chicago's First National. Leo had anticipated the need for a bank to work with in Botswana, especially with the project he had contracted Greshenko to spearhead for him, so he'd opened an account at the large international bank earlier. Transferring the funds had been simple enough.

Farrah had convinced him to change his mind about the dates on the documents and had him leave them blank. Probably just as well. The more he thought on the maneuver he and the boy were about to make, the more he wondered if he shouldn't slow down, take a step back, and rethink the whole thing. He didn't like the boy, and he was angry at Travis for playing Brutus, but that didn't mean he had to destroy them, not yet, anyway. He found his car and driver waiting for him at the hotel's entrance. He slid into the back seat with a grunt and gave the driver his destination. The Volvo pulled away and headed downtown. As often as he'd visited London and other drive-on-the-left countries, he still had a hard time getting used to it. He settled back in the seat, flinching every time the car turned into what his instincts told him was the wrong lane. He retrieved a cigar from his inside pocket, studied it and put it back. It held no appeal. He was tired. He didn't sleep well the night before, or anytime for that matter, and he felt old. His workload was killing him. That's what the quack said. Hell, he probably had it right.

If only…

How many men whose hearts can no longer be relied on and who, therefore, face a possible early and unpredictable end had uttered those words over the years? If only.

His phone vibrated in his pocket. It was not the Blackberry that he required all his employees to use, but one he'd purchased locally and which he used only for communicating with Greshenko.

"It's about time I heard from you. What have you got for me?"

"Several things you need to think about before we make any more moves."

"Go ahead, and please don't tell me we have trouble already. I just wanted you to make some contacts, set up appointments with the people who can make this project happen."

"No trouble in that department, at least not yet, Mr. Painter. That's not it."

"What then?"

"First, I spotted what I think must be a policeman on

my tail. He was with me from the time we arrived and ever since. He knows where I've been and to whom I've spoken. Is that a problem for you? It is for me. Police, any police, make me nervous."

"I don't know. Should it be?"

"We need to find out what he's after us for, I think. He was in Kasane waiting for me after I drove up here."

"He followed you?"

"I don't think he followed. He was here when I arrived. He must have flown up."

"He knew where you were headed?"

"Apparently. He must have talked to some of the people I met in the city, and they must have told him enough to figure out what my next step would be. But that doesn't explain why he's on my tail in the first place."

"I can't help you there. Use your contacts and find out. I want this thing to go through without a hitch. What else?"

"I'm having trouble meeting with Botlhokwa. He has layers of people around him, and getting through to him is difficult."

"I thought you knew him. What's different now?"

"That was a long time ago and before he slipped to the dark side, you could say."

"Do what you have to do, but be careful that if you spend money, you get value received."

Leo closed the phone and stared at the scenery as it flashed by. He was in an emerging country, that much was certain. The contrasts amazed him. He admired a shiny new glass and steel multistory building and noted the herd of goats grazing near its entryway. An enormous tractor trailer, larger than anything he'd seen in the States, a twenty-six wheeler, if he'd counted the axles correctly, blew by a crudely assembled wagon drawn by a troika of donkeys. Slick Japanese cars vied with battered pickups for parking spaces. And the road was lined with shacks, sheds, and rickety tin constructions in which entrepreneurs plied their trade—roast chicken for sale, haircutting, even a car wash that consisted of a man and a bucket of soapy water. Amazing. And all this juxtaposed against new high-rises and modern stores and shops. Every nation should have that sense of willingness to work at whatever was available. His country, he thought sourly, had too many people who were addicted to entitlements. They should see these people. He could work with them. He could build something with them.

SUPERINTENDENT MWAMBE TRIED hard not to show his annoyance. He did not like this member of the Gaborone establishment poking around in his jurisdiction. This man from the Directorate of Intelligence and Security, this Kgabo Modise, asked too many questions about his situation. What did he want? Mwambe had been at this post for many years. Longer than Modise had been a policeman or with the CID, he suspected. Too often these officials from the capital came to Kasane to inquire about things—things he could handle without their help. Now this man sat across his desk with an open notebook in his lap.

"What do you know about the Rra Botlhokwa?" Modise asked.

"He is a resident of this city in the winter. I believe he summers on a wine estate near Cape Town, or possibly it's a condo in Mauritius. We have reason to believe he is connected with some illegalities, but so far we have nothing to report. I have a man watching him." Superintendent

Mwambe sat back and graced the man from Gabz with a superior smile. He knew his job.

"He is more than that." Modise flipped though his notebook. "I assume you know he started out as a bright light in the country. Went into business instead of government. He has played fast and loose on the fringes of the diamond trade, perhaps dabbling in the darker markets. He has interests in hotels and casinos and some across-the-border enterprises that we are looking into. The Directorate on Corruption and Economic Crime has been closing the noose on him for some time. He was the first man in the country, black or white, to own a Rolls Royce. Of course you know all of this."

Mwambe didn't, but he was not about to admit it to the man from Gabz.

"The man you have watching him, he is good?"

"He is being trained by me personally. Yes, he is good."

"I found him asleep in his car this afternoon. He missed an important visitor to the chalet."

Mwambe straightened up. "What visitor?" There would be no reason to dispute the inspector's finding. If he said Derek was asleep at his post, it was so. He'd been given that assignment precisely because he was rubbish at everything else.

"We are interested in this man." He slid the photograph of Yuri Greshenko across the desk. Mwambe squinted at the picture. He did not recognize him.

"Reason?"

"He worked for the Soviets, which is what they were then, as a commercial attaché at the Russian embassy. That was when their presence in this country was highly problematical."

"Problem…what?"

"The Soviets provided a safe haven for the ANC/SA Communist Party. Gaborone was their listening post for the whole area, and Greshenko's countrymen provided a springboard for the Eastern Bloc which supported MK Freedom Fighters to infiltrate into South Africa. It was not a good time in our history."

Mwambe nodded. He remembered vaguely the bombings and Botswana Defense Force having to deal with insurgents from across all of its borders, particularly south and west. He'd been a young man then, but he remembered.

Modise went on, "So, now he returns as a member of an American party that is consulting the ministry about minerals. We do not think he has any interest in minerals."

"What then?"

"That is what we desire to find out. Interpol has identified him as a possible agent of the Russian criminal consortium. He had dealings with Botlhokwa in years past. Now he seeks him out again. If this business is to combine his American connections with the corrupt ones here, then we must take steps to see to it he leaves this country in pretty short order. If, on the other hand, his presence in an American delegation is something else, we need to know what that is, as well."

"What do you want me to do?"

"Put your nephew, Derek, on traffic duty or some task he cannot turn into *monontsha*."

Mwambe flushed and started to reply, then thought better of it. This man was from Gabz, after all. Mwambe had no interest in being reassigned to a lesser station like his friend Pako, and Derek's lack of competence could not be made into something it was not.

"I will put a detail on the house immediately." Kgabo Modise seemed satisfied. But was he?

"*No mathata,*" he added with more confidence than he felt.

TWENTY

BOBBY WAS STILL not in his room when Leo returned to the hotel. He would have liked to have the paperwork transferring the stock completed before they flew to Kasane, but it could wait. Patience was the one virtue that had sustained him over the years, and he would not press. He'd discovered in his years of running a company as complex as Earth Global that delay worked to his advantage more often than urgent action. His grandmother used to say things had a way of working out. For her it was an excuse to do nothing. For Leo, the axiom meant wait until the time was right, until all the other players had tipped their hand, until he knew beyond any doubt that he possessed a real chance for success, then act.

He called Sheridan Baker. It would be late, but he paid him a great deal of money for his services, and he assumed Baker would be there for him. Leo had him repeat what he'd told him about his son's condition. He needed to be sure.

"You're positive about the power of attorney? This Cavanaugh guy can execute business transactions on my son's behalf? If I wire money to him, he can pay the boy's bills, write checks, any kind of decision about expenditures and so on, all that?"

"Yes, sir, he can."

"Good, here's what I want you to do."

Leo laid out a series of steps he wished Baker to take,

papers he wished to be drafted, signed, and next-day mailed to his private box in Chicago with copies faxed directly to him, and finally an admonishment that absolute secrecy cover the whole business.

He sat back. He felt better. He called room service and asked for a pot of coffee and some pastry to be brought to his room. He then called for valet service to come and help pack his bags. He smiled for the first time in weeks. He could enjoy that cigar now.

THE GULFSTREAM V SEEMED empty with the reduced passenger load. The engineers and technical staff had all been sent home to Chicago, Denver, or Phoenix to prepare reports about what they'd learned and recommendations they might suggest if and when Earth Global determined it needed or could offer a presence in the country. The group traveling north to Kasane consisted of Rose Hayward, one of the engineers, Travis Parizzi, the Griswolds, Leo, and Henry Farrah.

Leo let his gaze roam over them all. Brenda had made a point of sitting away from her husband and was seemingly rapt in a fashion magazine. It was French, and he doubted she could read it, but then her only interest would be in the pictures. Bobby dozed in his seat, looking a little worse for wear. Farrah seemed nervous. He should be. Leo insisted he remain in the party, primarily to make it difficult for him to stay in contact with his co-conspirators. As long as Leo kept him under his thumb, his actions were limited. Time enough to drop the hammer later. Let him squirm. Travis stood and worked his way forward to take a seat opposite Leo.

"Leo, what happened to that consultant you hired… what's his name, Greshenko?"

He knew the name very well. Leo waited for what came next.

"I don't mean to tell you how to run your business, but—"

"Travis, you understand I pay you a great deal of money as my chief operating officer precisely because I want you to tell me how to run my business. What is it you're bursting to tell me?"

"Greshenko, did you know that he's Russian mafia?"

"I hope you didn't spend a lot of money to obtain that information." Leo was sure that he had. "I could have told you, if you had asked." The lines around Travis' eyes tightened marginally. Good, Leo thought, he realizes he's been trumped. There is still some hope to salvage this guy. "Why is that a problem?"

"Sir, it seems odd. Well, what can he be doing? I mean he's a crook."

"Ah, you are worried our reputation might be compromised if we are seen cavorting with alleged criminals?"

"Something like that, and I'm not sure alleged quite covers it."

"Travis, something like one third of the companies and CEOs we've dealt with in the past twenty years have been investigated or indicted by grand juries and a few even convicted of felonious behavior involving various borderline practices, insider trading, and outright consumer fraud. And that's not counting the misdemeanors and back door deals with regulators. Do you really think having a Russian with a wonky past temporarily on our payroll will remarkably change our public image?"

"Sir, I—"

"Rose Hayward is back there yakking to the stringers from all the press news services about all the wonderful things we might do for Botswana. Most of the public remembers what happens to them when there is an energy crisis, when the price per barrel of crude skyrocketed, and assumes we are robbing them blind and ought to be put in jail no matter what we do now or who we have on our payroll. They see us as predators, no, make that scavengers, hell, either or both will do. It depends on whether we're tearing up new land or reworking the old."

"I see but—"

"They may be right, by the way. We do make a lot of money exploiting resources we had no hand in creating. They think if it's in the ground or comes from the Almighty they ought not to have to pay through the nose to acquire their fair share. You have a problem with that line of thought?"

Travis started to reply and then must have thought better of it. He nodded. Leo couldn't be sure if he nodded because he agreed with the line of thought, with his overarching assessment, or just to be polite. It didn't matter.

"He'd know about ActiVox, of course. We could say something about that."

"We could. Very shrewd, but that's not why I brought him along. That process has departed this country and is buried deep in the Russian bureaucracy for the time being. There are problems in the economy, difficulties in distribution, and so on, and the Russians have taken it home for now." He shifted in his seat. "Enough about our Russian employee. As my COO, give me your thoughts on our move to acquire or license ActiVox. It is the scavenging end of the business, you see."

Travis scratched his chin and frowned. Leo studied his face for a sign. Oh, please, do not turn out to be a weasel, talk to me.

"I gather you think there is money to be made in some of the depleted mines we operate."

"Possibly, yes."

"It would be an undertaking with low profit margin."

"And the problem with that is…?"

"We normally work on a minimum of 15 percent net return on investment. This would be more like five, maybe less. The demand is not there, as you just noted. The bones may be picked clean."

"I grew up in the world that believed in two simple maxims, Travis. First, there is no such thing as a free lunch, and second, you'll never go broke taking a profit. Fifteen or five, money is money."

"Yes, surely. But if we were to put the funds we'd commit to the mines to some other venture, one with a better return, wouldn't it make sense to follow that?"

"It would, except for one thing you haven't thought of."

"And that would be?"

"The miners, the employees we have, the subs, the suppliers, and the whole array of resources we use to make money from those mines. If we shut them down and go haring off after some short-term cash-out, when it comes time to reopen the mines, the whole infrastructure will be gone. We'd have to rebuild it. That will cost. But if we continue to operate at some level, then when the demand for minerals returns, and it will, we will be ahead of our competition. It is not part of the corporate ethic anymore, but I still would like to think we owe the people who provide us with large profits in the good times a chance to stay above water in the bad. Especially if we can make some money when we do."

"I never figured you for a sense of altruism, sir. You're

worried about the miners and their families? That comes as a surprise."

"I see. You might just find I am full of surprises." Leo shrugged, graced Travis with a crooked smile, and continued. "And then, don't forget there's the real estate involved with the mining operations. I want to keep our options open on the lands whether we eventually close the mining operation down or not. Now, go back to your seat and think about what we just talked about. When we get to Kasane, we will talk again and discuss where you fit into the big picture."

If Travis felt a twinge of panic at this last remark, Leo thought he hid it well. He leaned forward and retrieved a sheaf of papers from his briefcase. Touching the tip of a pencil to his tongue he began totting up a column of figures. Travis took the hint and took a seat further back in the plane. Leo was enjoying himself.

TWENTY-ONE

BRENDA TRIED TO catch Travis' eye as he made his way aft. He nodded toward her snoring husband and shook his head. Once again he wondered what he'd gotten himself into by taking on Brenda as an ally. And what was Leo trying to tell him? He'd hinted that he might know something, but did he? If he did, he had to have talked to someone and that could only have been one of the Griswolds. He doubted it was Bobby, not that the kid wouldn't talk, but he didn't think he had sufficient brain power to grasp the significance of what Brenda and he planned to do. Besides, everyone knew that he and Leo were anything but close, and he would likely have no objection to seeing the old man taken down. That left Brenda. Would she have gone to Leo figuring there might be a bigger payday working with the top dog? With Brenda, anything was possible. He'd need to find out somehow.

He realized he had a dilemma to resolve. As exciting as another physical liaison with Brenda might be, he really needed to maintain some distance. The thought of being in proximity to her for any but the briefest interval set off all the alarm bells in his survival system, a system that had served him well in the past. And it didn't just involve the possibility of her husband finding out. No, women like Brenda were leeches. If they attached themselves to you and you weren't careful, didn't pull them off, they would bleed you dry. Still, there were worse ways to extract information. He pushed the image of a naked Brenda out of his mind. He'd deal with her later. At this moment, he had to assume that Leo might be on to him. He needed to shore up his position and make it unassailable. And that meant keeping Brenda and all the baggage she brought along.

He looked back at his boss, who seemed to be working out the arithmetic on a fresh sheet of paper. Like Leo, he had some adding up to do, as well. Griswold's shares were firm. Whether Brenda could raise the money to redeem them or not would be immaterial. If she didn't they were his. If she did and held them, he'd be sure she voted them his way. Either he'd have to keep the illusion of intimacy going until after the vote or persuade her she'd end up back on the street with nothing if she didn't. In the end, it didn't matter if she was loyal or trustworthy; Brenda would go along. Greedy people could be relied on in the short run. After that? So long, Brenda.

Added to Griswold's, there were his shares acquired over the years through the company's ESOP and the ones he'd bought subsequently from brokers eager to sell at a lower than market price as part of odd-lots. Then he had the proxies from board members he'd quietly picked up over the past months, and finally, the Reilly family shares. They would be the game breaker. Even if Brenda couldn't control her husband and bolted, he'd have what he needed. It would be close, razor thin, but he could still make it happen. Nothing Leo could do could stop it. He sat back in the leather captain's seat and relaxed. Done deal. What had Leo said? *Meet again and discuss where I fit into the big picture.* I think the reverse is what you need to be thinking about, old man. He signaled to the flight attendant and asked for scotch-rocks. He hoped Leo noticed.

THE GRAY MONKEY had been moving about the area for several hours. He'd tried begging for hand-outs near the lodge restaurant and attempted a grab-and-run from a table of late breakfasters. He'd been chased off by a cook wielding a meat cleaver. He'd swung over to the Sedudu Bar to see if any chips or a part of a sandwich had been left on a table from the night before. Even a half-filled bottle of beer would have been a welcome treat. He knew from past experience that his chances of finding one or the other were reasonably good. Today, however, he would be disappointed. He paused and surveyed the area, then scampered westward past the empty campground toward a stand of trees that hung over the river bank. Skimmers regularly visited the area. There might be a new bird's nest up there, and he could steal eggs or hatchlings. He was halfway up a vine when the corner of his eye registered the image of the lion. The resultant rush of adrenaline rocketed him into the tree's upper limbs and safety.

He hid behind a leafy frond and studied the big cat. He knew that if he had missed seeing it and wandered too close, he would have been that animal's next meal. Cats ate his kind. Some hunted them. The leopard could follow him into the tree if it chose. This cat, he knew was not a climber. A younger lion might try but probably would not.

The lion did not move. He broke off a dry branch and dropped it, hitting the lion on its side. Nothing. No movement, not so much as a twitch. He dropped another, larger stick. Still nothing. Curiosity has killed many more monkeys than it has proverbial cats. The monkey cautiously worked his way downward. When he found a limb about a meter above the lion, he positioned himself on it, snapped a large branch from the tree, and poked the lion in the ribs.

In one fluid, tawny, motion Sekoa cleared the ground, pirouetted, and swiped at the monkey, which escaped sure death from its claws by centimeters. Sekoa stood, and let out a terrifying rumble that seemed to rise from somewhere deep inside. It ended abruptly with a hacking cough. Blood dripped off his chin. He looked angrily at the monkey, who by then had managed to find a precarious perch in the topmost branches and sat chattering; all thoughts of eggs and hatchlings erased from his consciousness.

The lion dropped back to the ground and huffed his displeasure. He would liked to have pulled the monkey down from the tree. His hunger now caused him nearly as much pain as his diseased lungs. He licked the blood from his paws and stared off toward Sedudu Island and contemplated a herd of red lechwe grazing among a dozen elephants. Finally, his massive head dropped and he drifted off to sleep.

The monkey made its way limb-to-limb to an adjacent tree and edged carefully to the ground. He made a wide circle around Sekoa and galloped back to the hotel. A cook brandishing a meat cleaver posed a lesser threat to him than an angry and hungry lion.

TWENTY-TWO

THE PLANE'S DOOR whooshed open and the copilot had the stairs down while the twin jet engines' whine still carried across the tarmac at Kasane Airport. Brenda managed to be the first out, her BVLGARI sunglasses perched stylishly on the top of her head, her miniskirt flashing a bit more thigh than was usually seen in this part of the world. She seemed disappointed that there were no photographers. She'd expected a dozen or more when they'd landed in Gaborone and was amazed when there were none and she'd missed her chance to be featured on the front page of one, or more, of the country's newspapers. She didn't want to miss out this time. The absence of photographers, official greeters, indeed anybody of significance, annoyed her greatly. The shuttle from the Safari Lodge waited a short distance away and next to it sat an elderly SUV and an official-looking Volvo.

She turned to speak to Travis, who'd followed her up the aisle and whom she assumed would be close behind her, only to discover the next person off the plane was a man she recognized as one of the engineers. One who had not been sent home apparently but instead had managed to talk himself onto the plane for the ride north. He stepped around her, turned back, gave her a complete once-over, and with a grin that would pass as a leer in another age, walked to the shuttle. She smiled back and pushed her sunglasses down on her nose. After the air-conditioned chill of the Gulfstream's interior, the heat and humidity nearly knocked her down. She rooted around in her purse and found her cologne. She spritzed her neck and cleavage. It didn't help, but it did seem to entertain the engineer.

Leo exited the plane next and nudged her forward. "Don't dawdle, Brenda. We're scheduled for a river game cruise in a few hours and then dinner. You don't want to miss out on that."

Bobby, his eyes still crusted with sleep, nearly tripped coming down the steps. Travis hung back. She waited another few seconds and then followed the group to the shuttle. Leo, she noticed, veered off toward the SUV. A man she remembered as having been on the plane for the flight from Chicago, the Russian, stepped out of the vehicle and greeted him. They spoke briefly, and then Leo climbed into the right front seat, the man the left, and they drove away. Moments later the Volvo followed.

Travis fell in beside her and murmured something about staying cool. Not very likely in this heat.

"No, I mean keep your distance. Bobby is suspicious, I think, and could cause trouble. And Leo suspects something, too. I don't know what, but if he figures this thing out, we could have some difficulties."

Brenda stopped and faced him. "I thought you said this was in the bag. Anyway, I got options."

"You have nothing, Brenda. You go blabbing to Leo and he'll shred you like a wood chipper. He can bring a lot of not-nice folk down on you."

"Yeah? Like who?"

"Hired muscle, private eyes, and police. He makes really big contributions to all kinds of Chicago heavy hitters. They'd have your past plastered all over the front pages of the local papers and TV, and that's just for starters. Some of your former colleagues at the Golden Cage would not be happy with you, either, and you can imagine how they'd react to being shut down by Vice."

"Let them try. There's stuff I know that could send a lot of divorce lawyers humping up to the North Side in a hurry."

"Brenda, don't go there. Believe me, you do not want to get into a pissing match with Leo. Stick close to me, and when he's just the ex-CEO, we can have our fun."

Brenda couldn't be sure if Travis was blowing smoke up her skirts or not. Did he say that because he didn't trust her to stay in place, or he was on the level? She'd have to think about that.

"We gotta talk, Travis."

"Okay, but wait for my cue."

Brenda didn't like that idea either, but let it pass. She'd give it a day, two at most, but no more. Then she'd make her move. The party, minus Leo, piled into the van. She wondered where Leo was driving to. How come he didn't go with the rest of them, and what was up with that guy he was with?

Things were getting fishy. And then there was Bobby to contend with. Sheesh.

LEO SHIFTED HIS bulk on the front seat. The SUV had a bad exhaust system, and if the windows hadn't been rolled down, fumes would have quickly filled the cab.

"This has to be the only left-hand drive in the country. What is this thing, anyway?"

"It's and old LADA NIVA. Used to belong to a Russian delegation in Congo. They ran out of options. It cost too much to ship it out, so they left it. Some enterprising person here bought it. I have a certain sentimental feeling for it."

"Well, I like it. Feels like home. Isn't it tricky driving on the left with the steering wheel on the left, too?"

"It takes some getting used to. Remember, I'm European, sort of. We have to adjust as we travel."

"Okay, so fill me in. I can only talk on the way to the lodge. We will have to do the serious business tomorrow. How successful were you with the big man?"

"Something is not right, Mr. Painter. There are things happening here that I do not understand."

"What do you mean, something is not right? What's happening?"

"Well, for one thing we are still being followed."

"What? Now? Here? Is it the same guy you told me about?" Leo swiveled in his seat and tried to make out what was behind them.

"The funny part is they are not even trying to hide it. It's not a police car, mind you, but the way it has been hounding me I think it is safe to say it is CID or DIS. And lately, there has been a police car nearly everywhere I go. They stay three or four car lengths behind me, every day, all day. It's like they want me to know they're there."

"CID, DIS?"

"Criminal Investigation Department, Directorate of Intelligence and Security."

"Why would they want to do that? It doesn't make any sense."

"It does if they want to keep me, to keep us, from meeting with Botlhokwa. That old fox won't let us get closer than a kilometer if he thinks we'll bring the police down on him."

"That's it?"

"That or the government wants to make sure that I, perhaps we, don't embarrass them or the U.S. by mixing in where we don't belong. You are a guest of the country, after all."

"What can we do? I haven't come all this way to go home empty handed. Would spreading some money around help? I've made arrangements for that eventuality."

"These people are not easily corrupted, Mr. Painter. But perhaps...Here's your lodge. I'm staying at the Mowana Safari Lodge further down the road. I'll ask around and see if we can set up a meeting with a go-between in some out-of-the-way place. We just need to assure Botlhokwa we aren't wearing a wire, as you say in your detective shows, and any conversations we have are off the record. Reserve seats on as many game drives tomorrow as you can. I'll see if one or more of their people can be in the same areas on the route, and we can make at least a preliminary contact."

"How can you, or they, possibly know where we'll be on a drive? They tell me the park is about the size of Rhode Island."

"The guides talk to each other on radios. There is one pride of lions close by, and they almost always converge on it if one or another spots it. Tourists love taking pictures of lions. There is a chance we can use that as a starter."

Leo hoisted himself out of the passenger side and walked to the lobby as the shuttle pulled in. He left the details of checking everyone in to Rose Hayward.

"Listen up, everybody," she shouted. "The management has asked me to make these quick announcements. First, stay away from the river bank. There are spots

where the embankment is steep and people have slipped
into the water. There are crocodiles and they have been
known to attack people. Okay, second, there was an accident a short while back and a lion attacked a man."
There was a general murmur among the group. "Anyway,
the manager says they had to close their campground
temporarily. Apparently tenters and caravans are permitted to park somewhere around here, but they closed
that down until they catch the lion. Also, be very careful walking about at night. If you must go outside, stay
on the walkways and in lighted areas. And, finally, he
says to keep the sliders and windows closed and locked.
The area monkeys have been known to enter a room and
trash it looking for food and so on." It was not clear what
and so on covered.

In actuality, the Safari Lodge consisted of several
buildings. The main lodge had some rooms, shops, a
bar and lounges, as well as the dining area that stretched
across about one-fourth of its width. Below that, facing
the river were a large concrete esplanade with tables
and a modest swimming pool. To the west were several
structures designed to resemble rondevals, but their outward appearance was all they had in common with the
native huts. Inside were baths, air-conditioning, and soft
beds. In addition the lodge had built about a half dozen
multibedroom chalets, and beyond them were two buildings constructed much like two-story American motels
with perhaps a dozen rooms in each with doors opening
onto a walkway and small decks with sliding glass doors
facing the river. Each room had a large bed, a place to
hang clothes behind it, and a separate shower and water
closet. The end rooms had an extra, small bedroom attached as well.

Leo left the rest, and key in hand, marched away from the lobby area across wooden walkways toward the separate buildings. The path took him through a valley, and he noticed that the trees that pierced the deck near the lodge were, in fact rooted in the earth below it. His room was located in the far end building, and he was puffing from the exertion when he found it.

A man-eating lion! What a great bit of theater for the tourists. You had to admire these guys; they sure knew how to sell their product. He'd need to keep that in mind. His accommodation was on the ground floor and one of a series of similar rooms in a building that had two floors and that offered a view of the river. There was a small balcony at the rear with a sliding glass door, probably the one the monkeys were fond of.

He'd want to know the locations of the rest of the party eventually, but for now, this would do nicely.

TWENTY-THREE

BOBBY FOUND A small refrigerator in the room and he stocked it with beer. He had his third of the afternoon nearly downed when Brenda returned from the gift shop.

"Look at what I bought." She held a large bag aloft. Bobby swallowed more beer and grunted. He was feeling a little numb which was the state he'd been trying to achieve since they left Gaborone. Getting mellow eased the mental anguish facing difficult decisions made for him. And he'd never hit Brenda before. He didn't know how he felt about that. Not good, but…

"Count on you to find a way to spend money. What's in the bag?"

Brenda dumped her purchases on the bed and stripped down to her underwear. She held up and then put on her acquisitions: a khaki shirt with shoulder flaps and two breast pockets, which buttoned rather suggestively, a pair of matching cargo shorts, a sleeveless bush jacket and a floppy hat fastened on one side, Digger style.

Bobby grunted and popped open another can of beer.

She rummaged in the pile on the bed and pulled up a wide belt, which she threaded though the belt loops on her shorts—not a moment too soon as they were in the process of sliding to her ankles. As the *pièce de resistance* she folded a pair of gloves over the belt. She spread her arms and invited Bobby's comment.

"I liked it better when you didn't have any clothes on."

"Moron. Look at what else I got." She held up an iron spear point. "The woman at the store said it was a real Zulu *assegai*—you know, like in that movie we saw about those warrior guys trying to fight the English back in the day? I said I thought they were called *diassagai* but she said that was the, like, plural, you know—one, *assegai*, two, *diassagai*—only you don't say the two or something. See, they put a *d* and an *i* in the front instead of an *s* in the back. It's, like, Bantu and all."

Bobby had no idea what she was talking about, but the sight of the pointed spear point triggered something in his brain. What that might be did not register in its currently anesthetized state, but it would later.

"Do they have more of those spear things?"

"I think so. You gotta be quick if you want one, though. Travis and that engineer guy, what's his name, were looking at them when I left."

"I think his name is Polanski or something. He's, you know, Polish, maybe. I guess one spear is enough for us. You think you'll be able to get it back in the country?"

"Hey, it's, like, a private plane. If the pilot, you know, don't object, who's to know."

"What are you going to do with it?"

"I don't know. Maybe I'll hang it on the wall next to the Chinese lion mask we picked up in San Francisco. I could use it like a letter opener."

"When did you start reading letters? None of your ditzy pals know how to write."

"You are, like, so not right. Desiree writes poems and stuff all the time. And there's the bills I gotta look at every month."

Brenda removed and folded her safari outfit and put it away in the dresser. The soft breeze from the overhead

fan felt good on her skin. It was time to find out what
Bobby had been up to with Leo, and that meant she had
to be quick. One more beer and lover boy would not be
able to perform, and she needed him pliable. She perched
on the bed, batted her eyes, and smiled.

Bobby passed out.

THE GAME CRUISE boat was configured so that nine passengers could sit three across on the thwarts and the
guide sat in the stern. Neither Leo nor Bobby had made
it. Bobby because he was still asleep when the time came
to leave, and Leo begged off.

The guide took them out in the river and headed up-
stream toward Sedudu Island. Brenda was fascinated.
She'd seen movies and once, when she was dating a guy
from Northwestern—well, she called it dating, he might
have had different descriptor—she'd watched a lot of
PBS's *Nature*. But to see the real thing…

"Wow, look at those hippos, will you!" She unslung
her camera from her shoulder and began snapping pictures. She turned to the guide managing the boat's outboard motor. "Can you, like, swim with them?"

"Excuse me, you wish to swim with the hippos?"

"Yeah, you know, like in Florida, you can do it with
the dolphins."

"Oh, no, Miss. You see that old fellah there, that one
is the bull and very protective of his territory and his
ladies." The hippo in question opened his jaws wide to
display a set of tusks and a pink maw that was nothing
short of spectacular. "If he get you in that mouth, he
would snap you in half."

She'd never imagined hippopotami could be dangerous. She thought of them like panda bears. Big, only not as cute.

"That animal is not even bothered by the crocodile, you see. Now if you went swimming and managed to stay out of his area, then the crocodiles would find you; that is, if the tiger fish didn't get you first. No, no. Swimming in African rivers is not a thing you can do." He gunned the outboard motor to move the boat out of the hippos' range as the bull began to move toward them with a less than friendly look in its eyes. They cruised along the shore of the island. The guide pointed out the impala, gazelles, and elephants. The latter were hard to miss. There were two basking crocodiles on the Namibian shore that seemed uninterested in their presence. Brenda took their picture as well.

She turned to the passenger next to her. "You're the engineer guy that flew up on the plane with us. I know who you are, you're Polanski, or something, right?"

"Guilty as charged. Bart Polanski, right. That's me. And you are Brenda Starr."

"How'd you know that? I used to be Starr, but only now I'm, like, Mrs. Brenda Griswold."

"Congratulations."

Polanski seemed to be having difficulty keeping his eyes on her face, probably because her safari skirt had not been designed for sitting on the thwart of a boat.

"Yeah. So, what brings you up here?"

"Mr. Parizzi asked me to accompany him. We have some matters to discuss."

"Oh, now I got you. You're the Reilly grandson, aren't you? Yeah, Travis sort of needs you. Me, too. Without us he's crapola. Am I right?"

Polanski glanced nervously at Travis who sat three seats away.

"Probably ought to cool that, Mrs. Brenda Griswold formerly Starr. But, hey, if you'd like to have a drink with me later, maybe we could, you know, compare notes."

"Okay, but only if you think you can manage a conversation without staring down the front of my blouse."

Polanski blushed and backed off. She turned her attention back to the guide.

"Sir, how did those animals get out to the island?"

The guide smiled, displaying a set of the whitest, straightest teeth Brenda had ever seen.

"They swam, Miss."

"Aren't they afraid of the crocodiles and the...you said, tiger fish?"

"Oh, yes."

"So, what happens if, say, a crocodile catches them?"

"Then they become that croc's dinner."

"Really? So, you don't feed these animals?"

"Not unless we get careless."

"Then they, like, eat each other, you mean?"

"Oh, yes. Some are predators, some are prey, and once in a while, one of them will be both." He laughed, flashing those wonderful teeth again and added, "In this way they are like people, you see?" He turned the boat back downstream toward the lodge.

"Please understand, Miss, the bush is not a zoo and this is not one of your famous theme parks. These are wild animals living just as they have done since God put them here. We must observe and admire them. And stay out of their way."

TWENTY-FOUR

BOBBY HAD BEEN sufficiently awake, if not exactly alert, to join the game drive into the Chobe National Park the next morning. Brenda noticed that Leo managed to appear as well. She thought he looked really dorky in his wingtips. The golf shirt with the logo of a Palm Springs club on the front amounted to the only gesture he seemed to have made to the informality of the occasion. She drew what she interpreted as admiring looks for her safari outfit from the people waiting to board the vehicle. She'd added a leopard print scarf to the ensemble. After Polanski's misdirected ogling the night before, she figured she should do something about the cleavage. The truck, with its passengers packed three and four across in four tiers of forward-facing benches, rumbled out of Kasane to the park gate. The guide/driver dismounted and visited the building at the entrance, she guessed to pay their fees. She took a picture.

The next hour and a half was spent moving slowly through the bush. The driver rarely shifted from low gear. There were plenty of hoofed beasts to be seen. She tried to make a list of the variety but soon lost track. Bobby was no help. She asked him repeatedly to spell things like *lechwe* and he made a botch of it. An English couple made a nuisance of themselves asking the guide to stop for, like, every freaking bird in the world.

And then they had to take its picture. Brenda wasn't into birds.

The elephants were plentiful and really big. One juvenile followed them for a while trumpeting and wagging its ears. Brenda took a dozen pictures of it. The English just laughed at it. What was up with them?

"Hey, sir," she shouted over the grinding of the engine, "are we going to see any lions?"

"I hope so, yes. We are going to the place where they are often found. There is a pride that has its territory a kilometer or two from here. If they haven't moved away we should find them."

Twenty minutes later the truck rounded a clump of bushes and stopped. A half-dozen lions lolled on the ground like so many sleeping pussycats.

"This pride, you see has a new alpha male. Two weeks ago the old lion was driven off by this younger one that you can see over there beyond the termite hill." He pointed in the general direction of a tall pillar of dirt and sure enough the maned head of a male lion stared back at them. "We called the old one Sekoa because we think he was sick. *Sekoa* is our word for invalid, yes, a sick person? He was not so good and then this young fellah came along and sent him away."

One of the lionesses rolled over on its back as if waiting for a belly rub. Brenda started to climb down to take its picture.

"Do not move," the guide barked.

"I was only going to take a picture. They're okay."

One large female rolled into a crouch, set her back legs, her eyes riveted on Brenda's dangling leg.

The guide quickly maneuvered the truck to put

Brenda, who hung on to the side, away from the lions and out of their line of sight. The lioness relaxed.

"Hey, what was that all about?"

"The lady lion was looking to grab you, Miss. You must not leave the vehicle. I told you before, as long as you stay in this vehicle, she will not bother. The lion sees us as bigger than they are. But, if you walk away from the truck, you will be on their dinner plate before you can say your prayers."

Brenda sat back in her seat and endured the hard stares of the rest of the group. Two more trucks filled with tourists arrived. The lions barely acknowledged their presence. One smaller vehicle, which looked like the old SUV she'd seen Leo drive off in the day before, pulled up close beside them and on the side away from the lions. Leo muttered something to the guide, who nodded, and then alit and stepped quickly into the other car. One lion lifted its head and seemed aware of the exchange and then it closed its eyes again.

"What was that all about?" She asked Bobby.

"What?"

"Leo just got out and went into the car next to us. The guide just gave me hell for trying to jump down for a picture and then Leo just hops out and disappears."

"I guess he has his reasons. That's the Russian in there with him. I wonder who those other guys are."

Travis, she noticed, had his eyes locked on the SUV as well. Brenda took a picture.

When the clicking and whirring of cameras abated, indicating everyone had their fill of lions, the guide put the truck in gear. He looked toward the odd SUV and Leo, who waved, and they drove off without him.

"We will go toward the river now and see if the giraffe are waiting for us there today," he announced.

"You really think they wait for this truck?"

Bobby gave her a look.

"Well, they might. You don't know everything. I mean the pigeons in the park know when that old lady with the bread crumbs comes every afternoon. Animals aren't so dumb, you know."

"Right. Smart enough to stay in their seats rather than be eaten. Jesus, Brenda, what were you thinking?"

"Shut up, Mr. I'm-no-genius-either."

She turned and took another picture of the SUV, this time with the zoom all the way out.

"DID THAT WOMAN take our picture?"

"Probably, why?"

"There can be no record of this meeting, Mr. Painter. We agreed with Yuri to see you but it cannot be known."

"*No mathata,*" Greshenko said. "She is related to Mr. Painter. He will see to it that there is no picture."

"There are no police here, I take it. It is the police you were worried about. Is that not correct?"

"You do not know if there were police or not."

Leo cleared his throat. "The guide is temporarily in my employ. He assured me that the only passengers on the truck were tourists from the hotel. Rest easy. Now can we discuss a meeting with Botlhokwa?"

"Ah, as to that. Rra Botlhokwa asks if there is any remuneration in the meeting."

"He wants to know what's in it for him, is that the drift?"

"Drift? Ah, yes, I understand. Yes, that is the question."

"If he will give me an hour of his time, he will discover if there is something in it for him or not. We are not talking about a little over-the-border smuggling of proscribed substances. This will be a legitimate undertaking that he might find beneficial to his other enterprises."

The truck drove back the way it came. Leo would miss seeing the family of giraffe.

TWENTY-FIVE

MMA SANTOS TENDED a herd of goats. They represented her wealth. Her husband died in a mine accident in Kimberly many years before, when she was still a young girl. She depended on her goats and the support of her village to survive. Her children had fled south to the capital. One son died of HIV/AIDS, another in an automobile accident, and she had not heard from either daughter in two years. She did not know if they were alive or dead. She grieved for them as if they were.

Her goats replaced them. They provided milk which she sold to her neighbors and she used to make cheese. She bartered kids, milk, and cheese for the remainder of the things she needed to live. She owned nearly a dozen, more or less. When the kids arrived the herd grew, of course. She kept only the females, her girls, she called them. The boys, the males, she sold to the butchery as soon as they were weaned except, of course, the old ram, which she would keep as long as he could do his business. When that stopped, she would trade with a neighbor for a new male and send the Old Man, as she called him, to the abattoir with his most recent off-spring.

She gave names to her girls. She would look between their eyes and a name would come to her. She learned this method from her grandmother, who maintained she, in turn, had learned it from hers. Her friends said she shouldn't name them, as it would make it difficult for her to sell them later. They were right. Mma Santos had no close friends other than her goats. Her favorite she called Sesi, which means sister. She would have long conversations with Sesi, conversations she would have had with her own children had they been available.

When the LADA tore around the corner on its way from Kazungula to Kasane, scattering her goats in every direction, and ran over Sesi, she was beside herself. When her sons had died, they were far from her, away in Gaborone, and their deaths, as painful as they were, did not tear at her heart as did this last one. Sesi was her friend, her companion, her constant comfort. She tore her hair and wailed. The SUV skidded to a stop. She heard loud voices coming from the vehicle. Her English wasn't good and she could only make sense of a few words. The man on the passenger's side seemed angry. The other man sounded like he wished to explain something. The first one yelled and tried to move again. Mma Santos circled the vehicle and stood in front, her hands on her hips. She wanted to see the man who murdered Sesi. A man, not a *motswana*, leaned out of the right window and apologized to her for her loss in strangely accented Setswana. He begged her forgiveness. Before he could finish, the other man, on what she took to be the passenger's side, pulled out a fat wallet and threw some bills at her. The gears racketed and the car lurched forward, swerved around her, and, kicking gravel on Mma Santo's legs, roared away.

She picked up the bills and stared at them. They were not pula. The denominations were large, she saw, but she could not read the writing on the paper. She stuffed the money in her blouse and went to gather the broken carcass of Sesi and her other goats. She would take them back to the *kraal* early and mourn her loss.

"Tomorrow," she muttered, "I will see the *ngaka*, the witch doctor. He will know what to do."

"BAD MOVE, THERE, Mr. Painter," Greshenko said.

"What kind of crazy country lets goats wander all over the road? That woman should have to keep them fenced."

"People graze their livestock in the open. It is customary. Even if the government wanted them not to, it would take more than a law to make them stop. People learn to drive 'cattle conscious' here. Besides, they would tell you, the goats owned the road first. They grazed on that grass when the road was no more than a path or an elephant walk. The natives believe the cattle have rights. And so does the government. The people are only responsible for keeping their livestock fenced in after dark."

"Idiots. How in hell do these people think they'll get to tomorrow if they keep this up? Goats with rights? There is wealth here for anyone smart enough to see it, but they won't if they put goats' rights on the top of their list."

"Nevertheless, what you just did will get back to our decision-makers, and they won't like it."

"Then we'll spread some money around, offer an equity share for a few of them, and that should settle it. Besides, I left a year's wages with that woman. She should thank me."

Greshenko shook his head. Their project didn't appear that easy to move in the first place. Now...a step back. But it was Painter's money and as long as he paid, the work will go on. The meeting with Rra Botlhokwa had been cordial, but it didn't end with any commitments on his part. His help with the purchase remained at best, a distant maybe. And, of course, any move into the game park, they said, was out of the question. Painter had slapped the table at this news.

"But there is a lodge out there that is privately owned," he'd complained. "Why them and not us?"

"They were allowed into the game park because the tourism board wished it. There were villages in the park once, as well. The people of those villages were moved out, as well, and there are some private holdings along the river. But no new things can be added without the appropriate Ministry approval."

"We'll buy the Chobe Game Lodge, then."

"Not for sale, and if it were, you can bet the government would exercise a right of first refusal on it."

"Then why aren't we talking to the ministry in charge of this business?"

Greshenko looked away, his eyes narrowed, which only annoyed Painter more. Used to getting his own way and used to greasing the skids of any slow-to-move project with infusions of cash, both above and below the table, he'd left the meeting visibly irritated—at Greshenko and with the movers and shakers in the north country.

"Tomorrow you get back to those birds and get something moving."

"That may be easier said than done."

"What? Why?"

"They are suspicious of the police, for one thing. And there are other considerations."

"What's that supposed to mean? I pay you to use those

special skills I was told you possess to make this happen. You are here to help me."

"Yes, well, not entirely." Painter jerked his head around to look at Greshenko and nearly clipped a battered pickup. "I am here because you contracted for my services. My other connections—"

"You mean the Mafia."

"We do not use that term. That is what you call Italian gangsters. No, they permitted this trip away from Chicago so that I could take the pulse of the country, so to speak. They did not know about Botlhokwa, however."

"But you do. Yes, I see. You mean you're on a scouting mission for them to introduce the rackets."

"For them, for me, who can say how all this will play out. We do not do 'rackets,' by the way, Mr. Painter. We have other, more profitable interests."

"Like what?"

Greshenko did not respond right away. "It would be better if you did not know. If that DIS agent were to query you, you will be ignorant. One of your presidents referred to it as *deniability*, you see?"

Leo didn't see. He'd brushed Greshenko aside after the meeting and insisted on driving the LADA back to the Safari Game lodge himself. That put him mostly on the wrong side of the road and driving at an unacceptably high speed given the circumstances. If he even saw the goats, he apparently had no intention of slowing down or even sounding his horn.

Had he done the latter, the goats might have scattered and the Mma Santos would not have felt it necessary to solicit a *moloi's* curse.

TWENTY-SIX

AFTER DISMISSING GRESHENKO with the caveat he might need him later and asking that he investigate one or two of the smaller properties on the river, he returned to his room. The phone blinked at him as he stepped in. A message. Sheridan Baker had called and reported everything Leo requested had been done as asked. The paperwork was in the mail and should be in Chicago today. Faxed copies had been sent to the lodge. Leo called the desk.

"There should be some faxes for me. Would you please have them delivered to my room?"

"Certainly. And sir, you had a long-distance call from San Francisco while you were out. The caller left a message."

"Send that along as well."

Fifteen minutes later several papers were in his hands. He read through them to assure that the contents were correct on the one hand and useful on the other. The call from San Francisco had been placed by Cavanaugh. *Thank you*. You're welcome. More than you will ever know. At least I hope so. That bit of his program done, Leo settled into a chair and smiled. This could turn into a good day, after all. Now he needed a sit-down with Travis, but first, he needed Bobby Griswold's signatures on the transmittal forms. He called the latter's room. Not surprisingly, Brenda reported him as unavailable.

"You mean he's drunk or close to it, I assume. Throw

him in the shower and then tell him to get his lazy butt down here on the double."

He hung up and sat at the small desk. He arranged the papers he needed Bobby to sign on its surface and placed the others face-down next to them. He fixed himself a martini and settled in to wait for the boy. He liked the gin and wondered why the same label bought in the States didn't taste the same. This had more flavor, more body, if that could be said about gin. He did not consider himself a gin snob, but he could taste differences between the cheap stuff he bought in his youth and what he drank now. He guessed the British version, which would be sold in Botswana, underwent a different distillation process than the American. Hell, the Brits practically invented the stuff. He'd take a case home with him; that and a couple dozen Cuban cigars.

Bobby arrived thirty minutes later, bedraggled, his hair wet from the shower, a little worse for wear, but coherent. Leo sat him down and pointed to the places needing a signature. Bobby hesitated.

"Problem?"

"I'm just wondering, you know. Like, if I want to buy these shares back someday…They were my mother's and all, and well."

"I know that. Sentimental value is it? That's fine with me. As soon as you have the wherewithal to do that, they're yours."

Leo studied the boy's face for some hint at what really lurked in the dim recesses of his mind. He did not like what he saw, the slow, sly expression that Bobby could scarcely hide. Something was up.

"Suppose you, like, died. I mean, I don't think you will or anything, of course, but, you know, you had those heart attacks back then and…" His voice trailed off. Leo waited for what might come next. "See, I was hoping, like maybe, you could add them to the part of the will that's about me."

"Will? What will would that be?"

"Your will. I mean, Brenda said she talked to Farrah before we came over here and she thinks I'm in it, in your will."

"Ah, that will, my will, the one Farrah executed, you mean. I see, yes, of course. Well, as to that…" Leo considered what Bobby really had in mind. He didn't like where his thoughts took him. He didn't believe Bobby had the courage or audacity to take him on, but with idlers like this boy, you can never be sure.

"Very well, this is what I can do for you. Look, here is a bit of white space between the last paragraph in the paper in which you assign the shares to me and the signature line. There is enough room, if I'm careful and write small, to add a statement that will serve as a codicil, so to speak, in the agreement."

Leo sat at the desk and started to write in a cramped hand, paused, and looked up.

"It's important we get this right. The date on that will was…yes, the second week in February. We don't want some slick lawyer to find a loophole that will keep you from what you…" The greedy look on Bobby's face said it all. Leo left off. *What you deserve.* "That which is rightly yours. Let me see, I signed it on Friday, the week after the Super Bowl. Okay…The will of February…" he added the year, reread what he'd written, and handed it to Bobby to inspect. He, in turn, screwed up his face in concentration and read, silently, his lips moving.

"It says that in the event of my death, if these shares

are still in my possession, they will be added to the corpus of your inheritance under the terms of my will dated February, etcetera, etcetera. Does that sound about right?"

"Um, yes, yes, it does. I sign here?"

"Right there where I put that little check mark."

Bobby signed both letters of transmittal and handed them to Leo, who signed them also.

"You want to give me the money so I can pay off Travis now?"

"No, I think it would be better if I, as they say, cut out the middle-man. I have both these documents. When Travis sees them he will sign the first and that will be that."

"But I thought—"

"You needn't bother yourself about it anymore. If Travis balks, I'll call you. Now go enjoy yourself. Oh, and you haven't said anything to Brenda about either the divorce or this matter, have you?"

"No. Not yet. When would be a good time to do that?"

"Wait until you hear from me. I need to have a chat with Travis first. You understand, he may have something to say about that. It would be beneficial if he could be persuaded to testify about their relationship, at the hearing, I mean. Save a lot of legal maneuvering, right?"

"Um, okay, I guess so."

Leo doubted he did but it didn't matter. The ill-disguised look of disappointment on Bobby's face did concern him, though.

"Fine, now run along."

TWENTY-SEVEN

THE MEN HAD hunted with Sanderson most of the week. All they found of their lion were tracks indicating that he had not gone to Zimbabwe as they had originally supposed, but had veered off south and taken a path parallel to the Kasane road toward the Makgadikgadi Pans, the vast area of salt flats and ephemeral lakes, low scrub, the breeding grounds for tens of thousands of flamingos, and home to hundreds of varieties of birds and game. Rra Kaleke opined that if he made it there, he would not come back this way.

"How many more days, Sanderson, do you wish this hunting to continue?"

She considered how best to answer. She needed the appearance of a hunt at least until Mr. Pako took himself off to Maun.

"No much longer. Do me this thing and continue for a while longer."

Rra Kaleke nodded his agreement. He understood that stupidity often held things in place long after the time they seemed useful or sensible, but he liked this Sanderson, and he grieved for her son.

The sun began its descent in the west and the men gathered at the truck and piled into the bed. They had overcome their reluctance to ride with a woman at the wheel. She drove very well, they said, for a woman, and they admired the new coat of bright red paint she'd applied over the weekend.

Sanderson dropped the men off and parked her HiLux, Michael's HiLux, next to the door. Her daughter, Mpitle, had started supper. David Mmusi sat at the table as if he belonged there.

"Mr. David Mmusi, you are in my house, and I do not know why. Can you explain this to me?"

The boy started at Sanderson's tone. Mpitle stepped toward her mother.

"I asked him to stay a while. He has been telling us amusing stories and Michael has even had a laugh."

Sanderson looked through the open door where her son lay in bed. He smiled and gave a weak nod.

"It is so, Mma. This boy is telling stories, and also, so you know for sure, I have made certain no funny business has transpired while we are waiting for you to come home. I have asked this man to eat with us this one time but, of course, that is for you to say."

Sanderson sat wearily in the best chair that had been kept vacant for her.

"Yes, you stay, David, it will be an honor." She turned to her daughter. "And what have you prepared for this wonderful occasion?"

Mpitle grinned and showed her the stew she'd concocted from vegetables and impala, meat that Sanderson had brought home the day before. Rra Kaleke had insisted she have a share of the "hunt."

"When we are finished with this cookery, you and I must have an important talk together, Mr. David Mmusi."

THE KNOCK ON the door interrupted Travis' study of Earth Global's most recent annual report. There wasn't anything in it he hadn't read many times before. And as he'd composed most of it himself, it wasn't that he was enchanted with his own prose. After his brief chat with Leo, he looked for something he might have missed in the minerals and mining section. He shuddered at the thought of who might be calling. He believed he knew and considered remaining seated and not answering. Instead, more out of a concern she might cause a scene than out of a desire to see her, he answered the door.

He'd guessed correctly. Politics, they say, makes strange bedfellows. Business has its own version of that axiom, and Travis now contemplated a personal application of it. He'd assumed correctly, and Brenda Griswold stood in his doorway, her fingers already at the buttons on her blouse. Travis never married and had no intention of entering that blessed state until after he'd secured the presidency of Earth Global, perhaps not even then. He found himself at the brink of accomplishing that coup, but to do so required him to accommodate the woman standing at his door. She hesitated for a second and then pushed past him into the room.

"Bobby's out talking to Leo or something. I told him I would be on another game drive, so we have all afternoon."

"How about we just talk for a minute?"

"What's to talk about? You need me, Bobby's a loser, and since I control the shares you need to get what you want, we're a team. Simple." She finished unbuttoning her blouse and slipped off her shorts.

Travis had no objection to conducting an affair. He'd done so in the past and guessed he would in the future. The fact that Brenda married Bobby Griswold and therefore should be off limits did not concern him in the least.

He'd discovered affairs with married women to be a far safer undertaking than with singles. The former had more to lose if caught and tended to be discreet. Similarly, ending the liaison took far less effort, for the same reasons. Brenda, unfortunately, did not fit the married woman profile. No one would ever describe her as discreet, and terminating any liaison with her, should he wish to, could be very difficult. That ending would have to happen.

But, for the moment, he needed her.

"What's your husband talking about with Leo? If he spills what we're up to, this could all go south. I'd be out. You'd be out, and we'd have no future."

"Bobby doesn't know squat. I mean, he knows I have the money lined up to redeem the shares, and he knows I'm fixing it so we have a payday and you're involved in it. That's all. He won't tell Leo anything to screw it up. He's not that quick."

"I don't like it. If he finds out about us…"

Brenda turned her back to him so he didn't see the look that crossed her face. Had he, he would have had no compunction to toss her out of the room, half naked or not.

"No problem, Travis. I have him under control."

He hoped so. He strolled to the slider and pulled the draperies across it. The room, without the sun streaming in seemed smaller, and Brenda's perfume seemed to fill it. The scent was pleasant enough but, as Brenda apparently did not stint in its application, overwhelming. He returned to the bedside.

Strange bedfellows, he thought.

TWENTY-EIGHT

LEO PAINTER DID not achieve success by being stupid. If anyone were to ask him for the keys, he would say that any jackass can run a company; just look at the idiots running the banks and Wall Street. To make money, however, required a person both to have a feel for the doable and a willingness to do it. He might have added that it didn't hurt to have a streak of ruthlessness as well. Sometimes that characteristic played out in the board-room, in the hurly-burly of power brokerage. But more often it allowed one to recognize it in an opponent and take anticipatory measures. Thus, Travis did not realize it, but he would soon have his ears pinned back.

Leo picked up the sheaves of papers he'd placed face down and read them carefully. Early that morning, before he'd met with Greshenko and had the disastrous meeting with Botlhokwa's people, he'd called his office and had his administrative assistant pull all the statements from the phone company for the past three months for both the office sets and the Blackberries used by Travis and Farrah. He asked her to copy them and fax them to the lodge. Since the company paid those bills, he assumed he had the right to access the records. He'd supplied all his chief executives with the devices precisely for that reason. *Lex facit regem.* Actually, at Earth Global, it's the other way round: the king makes the law, and until he said otherwise, he would remain king.

Farrah thought Leo bugged his Blackberry, and Leo did not disabuse him of the notion. He hoped it would discourage disloyal behavior. It seemed it had not. As it happened he did not have direct access to their devices, but he could review all the calls in and out, and that is what he occupied himself with for the next hour. He mixed another martini. He recognized most of the numbers. Farrah, since his divorce, had few friends and not much of a social life. It did take some study to figure out some of Travis' calls. He had to check his own pocket diary to identify a half-dozen.

"Travis, Travis, you are breaking this old man's heart. Is there any hope for you, or must I toss you to the dogs?" He glanced out the window at the river. "Make that the crocodiles." Leo shook his head and sipped his martini.

"Why are you young people in such a hurry to go to hell? Patience is not only a proverbial virtue, but in business, it is an absolute necessity. Take a lesson from the great poker players. Fold more hands than you play, and know that all the big pots are won after midnight."

There was no one in the room to hear Leo's musings, and even if there had been, it's unlikely it would have mattered. Leo sighed and drained his glass: time to go to the main lodge for dinner.

"Mark Twain said, 'There are some things a man can only learn by swinging a cat by its tail.' Travis, my boy, with my help, you are about to swing a cat. And when I'm finished with you, I will have a long chat with Henry Farrah."

THE GRAY MONKEY, after his near miss with the lion, made a point of staying close to the lodge and would do so until the memory of his close encounter with death faded or

his innate curiosity overcame caution and he ventured
out once more. But now, his interest centered on the
lodge's many rooms and chalets. He'd come to Leo's
sliding glass door on the balcony side of the room in the
hopes of prying it open and executing a grab-and-run on
the contents of what he took to be a bowl of fruit. He'd
done it many times before. If he'd thought about it, he
would have been thankful that the tourism board en-
couraged so many absentminded visitors to explore his
territory to be charmed and cajoled out of food. He sat
staring through the door, watching the man rifle through
his papers and mutter to himself. And then, watched as
he straightened his shirt, donned a jacket, and left. As
soon as the door closed behind him, the monkey went
to work on the slider. Fortunately for Leo, he'd secured
the papers in his briefcase and well away from the bowl
of fruit.

BOBBY DID NOT, for one second, believe Brenda had joined
another game drive. He'd seen the truck pull out, and she
wasn't in it. She would be back with Travis. Okay, let her.
He had a plan, and then she, no all of them, would get
what they had coming. He rummaged through the pile
of clothing and parcels Brenda had piled up on the bench
at the foot of the bed and found what he sought. He hesitated. It wouldn't do to touch it with his bare hands. The
gloves from her ridiculous safari outfit lay on the floor.
He retrieved one of them and forced it on. Too small to
fit over his hand but he did manage to insert his fingers.

He picked up her *assegai* and laid it on the leopard-
patterned scarf. He folded the edges of the scarf over
the spear tip and walked to the slider, opened it and
stepped out onto the balcony. He hid the scarf and its

contents along with the glove under the bottom step and returned to the room. He'd show them all who was a "boy," who didn't have the smarts, who didn't have the guts. They never thought he'd make it. He would show them. All of them would pay: Leo, Parizzi, and Brenda, especially her. And then they'd see who the top dog at Earth Global was.

They'd all be at dinner now. He didn't want to see them. He flopped down and cracked the last beer. He'd need to call for more.

He'd fix them.

TWENTY-NINE

LEO TOOK IN the company seated about the dining area. He didn't see the Griswolds or Travis. Perhaps they'd eaten earlier or would be coming in later. He'd heard about a rustic restaurant east of the lodge, The Old House. Perhaps they'd gone there for a change. He sipped his soup and considered how he should approach Travis. On the one hand, it would not do to seem weak, but, on the other, if he acted too aggressively, he might precipitate something that would be at cross purposes to what he had in mind as his closer. He hoped the man's common sense would at least temper his ambition—"vaulting ambition"— as Shakespeare might say. Travis had a great deal in common with Lady Macbeth. The future of Earth Global hung on the tenuous thread of his next move and Travis' response to it.

Henry Farrah entered the dining area somewhat unsteadily. Leo waved the lawyer over.

"May I join you?" Farrah said.

Leo could smell the booze from five feet away.

"Actually, I intended to dine alone, Henry. I have some planning to do, you might say." Farrah seemed disappointed. "However, I would like you to join me in my room for a drink later, if you will."

"What time?'

"I'll give you a call. And Henry? Try to be sober when you arrive."

Farrah wandered off to another table and, in a display intended for Leo, ordered another drink. Leo pretended not to notice. He was halfway into his steak when Travis and Brenda Griswold entered. Interesting. She must really have sunk her hooks in him. Well, that would change in the next hour or so. As he had done with Farrah, he motioned for Travis to join him.

"Yes, Leo? It appears you are nearly finished. Mrs. Griswold and I met on the path coming over. She thinks her husband may join us later. Did you want to speak to me?"

Very cool. He thinks he has me. Perhaps, and then again, perhaps not.

"I thought you might drop by after dinner. There are some things we need to discuss."

"I'd like to, but I'm afraid I may be otherwise engaged."

"Then I suggest you become disengaged." Leo cut a look at Brenda who, in turn, appeared as smug as the cat who licked the cream. Travis started to speak, but Leo waved him off. "It's not a request, Travis, it's an order. Eight o'clock, my room."

Travis studied him for what seemed a full minute, eyes narrowed and a small crease bisecting in his forehead.

"Eight o'clock it is, then."

So far, so good. Now if he just knew where the boy had gotten to and whether Greshenko had made any progress with the land deal. He finished his steak, ordered a cup of decaffeinated coffee and turned his attention to the "odd couple." Brenda was bending Travis' ear. He on the other hand, seemed lost in thought.

WHEN LEO RETURNED to his room and opened his door, he looked at what appeared a war zone. He hadn't seen anything like the state of his room since his twenty-first birthday and he had had to repair his grandparent's house after a semi missed a curve on a snowy night and plowed into their living room. The place was a shambles. He glanced at the slider, which stood open about a foot. He'd forgotten to lock it. He first thought Henry Farrah must have come in a drunken stupor, looking for something, but he'd left him in the dining area. He strode to the closet and checked the status of his briefcase. It lay undisturbed and intact on its side. He called the front desk and asked for someone to come and straighten up the mess.

A crew from housekeeping arrived five minutes later.

"Ah, you have met our monkeys it seems, sir," a tall woman in a uniform said with a grin.

"Monkeys? What monkeys? Monkey business if you ask me."

"No sir, you must remember the warning the man gave at the time you registered? And look there." The woman pointed to the small sign over the slider. In bold, red letters on a white background it stated that guests should keep the sliding doors closed and locked. The standard warning about the area's monkeys that would surely come in and could cause damage and perhaps even physical harm if the residents were careless about keeping the sliders closed and fastened.

Leo had heard the caution and had been amused at the sign but, in his innocence, or rather his cynical mindset, he assumed they, like the man-eating lion story, it represented another marketing ploy to scam the tourists. He allowed the crew to remake the bed and straighten the room as best they could and then sent them on their way. He wanted to prepare for his visitors.

"WHAT DID THE old coot want?" Brenda attacked her salad. Sex, she'd told him earlier, always made her hungry. Good or bad, and his performance rated somewhere in the middle on that one, but either way, good or bad, it produced an appetite. That being the case, he supposed, it constituted nothing short of a physiological or metabolic miracle she hadn't ballooned up to two hundred pounds by now.

"He wants to meet me in his room and talk over some business." He sat back and watched her, marveling how she could shove greens into her mouth in one continuous motion. "Are you sure your husband hasn't tipped this deal?"

She paused, fork piled high, and looked up at him. "He's been mostly buzzed or blotto for the last coupla days. He ain't said diddley squat to anybody."

"You're sure?"

Brenda nodded and dug into her roast. "This tastes like deer or something. One time my stepfather, the son of a bitch, came home with what do you call it, deer meat."

"Venison."

"Venison, right, and my mom got herself sober enough to cook it. When she wasn't drunk out of her gourd, she could cook, I'll tell you. Anyway that venison tasted like this here."

"It should. It's impala, I think. The old man is up to something. I wish I knew what."

"Who cares? You have the votes. You have your meeting thing, and bip, bop, he's on the street and you're the boss. Then, you and me—"

"Don't get ahead of yourself. There's a way to go before that happens, and when it does, then we'll see."

"Then we'll see, nothing. Like it or lump it, we're a team, pal."

Travis let the last remark slide. He'd need her to secure his position for now. But after that happened, well, the lady had marketable skills. She'd survive somehow.

"Maybe I should go to see him with you. Just so he knows he's over a barrel. I can say some things that will really get him, you know?"

"That is a very bad idea, Brenda. You go back to your room and amuse your husband."

"Amuse? What do you mean?"

"Keep him happy for a few more days. You know what I mean."

Brenda made a face and tackled a second portion of impala.

"And I'll handle Leo Painter. I've been doing it for years. This will be just one last time before it all comes to an end."

"Well, good luck with that. I still think I should go with you."

He smiled at her and concentrated on his dinner. It promised to be a long night for both of them, one way or another.

THIRTY

TRAVIS ARRIVED AT Leo's door precisely at eight o'clock. Leo let him in and offered him a drink. Travis waved him off, scanned the room, seemed to notice the disorder, and raised an eyebrow.

"Monkeys. They came in through my slider and almost wrecked the place."

"Monkeys?"

"Yes, monkeys. I saw that sign over the door but thought they were being over the top on their warnings. Look out for the crocodiles, beware the man-eating lion, keep a sharp eye out for monkeys. I guess they were serious about the last one."

The two men sat across from each other in two wicker chairs. They could have been two lions sizing each other up. The faint aroma of cigar hung in the air. Leo smiled, a little smile, a confident smile, like the crocodile lurking in the river just beyond the deck.

"Do you know how I spent my afternoon, Travis?" Leo didn't wait for an answer. "I spent it poring over phone records, yours for one. That would be records for your office phone and your Blackberry." He paused waiting to see if Travis would react. "You have been a busy little beaver, Travis. Do you have something to tell me?"

Travis narrowed his eyes and thought for a moment before answering. Getting his ducks in a row, Leo assumed. He hoped Travis would be careful in answering. Not jump too quickly.

"You are playing me, Leo. Why don't you just say what's on your mind."

"Very well." Leo paused and scrutinized his COO. It's in the eyes. The eyes never lie, even when the tongue does. "Did you know that I had planned to turn the company over to you when I thought the time was right? I thought we'd have a conversation about that on this trip, after we were finished with the official business. But, as I said, you've been busy, it appears. It seems you are ahead of me and are convinced you've managed to corral enough votes to push me out of the company all by yourself. Have I got that approximately correct?" Travis opened his mouth and closed it.

"I know some of those people you've called…most of them, in fact. Tell me, exactly what made you want the job now rather than, say, in a year or two?"

Travis shifted in his chair. "Very well, since you know what I planned and since, as you indicated, I have the means to do it, I'll tell you. With respect for what you have accomplished in the past, I think you have fallen behind the times. Hell, you've spent your life building the company, and it's become a habit. So much so, you are missing things."

Leo smiled and circled his hand, inviting Travis to continue.

"I think it's time for a change. You, it seems to me, are like the man standing on the platform waiting for a train that's already come and gone. You're missing the thrust of the future, Leo. It's in energy, not minerals and real estate."

"The thrust? Mercy. And what do you propose to do about this missed thrust, if I may ask?"

"I intend to sell off the less profitable subsidiaries, concentrate on high-margin projects, and make the company smaller and more nimble."

"Did you say nimble? Gracious, what a description. Nimble. Is that the new hip business buzzword? What happened to robust? Never mind, I don't want to know.

"Travis, ballerinas are nimble. Jack jumping over the candle stick needed to be nimble. Professional football players, on the other hand, are not nimble, although you might say they are robust. No, footballers are quick. They move to the ball and smother their competition. There's an important difference. Business is a tough, in-your-face undertaking. Business is football, not ballet. I won't let you pull this company down because of your addiction to the banality of MBA double-speak."

Travis' face reddened. "It's not for you to say anymore, Leo. May I remind you that you did this to Harry Reilly. Did you really think the same thing couldn't happen to you?"

"What do you believe I did to Harry Reilly?"

"Shoved him under the bus, dumped the daughter, and took over."

"You are repeating water-cooler gossip." Leo let out a sigh and shook his head. "Let me tell you what really happened. It may help you understand what I have to say later. Harry Reilly was an old-fashioned oil man. He grew up in the Texas oil fields working for his old man, Jack—Black Jack Reilly—who made his fortune and started the company as a wildcatter. Harry worked as a roustabout, manager, even briefly with Red Adair putting out wellhead fires. He took options on real estate as part of his desire to drill new oil wells. The mining turned out to be an accident. If the minerals were there, he might or might not dig them up. That's all. I couldn't get him to see the future as, I suppose, you don't think I can.

"Well, I pleaded with him, begged in fact. He threatened to fire me; would have, too, if I hadn't been married to his daughter. So, I met with some stockholders, told them what we were missing, and they asked him to step aside. I wanted him to stay on as chairman of the board, but his pride wouldn't let him, and he left with a black Irish curse. The daughter followed. She dumped me, not the other way around."

"Are you asking me for the chairmanship?"

Leo lit a cigar and poured himself a drink. He was enjoying himself. "Sure you won't have one?" Travis shook his head. "No, Travis, I am not asking you for anything. I don't have to, because I am not going anywhere."

"You plan to fight me on this? Leo, don't make this hard on yourself. I have the votes. You know I do."

"I don't know. Show me."

Travis shook his head as he might if he had to instruct a recalcitrant child in his ABCs. "Very well, I have my personal holdings to which I have added Robert Griswold's. I have commitments from three board members to vote their shares for me, and…" He paused for effect, "I have the Reilly family shares committed as well."

"Do you now? The Reilly shares, well, well. That's very interesting. I knew about Bobby's foolishness, of course, and the board members are the same ones Farrah talked into the IPO, greedy bastards, looking for a quick payout instead of long-term profits. Oh, well." Leo fished in his briefcase and pulled some papers which he handed to Travis.

"Have a look at these two documents. The first is an agreement by which you surrender Robert's shares to him on the payment of a certain sum. He has that option, as we both know." He reached into his jacket pocket and withdrew another slip of paper. "Here is a check drawn on a local bank for that amount. I can ask the boy to come in here and see to the transaction, but you'll agree that would be a waste of your time and mine."

Travis swallowed. "His wife declares he will vote them for me anyway."

"Brenda? Oh no, no, no, Brenda is not part of this equation. Look at this second document, please. It's a similar agreement but transfers ownership of those same shares to me."

Travis mopped his brow.

"Problems, Travis? I assure you the documents are all in order or, if you decide to push, can be made public and very airtight. It is not in your best interest to do that, I don't think."

"Okay, I wondered what you and Griswold were up to. Now I know, but I don't need his shares except as insurance. As I said, the Reilly people will vote as I direct them."

"Will they now? You're sure of that, son? You have the commitments from all the share holders?"

"I do."

"You're sure, absolutely sure?"

"Absolutely sure." Travis didn't look so sure.

"Alas, Travis, you don't. One more piece of paperwork." Leo handed him the fax from Sheridan Baker.

"The Reilly grandchildren now hold those shares in

unequal amounts. They have steadfastly refused to sell them to me. However, a significant number of the Reilly shares are held by my son the majority, to be precise. He is very ill and may not live long enough to see the New Year. The man who holds his power of attorney, for remuneration specified elsewhere, has given me his proxy as well as the right to buy them all, if that becomes necessary. You have that engineer Polanski's shares and are counting on his assurance he can swing the rest. He might have been able to do so in the past. He can't now. So, you do not have all the Reilly shares."

Travis stared at the man across from him and shook his head.

"It seems you've been busy, too. So now what? Am I fired?"

"Not so fast. Let me tell you a story. When I was young, before I went to work for Reilly, I worked construction downstate. Well, we hit one of those recessions that come along every couple of years, and business just dried up. I urged the owner to lay off the crews and cut back on inventory, ride it out. You see, I had in mind to create some job security for myself. And that would be the prudent thing to do, I thought. You would probably agree, but do you know what he did?"

Travis shook his head.

"He kept them all on the payroll and bid the little business still out there. Bid at cost or below. Took big losses. I asked him what he was thinking. He said he wanted to keep the crews working and the subs happy against the time when the economy turned around. Well, it did turn, as it always does, and the jobs started to flow. While all his competitors scrambled around looking to rehire workers and reassemble the gangs they'd just fired, he was able to grab off nearly all of the building contracts in the Springfield area. Made a fortune."

"And this is related to me, how?"

"Ah. You believe there is no money to be made in mining, is that right?"

"Very poor margins, Leo."

"There is an important difference between a poor margin and no margin. Do you think the world is finished with copper, or nickel, or molybdenum, or any of the stuff we dig out of the ground? You know it isn't. I want to keep the crews working, and I am even willing to run the mines as a not-for-profit or at a reasonable, tax-deductible loss in order to grab the market when it rebounds. And, if you factor in a possible license for ActiVox, assuming we can get it, we clean up. As for the real estate, you know the old saying, God isn't making any more land. That's not true on Hawaii, of course, but you get the point. We are drilling on that land, Travis, but not for the oil that Reilly hoped to find. We're looking for water. It will pay out. Do you understand what I am offering you?"

Travis shrugged. "Is this the wisdom that comes with age?"

"Crap. Wisdom is overrated. Every old fart in a rocking chair thinks he's a font of wisdom. Usually it's just mellowed prejudice. Old people invented revisionist history, by the way, not academicians. We remember selectively and sometimes foolishly, making our lives more heroic, or more meaningful. No, what we really get from living a long time, if we're honest with ourselves, is not wisdom, but perspective. We can measure things and place them in space and time. Remember that, the next time some old guy wearing a dorky tee shirt offers you advice."

"And me? What advice do you have for me?"

"Well now, what shall I do with you? I meant it when I said I wanted you to take over the reins. You must learn patience, Travis. You're good, but you're in too much of a hurry. That could spell trouble for the company. I've worked too hard and too long to see it crash and burn because you couldn't hold your water."

Travis leaned forward.

"That said, you will stay on. Beginning July 1, you will be named president and CEO of Earth Global. At that time, I will assume the chairmanship of the board. Do not be deceived. You will feel my heavy hand on your shoulder every day until I'm sure you're ready to run it on your own or I drop dead, whichever comes first. If you're smart, you will not pray too hard for the latter."

"You're serious?"

"Serious as a heart attack. Oops, bad figure of speech. But there is one condition."

"Name it."

"I want to develop some small projects, here and there, through the real-estate division. Principally, I want to build a lodge-casino on the Chobe. I think I can persuade the government to let me build the lodge. I'm not so sure about the casino. But, I'm a patient man. That's why I brought in the Russian wheeler-dealer. He knows people."

"I'm overwhelmed."

"And you should be. Now go back to your room and kick that tramp out of your bed. Get some sleep. We will be meeting with Yuri Greshenko first thing in the morning to help set up the deal locally."

THIRTY-ONE

LEO USHERED TRAVIS to the door. It closed behind him and Leo sat down. It was time to call Farrah. That conversation would not take as long. He called Henry on his Blackberry and got his voice mail. He tried his room and had no luck there, either. He finally tracked down his errant legal advisor in the main bar.

"Henry, I need to speak to you on a matter of some urgency. Please come to my room as soon as you can." He hung up before Farrah could make his excuses and sat back to wait. The phone rang.

"Henry...oh, sorry it's you, Robert. What do you want?"

"I need to talk to you about something pretty important, Leo."

"I can't talk now, sorry. Can't it wait until tomorrow?"

"No, like, it's about the shares."

"That's all taken care of. If you want the money I promised, it will have to wait until we return to Chicago. Besides, you don't want that on your books until after you divorce Brenda."

"Well, I'm not too sure that's what I should do. Brenda is, like, okay in her way."

"We've been over this already. You think about it some more." There was a knock at the door. "I have to hang up now, there's someone here I need to speak with more than I need to talk to you."

"Listen, this is really important. Can you meet me at the Sedudu Bar?"

"The what?"

"It's that bar where we went for a sundowner. You walk out that path away from your room past the camp-grounds. They're empty now, and the bar is, like, this little building on the river."

"Wait for me there. I'll be along when I can."

Leo hung up and promptly forgot the conversation. He had Farrah at the door, and his heart was not behaving. He slipped a nitro under his tongue and answered the door. Henry Farrah swayed in the entryway and then stumbled into the room.

"Henry, you're drunk. I asked you to stay sober at least long enough to have a meeting."

"I am unsteady, Leo, but not drunk. There is a difference."

"I see. Well, sit down. I won't offer you another drink, however."

Farrah collapsed in a chair and looked balefully at his employer. "So, what's so important we have to meet in the middle of the night?"

"Nine-thirty scarcely qualifies as the middle of the night, and you *are* drunk. Very well, I will ask you a question. Why did you refuse the retirement package I offered you three months ago?"

"I thought I should be treated better than to be unceremoniously shoved out the door without so much as a fare-thee-well." Farrah waved his hand vaguely in the air and looked smug.

"It was a very generous package and as for the 'fare-thee-well'? We don't do that." Leo withdrew the sheets of phone calls. You've been very discreet in your attempts to cash out on the IPO, but not quite enough, I'm afraid. Your friends on the board were able to force the decision to create it, but the landscape has changed lately. I offer you the same package as before, but this time it is a final offer, Henry."

"You can't stop the IPO, Leo."

"There will be no IPO, at least not right away. Final offer, take it or leave it. As of this moment you are fired."

"You can't fire me. The board won't permit it. They want the IPO and they will support me."

"There will be some significant changes in the board's make-up when we return to Chicago. I have recently come into sufficient voting shares to replace some key members, your friends, to be precise. So I *can* fire you and I just did."

Farrah blinked. His mouth fell open. Any thoughts he may have had about a financial windfall evaporated. He was suddenly very sober.

"Leo, you can't. We go back...help me out here."

"Game's up, Henry. Some disloyalty I can abide, if it is in the company's interest to do so. In your case... well, you have not been earning out of late, and you had your chance to exit with some measure of grace earlier. Now, you're out of chances."

Farrah stood and walked to the door.

"I gather there is a bar down near the river. Why don't you go there and have a think. Not a drink, Henry, a think. We'll talk again in the morning."

Henry left without a word. Leo slouched back in his chair and took some deep breaths. His angina seemed a bit more painful. He popped another nitro and closed his eyes. He would rest for a while and then, when the pain subsided, he'd get to bed.

Sanderson had her talk with the pretty David Mmusi and then another with her daughter. David assured her he was not that sort of man, an affirmation which she doubted, and Mpitle said she wasn't that sort of girl; one which she hoped was true.

"So, Michael, what must I do about these two young people?"

"Mma, you must trust Mpitle. She sees how it is with me. She saw our father waste away. She will be very careful. David? Well, I don't know about that boy, but Mpitle will be careful."

"I wish she would be more than careful. She says to me, 'Mma, I am not that sort of girl,' but I don't know."

"You will never know. It is the hormones, I think. They sometimes will muddy up the river of your mind."

Sanderson thought back to the time when she was her daughter's age and nodded. "Yes, that is so. If it were not so, there might not have been a Michael for me to weep over this night."

Michael smiled. "It is not weeping I wish to have. I made a mistake and that is that. I cannot take it back." He closed his eyes and sighed. "I am ready to die, Mma. I have done what I can and," he attempted a grin, "and now you have your *bakkie*. It is enough."

"It is not enough, Michael. I would give a hundred trucks to have you back and healthy. I pray to the Lord God every night. I ask this of him, 'Jesus, you say, ask and it shall be given, and I want to know why this is not being given to me.'"

"And I ask him, 'Please let me go so my mother may not cry so much.' You see, we are at odds. How can God answer both of us? I think He has decided to listen to me."

Sanderson wiped her eyes. "You must not ask Jesus for that anymore, Michael."

"It is too late to change it now, Mma. So be at peace."

THIRTY-TWO

HENRY FARRAH WAS not as sober as he had appeared when he stormed out of Leo's room. As with many of his generation, he'd grown up in an era that partied hard, played hard, and blew off the potential consequences. He thought he'd developed a high tolerance for alcohol. In fact, as a young man, he had. He could drink many lesser men under the table. But age plays tricks on one's body. The ability to metabolize alcohol decreases inversely with the years, which is why there are so many old people diagnosed as alcoholics by their families. It's not that they drink more, or even to excess. Two martinis before dinner might have characterized a couple's preprandial drinking for years with no untoward effects. Then one day the roast burns to a crisp, or they miss dinner entirely, or…worse.

Henry would have been over his limit even if he had been twenty. He staggered from Leo's room and headed down the path that led to the Sedudu bar. His intent was to get thoroughly blotto and then he'd have a few things to say to that bastard, Leo. It was very dark and the path was uneven and he stumbled a lot. He had to pass by a copse of trees whose hanging branches hung over the narrow walkway. As he came abreast of them, he could just make out the bar's dim lights ahead. A figure stepped in front of him.

"Take some advice from someone who knows, don't

sell your soul to the company. It'll kill you," he mumbled to himself and paused, peered into the darkness in an effort to make out who stood in his way.

They were the last words to leave his mouth, for at that precise moment he experienced the most excruciating pain he'd felt since he passed a kidney stone. It quite literally took his breath away. The pain centered in his abdomen just below his breastbone. In the fraction of a second between the onset of the pain and his reeling away, he wondered if this was what a heart attack felt like. The image of his wife and daughter flitted through his mind. There was the life insurance. In the seconds before the damage to his left ventricle caused by Brenda's spear point resulted in a massive hemorrhage into his cardiac cavity, he managed to stagger forward, arms flailing. His thought, which he never completed: seek help at the Sedudu bar. Instead, faculties fading, he careened across the campground and collapsed in the scrub at its edge.

The last thing Henry Farrah saw before he departed this life was the enormous maned head of the lion. Its golden eyes seemed soft and strangely sympathetic, as if it, too, faced death and understood his anguish.

THE SOUND OF the struggle had aroused Sekoa, that and the metallic scent of blood that quickly wafted across the space between him and the sounds of distress caused by Henry's death. He listened to the pounding of feet going away in one direction, the crashing about in the bush closer in. He heaved himself up on quivering legs and cautiously padded forward toward the inert man. He stood over him, poised and ready to give chase if by chance it should try to rise. He sniffed and snorted. The thing was dead. He would not have to kill it. He closed his jaws on the man's shoulder and dragged him a dozen meters far-ther into the bush. This small effort so exhausted him he dropped to the ground next to his prize, panting. His starv-ing body told him he must feed but he could not summon the energy to do so. He would rest.

Back along the trail he'd made dragging the corpse, the spear point had come dislodged and lay partially hid-den in a clump of grass. Sekoa huffed and dropped his head on the man's chest and closed his eyes.

There is some evidence, mostly anecdotal, that ani-mals anticipate their deaths. Tales of elephant grave-yards, cats who wander off to die, a dying bull who charges one last time. Who can be sure? It is equally uncertain if humans have that same sense. If so, the ev-idence for it is even scanter. So, one cannot say whether Sekoa knew his time had come. Henry Farrah certainly did not. The only certainty was that the two of them would be found together the next day by the hotel's em-ployees who'd been sent out to search for the missing Henry Farrah.

BRENDA SAT BY the bed, obviously angry, her face flushed and her foot tapping a staccato beat against the floor.

"Where've you been?" she demanded of Bobby as he slithered in through the sliding glass door.

"I could ask the same thing about you, only I already know. You've been with Parizzi."

"Don't be an idiot. Why would I be seeing him? He's a jerk."

"He's a jerk now? Woo-hoo, what happened to the hot financial deal he was going to do with the stocks? My stocks? Weren't you supposed to be his partner or something?"

"The deal's off and it's your fault. You had to go and tell Leo about how Travis had bought them and now Leo has them and Travis doesn't need us anymore."

"He dumped you, Brenda? Gee, I'm so sorry." Bobby's grin only infuriated her even more. She launched into a tirade that made all of her past efforts pale by comparison. Bobby cracked a beer and waited until she wound down.

"You got what was coming to you, Brenda, so stop your bitching."

"What was coming to me? Listen, I busted my ass to put this thing together. And what about you? You're out in the cold, too. Didn't you tell me Leo fired you? So what do we live on now?"

"We? What's with we? You and me aren't a *we* anymore. It's, like, just me."

"Yeah? You thinking about cutting me out? Let me tell you, it can't happen, Buster. You'll end up losing the farm. See, I know things about you—a certain thing. I have alternatives, and I'll hire me a lawyer."

Bobby giggled and then composed himself. "You'll need a good one, maybe local at that?"

"What does that mean?"

"Nothing. Nothing at all. But you'd better believe I am not going to suffer, now or ever again. That company? I figure its going to be mine soon."

"Yours? That's a laugh. Leo thinks it's his company. Travis says it'll soon be his, and now you say it's yours? How do you figure that?"

"Let's just say I fixed it."

"Fixed what?"

"All you people, even my own wife, you all think I'm stupid. Well, I am not the stupid one here. You want to stick around, Brenda, you'd better be real nice to me from now on. Calling me stupid could be, like, hazardous to your health."

Brenda studied him closely, weighing her options, all of which had been drastically reduced in the last hour, and calmed down. She thought she knew how to manipulate him.

He giggled again. She was stuck, and he was going to enjoy this, it seemed.

"Nice, how?"

"What, I have to spell it out for you? Go take one of those long showers you like so much. You need to wash Travis off so take your time and make sure you do it right. Then, come out. You know what I want."

She hesitated, seeming to weigh her chances one way or the other, shrugged, and did as he asked. When the shower door closed he slipped her bloody glove in the trash can under a supply of tissues she'd deposited earlier. He noted that some of the blood oozed onto two of the tissues, her tissues, with her DNA.

Sweet.

THIRTY-THREE

DAWN BROUGHT BACK the birds yammering in the trees. Farther away, toward the park, an elephant trumpeted, ushering in the rising sun. Mist drifted across the river, and the day broke fresh and new. Near the river, the herbal scent of the river seemed to rise with the mist. David Mmusi considered himself a very lucky fellow. He had a beautiful girlfriend and a part-time job at the Safari Lodge. Each morning before school, he would walk to the Sedudu bar and straighten up. His job was to remove the empty bottles, empty the dust bins and ash trays, and sweep up. In the afternoon he would return and help fill the ice buckets, place the tables and chairs in order, and set out the bottles of liquor for the evening's consumption. It did not pay well, but it would serve as a foot in the door for the future after he finished his education. Jobs at the lodges in Kasane were difficult to obtain. He had a head start.

He quick-stepped down the path from the main lodge, humming along with the latest song from America that he'd downloaded to his MP3 player. At the turning in the path, where tree limbs hang over, something bright and colorful caught his eye. He stopped and looked into the deeper shadows against the tree trunks. A leopard patterned scarf apparently dropped by a guest fluttered weakly in the freshening breeze. He picked it up and folded it carefully. It will be a very fine present for Mpitle, he thought. He put it in his pocket and continued on his way to the bar. He had work to do and a long walk after that to school. He would present this fine scarf to Mpitle during lunch break.

TRAVIS SAW THE DAWN. He had not slept. Too much had happened in the last few hours, and his excitement had kept him as alert and wide awake as a triple shot cappuccino. Getting rid of Brenda Griswold had been easier than he'd expected. Once she realized she no longer had anything with which to bargain and therefore he had no further use for her, she'd left, but only after making some very explicit suggestions as to what he could do with himself in the future, several of which were neither gracefully stated nor anatomically possible. He guessed he'd gotten off easy. He hoped she would find her way back to her husband and former life. She certainly seemed capable. She'd hooked Bobby once, she could do so again.

Candor was not a virtue in the circles in which Travis moved, but he had to concede he felt no remorse. Schemers like Brenda always landed on their feet. She would this time as well. He turned his attention to the papers he'd brought from Chicago. He didn't need half of them anymore. They dealt with a now no-longer-operative, the who, what, and how of his take-over plan. The rest were detailed performance ratings of the company, its divisions, and subdivisions. He'd need to memorize the figures. If he and Leo were going to work together, he'd need to know as much as he did—no mean feat. Leo might not have the benefit of an MBA, nor, Travis believed, a baccalaureate, but when it came to the company and its myriad pieces and parts, he was a walking encyclopedia. Whether or not people thought Leo was over the hill, they conceded he knew his company—all of it.

Real estate? Leo said he wanted a piece of it to build his lodge and casino and maybe a few other projects. Well, why not? The old guy could not last much longer. Why not give him a hobby? And the way this country was progressing, a tourist spot on the Chobe River could pay. He'd have a conversation with Greshenko about that. Perhaps the company could hold its retreats here.

Overall, it had been a stupendous night. He flopped on the bed and dozed. Meeting with Leo and the Russian—when? Leo hadn't said. Soon.

SANDERSON AWOKE EARLY. She'd had a dream that frightened her. Something about death. She couldn't recall exactly what, but it felt close. She crept to Michael's room and listened to his ragged breathing. Not Michael. Who? Who was going to die? She could not get back to sleep, so she dressed and prepared coffee and porridge. Today she would have to stop the hunt. She could not justify the time anymore. Mr. Pako would be leaving in the afternoon and that would settle it at last. The game drivers had reported that a new male lion had assumed the rule over the Natanga pride. That made her sad. She would miss old Sekoa.

Mpitle stirred and asked if something was wrong.

"No, nothing's wrong, girl. You go and sleep some more, then you must get yourself ready for school. Your breakfast is on the burner. Make sure Michael eats something. I must go and see about this hunting we have been doing."

She stepped out into the dawn, took a deep breath and climbed into her truck. The anxiety she'd felt ear-

lier would not go away. What could it be, all this thinking of death? Rra Kaleke approached her.

"*Dumela, Mma,* will we be hunting today?"

"*Dumela, Rra,* no, no hunting today or anymore, I
think."

Rra Kaleke nodded. "That lion is gone far from here.
But I thank you, Sanderson, for the opportunity to hunt
again. You are a good woman."

With that he turned on his heel and strode away. She
recognized that he'd paid her a high compliment. He reminded her of old Sekoa, and she wondered how many
months or years either had left on this earth.

BRENDA SPENT THE early dawn staring at the bare back of
her sleeping husband. It had been too easy. Bobby was
up to something. What had he meant when he said he'd
fixed it? Why so confident all of a sudden? She wished
she knew. She'd go through his stuff and find out, but
first she needed a shower. She slipped out of bed and
into bathroom. She inspected herself in the mirror. Her
mascara had run and she looked like a raccoon. Her hair
could have served as a nest for a pair of storks. She was
a mess, and really hungry.

THE GRAY MONKEY sat on his haunches and studied the
lion and the man. He had no fear of either. He knew they
no longer posed a threat. The sun warmed the ground,
and that woke up the flies. They began to arrive, first
just a few, and then they came in swarms. The vultures
would be next and then the rest of the carrion eaters. A
dead lion, a dead man. The inevitable sequelae of scavengers soon to come frightened him more than either
the man or the lion would, if alive. He galloped away.

A kilometer to the west, the hyenas began yipping and chortling. The pack waited. They had tested the air and knew their enemy lay dead nearby. There would be food, but did they dare go so close to the humans? They'd found the gap in the fence and had even made a protracted sortie in the direction he'd gone, but caution quickly overcame hunger, and they'd retreated. But now?

The pack circled, barking and yipping, awaiting a decision from their leader. The pack's matriarch lifted her head and turned eastward, toward the scent. She snapped her jaws, made a noise that sounded like a cross between a gargle and a bark, and then turned and trotted west. Some of the pack milled about, reluctant to follow, and yapped their frustration at having to pass on this easy feed.

THIRTY-FOUR

LEO PAINTER'S MORNING started slowly. He'd slept fitfully at first, until the four extra-strength Tylenols and the nitro finally kicked in, easing his chest pain. Bright sunshine and singing birds finally pulled him back to consciousness. He arose, splashed water on his face and confronted the day. He didn't like what he saw. A shower and shave only marginally improved his mood. He dressed and contemplated an early breakfast. His sour stomach vetoed the idea. He brewed a pot of hotel room coffee and nibbled at a mango, the only item left from the basket of monkey-purloined fruit. It had apparently rolled under the bed during the simian rampage and been found by the cleaners sent to restore order. The coffee was bad, the mango stringy, and his disposition elevated only slightly from this attempt at nutritional discipline. He looked at his watch. Both Greshenko and Travis were late. He could forgive Travis. He had neglected to specify a time when they spoke the previous night, but Greshenko knew better.

A noise at the sliding glass door momentarily drew him away from his annoyance. A gray monkey sat in what could pass as a slovenly lotus position on the deck, contemplating Leo. Leo stared back. He'd once tried staring down a cat and lost. In the absence of anything better to do he took on the monkey. The latter, evidently satisfied he had Leo's complete attention gravely pointed with its right arm and long fingers toward the path that led to the Sedudu bar. He rolled his head clockwise, grinned and gamboled away on all fours.

"Thank you for the suggestion, friend, but it's a bit early for a drink."

The monkey did not respond. A knock at the door. Leo swiveled around.

"It's open."

"I am sorry I'm late," Yuri Greshenko looked hot and sweaty. "But on my way over here I had a flat tire. Actually, I had two."

"Two? How'd you manage that?"

"I don't know. The tires were fully inflated when I left the Mowana Lodge, and just after I pulled around the corner by the golf course, the left front tire just went flat. I didn't see an obstruction, no pothole, nails, nothing. I went to get out the jack and spare. The jack was missing and the spare was flat as well. And I found this." He held up a dark leathery thing. "I called the rental company and they are sending someone to fix it. I didn't think I should wait, but I had to walk the last kilometer and a half."

"What's that?" Leo pointed at the thing dangling from Greshenko's hand.

"I don't think I want to know. The last time I was here, I heard tales about witches and magic and ritual sacrifice of prepubescent girls and boys, and I'm afraid this might have something to do with that."

"They killed kids?"

"It was said so. I don't know. I never had it confirmed or authenticated. It's just what people said."

"You don't think someone wanted to cast a spell on you, do you?"

"Not me, I don't think. On you. Remember the old

lady and the goats? She was yelling at me when we stopped. We were driving a left-hand steering car and I was seated in the passenger seat, which would have been the driver's side in the right-handed variety. She is used to seeing right-handed cars, so she probably thought I was the driver. I think she may have spent some of your money with an *ngaka* and this is a bit of *boloi*, witch-craft."

"So you believe that piece of whatever caused your flat tire?"

"No, I don't, but it is not important what I believe. It only matters what the person who put this thing in the car believes. Judging from the look on that old woman's face, we got off lucky. She wanted you dead."

"Take more than a piece of hairy leather to pull that off. I'd offer you some of my coffee, but it's really awful. As soon as Travis gets here, we'll go for breakfast at the lodge."

"The young man knows what you want to do up here?"

"Not all of it, but enough. Also, he is unclear why you're here. I suspect he had some intel on you and suspects the worst."

"No doubt. He must think you're off your rocking chair. Is that how you say it?"

"Close enough."

"You are a very trusting man, Mr. Painter. Most people would not have had the, what do you say…the stomach—"

"Guts."

"The guts to engage my services. I have a reputation, you know. I am guessing, but I think that policeman who has been on my tail since the day we arrived has a dossier on me and is waiting to see who I contact. Approaching Rra Botlhokwa could easily be misinterpreted."

"As long as you don't break any laws..."

"It is not a matter of breaking a law. This country is very proud of the fact it is considered one of the least corrupt countries in the world. It ranks above most European nations and a long way above the United States. They will react to even their suspicions."

There was a commotion outside followed by a knock at the door. Again Leo invited the caller in. Travis entered followed by another man. Greshenko sat a little straighter at the sight of the second.

"Leo, I was held up, sorry. This is Mr. Modise. He wishes to have a word with Mr. Greshenko and with you."

Modise stepped into the room and surveyed it like a man about to repossess the furniture. Nothing seemed to escape his notice.

"Inspector, what can I do for you?" Leo would be polite and careful. Greshenko could very well become a problem, and if he were to leave town it could certainly put a hair in the soup.

"I must ask you a few questions. But first let me say that we are honored with your presence, Mr. Painter. I am told of the many things you have done, and we, in this country, hope you can teach us much about minerals."

Leo nodded and wondered if polite pleasantries were always part of the drill in Botswana, or if this man was treading lightly because someone higher up told him to be careful.

"But I must also put a question to you as it respects the man they call Rra Botlhokwa."

Here it comes, Leo thought. Greshenko edged forward in his chair. Travis lifted one eyebrow.

"You see, it is thought that this man may be dealing in matters that would attract the attention of my police department. That is the truth of it. And then there is Mr. Greshenko here, whose most interesting file is sent to us by Interpol. So, we must ask if there is anything that you are about that will cause me to suspect you of some behavior that might possibly embarrass our two governments?"

Very neatly put. It was just the right combination of circumlocution to stay within the boundaries of diplomacy and just a little steel at the end to make us sit up and take notice.

Leo pondered how to frame an answer when someone else knocked at his door.

THIRTY-FIVE

BRENDA WANTED BREAKFAST. Bobby was dead to the world. She thought it would be neat if she gave him a poke with her *assegai* to get him moving. Serve him right, too. He couldn't be the only one doing the poking. She smiled at her joke—good one. Rummaging through the pile of parcels, discarded clothes, and underwear that had accumulated on the bench at the foot of the bed produced nothing. She scratched her head and tried to remember where she'd seen it last. She attacked the pile a second time. She did find the paper bag it had been in and the sales slip, but no spear point.

She found a ball point pen, a poor substitute for an *assegai,* and used it to give Bobby the poke in the ribs. He moaned and called her a name. Maybe she should, like, go to breakfast without him. And maybe she'd take some pills and poison Travis' coffee, the rat bastard. She wondered idly how many Percocets it would take to snuff him. She went back to the heap on the bench and pulled out her safari shorts. She put them on. Added the blouse and tucked it in. The belt was on the floor. She found one glove but not the other and the scarf was missing. She wondered if she'd left them in Travis' room. Probably, but that didn't explain the spear point going missing. She frowned. She knew she wasn't exactly a neatnik, but also she always knew where things were in the piles and messes she made, and that *assegai* should have been in the bag on the bench. So what happened to it?

"Where do you think you're going?" Bobby had woken and was watching her with one eye.

"Breakfast. You know how I am after. I could eat a whole, whatever that thing was they served last night. Kubu? No that's not right. That's what I called it and the waiter laughed at me. He said *kubu* meant hippopotamus and they didn't serve hippo. But it sounded like that."

"Kudu."

"What?"

"The meat was kudu, not *kubu*. Kudu is like a big deer thing only with different horns. I saw a picture."

"Big whoop, Bobby, you know, like, big freaking deal. So you know your animals. I knew it wasn't a hippo steak. Look, if you want to eat breakfast with me, you'll get your lazy ass out of bed."

Bobby rolled off the bed and made his way to the bathroom. His back was crisscrossed with red scratch marks where she'd clawed at him the night before.

"Hey, it's all steamy in here. What have you been doing?"

"Taking a shower, stupid. You could use one, too, but hurry up. I'm starving. Hey, you haven't seen my spear thing anywhere have you? I can't find it."

"I didn't take it. What makes you think I had anything to do with it? What did *you* do with it, is the question. I think you better be thinking about that."

"What the hell are you talking about? I just asked you if you'd seen it anywhere, that's all. What's with the third degree? Jesus, you sound like a cop or something."

"Maybe you ought to get used to that."

"And what's that supposed to mean? Bobby, what have you been up to? I know you, there's something."

"Nothing."

"Yeah, yeah. Listen you better hope I find out in time so I can square it with whoever, or whatever, is going to be, like, after you."

"You're on the wrong cart path there, sweetie. You're the one who…"

"I'm the one who what?"

"Nothing. Are we going to breakfast or do you need an appetizer first?"

"Don't need an appetizer. And if you want any more of me anytime soon, you'll tell me what you did that has you so, you know, defensive."

Bobby, she noted, dummied up. Something had happened lately, and he didn't want her to know what. Pretty typical. They left for the lodge, Brenda plotting how she'd wangle the thing out of him and then how she could sneak into Travis' room without him knowing so she could get her glove and scarf and, oh yeah, her red thong. Who needed Travis anyway.

As they stepped from the room, the housekeeping staff, which had been loitering a few steps away, picked up their equipment and moved toward them.

"Great, give it a going over only don't screw around with my crap." Brenda stepped aside to let them enter. "Sheets, towels. Lots of towels. Like, we're always running out of them, and stuff. The bed is a mess, too. You might need rubber gloves to change it. Junior, here, isn't exactly Mr. Sanitary."

The staff showed some more of those amazingly white teeth. How do they do that? Their dentist bills must be out of this world. They hadn't a clue what she was saying.

"Hey, Babe, while you're at it, look around under the bed, and here and there, and see if you can find my other glove. I lost it in there somewhere."

Bobby surfaced from his morning stupor.

"What are they doing?"

"Cleaning the room and all. Where you at, Bobby? It's nearly nine-thirty. They have a job to do."

"I don't want the room cleaned." He gestured at the women and raised his voice. "No cleanee the roomo, you understandee?"

"You jerk. They, like, speak English and they ain't deaf. They gotta clean the room. It's their job. Even if it wasn't, I want them to. They should, like, fumigate the place. It stinks from too much bed wrestling." She turned back to the crew. "Clean it. He's still drunk, you know?" She mimed tilting a bottle to her mouth and pointed at Bobby. The women laughed.

"No, no, not now, later." Bobby sounded desperate. What was up with him?

"Okay, hot shot, they can do it later. But if you have any ideas about getting back in that bed anytime soon, you can forget it, for sure."

Bobby seemed mollified and turned back toward the lodge. Brenda made a shooing sign to the crew indicating they should go on in the room and clean it anyway. Bobby was an idiot. She really needed to get a better deal somewhere. She almost had it with Travis until Leo stepped in and ruined it. Leo and idiot boy. But there was something else in the wind. She was sure of it and her antennae were up. Bobby couldn't fool a two-year-old. He'd done something, and if she could just find out what it was, she might have the upper hand again. That would be good.

All she knew was there was something in the room he needed intact, and there was something about her and… who? Not Travis. He'd dropped that. Leo? She'd find out and then, ladies, hold on to your panties.

THIRTY-SIX

THIS TIME LEO stood and answered the door. Two anxious looking men waited on the doorstep.

"Mr. Painter, sir, can you help us?"

"I don't know. I suppose it depends on what you want?"

"Your friend, Mr. Farrah, is missing. We are concerned, and thought he might be with you."

"Oh, excuse me. Come in." The men sidled into the room. "This is Mr. Greshenko and Mr. Parrizi, my associates. Perhaps they can help, and police inspector..."

"Kgabo Modise, from Gabz. What happened?"

The two men exchanged worried glances and one, probably the more senior of the two, said, "We are the management. We are concerned about Mr. Farrah?"

"Henry? No, he's not with me. Why? Is something wrong?" Leo tried to remember if Farrah said anything the night before.

"We are not sure. You see, it is like this. Mr. Farrah engaged to go with a group to Zimbabwe to see the Victoria Falls. We do not recommend our guests go alone because of the situations in that country. He failed to meet the bus. We placed a call to his room, and no answer. The driver, he is getting impatient. We knock on Mr. Farrah's door. Again no answer. So, we think, maybe this man is, perhaps, sick. So, we open the door. By now the group has left for the Falls without him and the driver is not so happy to do that. But, you see, Mr. Farrah's bed is still made, not been slept in, and he is not there. We are worried he might be hurt or…" The manager's voice trailed off.

"I can't imagine why he did not return to his room. He seemed all right when he left here."

"The barkeep says he was unsteady when he received a call from you, he thinks, and then Mr. Farrah leaves."

"You mean he was drunk the last time anyone saw him at the bar."

"It is so. And because of this unsteadiness, it is possible he could have fallen. If he goes too near the river, or…" The manager shrugged and rolled his eyes.

"Or what? You think he might have fallen in? The water would sober him up in a big hurry. He wouldn't go near the river no matter how drunk he was, and if he fell in, he'd fly out of there like a rocket. Henry was terrified of your crocodiles."

"I was thinking of the lion."

"The lion? Don't tell me that it's real, too. There really is a lion on the loose? Christ, I thought that was just a PR ploy."

"No. Mr. Painter," the manager looked hurt, "I assure you there is a lion threat. Not three kilometers from here a young man was taken. It was very sad. We warned you when you arrived to be careful, you see. Even now, they are hunting it."

"Well, I'll be…"

"So if you can help us find him, Mr. Farrah, I mean, we would be grateful."

"I don't know what I can do, frankly. Farrah spent about an hour here last night, He left about ten, and I think he was headed to the Sedudu Bar. Maybe he passed out down there."

"The boy has already been there to clean, and he does not report your friend being there. Perhaps he is nearby."

"Sorry, it's the best I can do. Say, do you think you could have a pot of coffee and some Danish sent down? I am in the middle of a meeting here with my associates, and Inspector Moeasy has some questions he wants to ask us."

"Modise."

"What? Oh, sorry, Inspector *Modise*. When he's finished perhaps he can help hunt. Isn't that what you do, Inspector, hunt for things?"

Modise gave Leo a chilly smile. "It is one of the things we do, Mr. Painter. Stopping crime is often about hunting."

The two hotel employees left with a promise to send over food and drink.

"Inspector, you asked me a question before we were interrupted. In the confusion I lost my train of thought. What was it again?"

"You are not concerned about your missing friend?"

"Henry Farrah is not my friend. He is, or I should say, was, an employee. I do not make friends of my employees. To my mind it is bad business. I work with them, am cordial most of the time, but I learned early in my career that it is much easier to fire an acquaintance than a friend. Furthermore, the man was preparing to stab me in the back, metaphorically speaking. One of several with that idea in mind, I might add." Leo shot Travis a look.

"I am sorry to hear that. You are correct, I did not ask about your friend before, I asked if there was anything you and Mr. Greshenko, and now Mr. Parizzi, were about here in Kasane that could cause either of us to be concerned for your future stay in Botswana?"

"No, Inspector. There is not. Our dealings with Mr. Botlhokwa, were aboveboard. We were led to believe he had certain connections that might expedite our business here. That is all."

"I am happy to hear that." Modise did not look either happy or convinced. He rose to leave, and his eye fell on the bit of *boloi*. "Where did that come from?"

"Had a flat tire on the way over here, found that in the back of the LADA when I went to look for the jack. I think somebody doesn't like me."

"So it would seem. You say you had a flat tire?"

"Two."

"Then it must have worked. May I have it?" Greshenko nodded. "We have an open case concerning the disappearance of a young girl. We will take this to the lab and run a DNA scan."

"You think that's human?" Leo found the idea appalling.

"I think this is monkey, but I must be sure. The lab will know. And if it isn't then we will be back to find out who purchased it and, from whom."

"Well, good luck with that."

Modise produced an evidence bag from his coat pocket and placed the charm in it, marked the time, date, and place it had been recovered. He walked to the door, paused and faced the three men.

"Please do not require me to return to you. Take some advice. Do your business without the famous Rra Botlhokwa."

When he'd left, Leo turned to Greshenko, "Can we?"

"Maybe yes and maybe no."

"Leo," Travis said, "would you fill me in on what you've been doing. If I'm going to spend time in a Botswana jail, I'd like to know why."

"Here's our coffee. Have a cup and then we'll talk." He let the staff person in and waited until the man set up and departed. "All right, Yuri, fill Travis in on what we've been doing."

THIRTY-SEVEN

SANDERSON LOOPED BACK to her village after reporting to her supervisor. Pako seemed preoccupied with packing, unpacking, and repacking boxes in anticipation of his move to Maun. He said he did not have time for her this day or to give her any direction.

"You should be out hunting the lion. You should understand that if there is failure doing this thing, there was nothing I can say to my successor to help you keep her position."

He looked very smug when he said that. She excused herself and left.

She checked in on Michael. He seemed better, stronger. He smiled and assured her that his sister had made him eat.

"Too much, Mma. Tell my sister I will die of overeating before this disease gets me."

She made a face at him. Making jokes like that did not please her at all. Still, it showed he was stronger. Maybe…No she would not think it.

She made an early lunch of some cold meat left over from the previous night and the bit of breakfast porridge still in the pot. Her mobile beeped just as she finished.

The hotel was calling. There had been an accident with a lion. She must come immediately. A lion? Her lion? That could not be. Her lion, as everyone in the village knew, was in the Makgadikgadi Pans by now. What is this? She called a goodbye to her son and raced to the Land Rover. Rra Kaleke stood in front of his rondeval. She waved to him.

"Rra, you must come. There is another lion taking a man."

Kaleke shuffled as fast as he could and slid into the cab next to her. "Where is the lion doing this?"

"At the Safari Lodge near the Sedudu Bar. It is all I know. But they are thinking it is the same animal that took that Zimbabwe boy. But it cannot be the same one."

Kaleke shook his head. They raced to the Kasane road and turned toward the lodge. Three police cars were drawn up in front, but as they arrived, two of them drove off toward the end of the hotel property to park nearer the bar. She followed.

A crowd had gathered at the camping ground that covered the space between the hotel's separate lodge buildings and the Sedudu Bar. Police were busy urging them back. Anxious faces turned toward her as she strode forward through the crowd. She was the gamekeeper; she would know. Sanderson pushed ahead and, followed closely by Rra Kaleke, made her way through the crowd toward the spot where two men stood talking animatedly to a third. As she approached they turned and seeing her uniform, pointed further into the bush.

She saw the lion first. His huge body stretched out and his head rested on the man's chest. He appeared peaceful and asleep. The plethora of flies indicated he wasn't. She drew closer.

"It is Sekoa," she said. "It is the old lion from the Natanga pride. So this is where it ends, old man," she said to the lion, then realized Rra Kaleke might think she spoke to him.

He did not. "This *tau* did not kill this man," Kaleke said. He shook his head. "That is very strange. It looks like he just put all his energy in bringing his prey to this spot and then he says goodbye to the world."

"He was a sick lion. His poor body must have just given out. But why do you say he did not kill the man?"

"You see, there are no wounds to the man's neck. If this lion did take this man, he would close those terrible jaws on his *kgokgotsho*, his…what is it? His throat? He would close down on it until he is dead. Then he would bring him to this place. But look here. There are only the marks on the shoulder, but, you see, his wind-pipe has no marks. Then he drags this body to this place from over there." Kaleke pointed back the way they'd come at the disturbed grass and scarred earth on the camp ground.

Sanderson looked back the way he'd indicated and then back at the man.

"Maybe this man had a fall or a heart attack and old Sekoa came upon him and say, 'Here is a fine meal for me,' and dragged him in the bush to feed. Only he is too sick and so he dies."

They signaled for help and the man who'd been talking to the hotel staff came over.

"We must move this body away from the animal," she directed the man to grab the shoulders and she his feet. On her count Kaleke lifted the lion's head and they slid the body out from under it.

"What is this?" She studied the angry gash on the man's abdomen. "That does not look like a lion wound."

"What then?" The man who'd come to help said.

"I do not know, but that is not from this old man— the lion, I mean."

"I am Inspector Modise of the Gaborone Police. What are you suggesting?"

"I am saying nothing, only that this lion did not kill this man but he has some sort of wound."

Superintendent Mwambe strolled over to the group.

"Where is your boss, Sanderson? Where is Mr. Pako?"

"He is busy preparing to depart. He says I must handle this."

"Well, it seems you have found your lion at last. It is unfortunate for this man you did not find him sooner. Were you hunting in the wrong place, Missus?"

Kaleke faced the police superintendent. "This is not the lion that took that boy."

"Nonsense. And who are you to make such an assertion? Of course it is the lion. I will tell the hotels they can relax their vigilance. The lion has been found and is dead, no thanks to Sanderson."

"But—" Sanderson felt Rra Kaleke's hand on her arm and glanced at him. He shook his head. Mwambe marched away to direct his officers in their duties and give the hotel manager the good news. Modise frowned and followed him more slowly.

"Sanderson, accept the lion. It will relieve you of pretending to hunt. That other lion is gone, and this one will do, you see? That Mwambe cannot be told anything; he is so puffed up, this man. Do you know what he is named in the village? *Tshwena*, the baboon."

She saw Kaleke's point. If luck gives you this chance, you must go for it.

A truck arrived to take the body away. People milled around waiting to see what would happen to the lion. A dead lion was worth much pula. His pelt alone would bring a big price in the right places, and certain of his parts, like his heart, could be sold to the witches for money or favors. If they buried it, surely someone would return and dig him up. Sanderson called for a second truck to come and collect the lion. Sekoa belonged to the government now, and severe penalties would fall on anyone who tried to interfere.

The hotel manager walked over to Sanderson and Rra Kaleke. He nodded to her but addressed him.

"Rra, what do you make of this situation? This man was a guest from America, a Mr. Henry Farrah."

"It is a confusion. We see this lion, and he is with the dead man, but he is not the cause of this man's dying. At first I believed he has seen this old lion coming at him and his *pelo* just stops from fright."

"You think the lion jumps out of the bush, and the man, this Henry Farrah, had a heart attack?"

"Yes, that is what I think it must be at first, but then I see that this man has come across a very strange thing. He has had a meeting with something very sharp and it did him a disservice. I think he falls over there," he pointed back along the route marking the broken brush and flattened grass. Rra Kaleke gazed sadly at the departing truck carrying the last remains of Henry Farrah. "And then this poor lion found him and dragged him in the bush for a meal, but he didn't live to eat it. Maybe it is the *tau* that has the heart failure, instead."

"You do not think that the wound was made by the lion?"

"No. If the lion bites him, there will be many punctures. His teeth are in pairs, you see?" Kaleke bent over and pulled back Sekoa's lips to expose his incisors and massive fangs. "You see this one on the right side of his mouth is chipped. He must have had a disagreement

with a *nare,* you know, a big buffalo, and broke off a
piece when he tries to bite on his *kgokgotsho* to bring
him down."

"He fought a buffalo you think?"

"Of course, many. This one is a proud animal, he
would bring down buffalo, anything except a grown elephant, I think." Rra Kaleke surveyed the nearby trees.
"If the *manong* had found these two sooner, there would
be no evidence to tell us these things."

"But, why did the vultures not come until now?"

"Who can read the minds of all these creatures that
Modimo gives to us?"

THIRTY-EIGHT

EVEN THOUGH HE was on edge, somehow Bobby managed to eat his breakfast without starting a quarrel. He needed to be Mr. Cool this morning. At any moment he expected police cars and detectives to come crashing into the hotel, throw handcuffs on Brenda and haul her away. He did notice several employees dashing toward the walkways that eventually led to the path to the Sedudu Bar. If Brenda noticed, which he doubted, she gave no indication, but happily wolfed down a huge breakfast and several cups of coffee. He would have to wait, he guessed.

They were nearly back to their room when a policeman approached them.

"What's with the police cars, officer?" Bobby kept Brenda close.

"Ah, I am *Superintendent* Mwambe, not 'officer.' And the excitement is about a death."

"Somebody was killed?" Wherever Brenda's mind had been, it quickly returned to the present.

"Alas, I am afraid it is so, an American tourist, one of your party, if I am not mistaken."

"Name?"

"I do not know. He was a large man in a suit…"

Bobby's eyes lit up. "That would be Leo Painter, then."

"Leo's dead. Wow. Where?"

Mwambe pointed back along the walkway toward the bush. "Just by the Sedudu Bar, Miss. It is very terrible."

"This I gotta see. Bobby, we could be in for some serious money soon." Brenda rushed away. After four steps she paused and bent her knees and lifted her feet, first one and then the other, to remove her shoes. Bare footed, she hurried down the walkway, pausing momentarily to drop her shoes and her purse by their door.

"Put those away for me, will you?" she called over her shoulder.

"Leave it to my wife to wear stilettos with a safari outfit. She's strange, you know?"

"I'm sorry, you were saying?" Mwambe had had his eyes and mind on the show of legs and thighs and missed Bobby's remark.

"Weird, she is. Say, you know, she's been acting kind of strange lately. Now that you tell me Leo's bought it, it makes sense, sort of. See, I came in last night, like, I was at the bar, and she's all jumpy, you know?"

Mwambe did not know. His confusion altered his usual scowling expression.

"See, she really hated Leo, and it wouldn't surprise me if she didn't have something to do with him getting killed."

"I hardly see how that is possible, Mister…"

"Sorry, I'm Griswold, Bob Griswold. Oh yeah, she could. You don't know it, but back in Chicago? Like, she used to hang around with gangsters and all. Worked in a night club as an exotic dancer."

That revelation brought another shift in Mwambe's expression. Exotic dancer added to the bit of leg he'd seen…"That is quite fascinating Mr. Griswold, but I still don't see how."

"Look, step in our room for a minute. You just might be interested in something I saw in the trash can. It, like, didn't mean anything at the time but, you know, I thought she might have cut herself shaving her legs and so I didn't pay any attention but when you add in Leo's been killed, well. . ."

Mwambe's mind had stopped inputting with *legs*.

They reached the door. Bobby stooped and collected Brenda's shoes and opened the door. "If you'll just have a look." He stopped in his tracks and dropped the shoes. Mwambe had to sidestep around him.

"They cleaned the room. I said not to and they did anyway. Now it's gone." He turned to the policeman. "You'd better check the trash for the evidence."

"Sir, I am confused. You say your wife had something to do with the death, is that correct?"

"Yes, no, I'm worried, you know. Like, she is my wife and all, so I have to support her and..." Bobby ran out of words. He didn't want to sound too pushy, but he did want Mwambe to start to check her out. Only the room was clean and the glove gone.

"How could she have done such a thing? I cannot see how this woman in her high heels and short dress could have incited a lion to attack your friend. A man perhaps, but not a lion. How would she do that?"

"Whoa, you said lion? A lion killed Leo?"

"But yes. I thought you knew."

"You just said he was killed, and I thought you meant he was murdered."

"Well, by the lion, yes. We do not think of wild animals as murderers. Hunting and killing is what they do. But I suppose you could say that."

"No, wait, you're sure about the lion thing?"

Superintendent Mwambe backed out of the room. "If there is nothing for me to see…your dust bin is empty and…well, good day to you." He scurried down the walkway toward the lodge. Bobby kicked the door shut. He went over to the trash can and peered in as if to be sure his eyes were not playing tricks on him. Still empty.

He sat down heavily on the bed and contemplated his reflection in the mirror. Leo was killed by a lion. What was he to do now? He'd inherit all that stock and would be in a position to have an important position in the company for sure, but the divorce was out. Brenda would get half of everything if he did it, and she wouldn't cut him any slack. He'd have to stay married. Maybe later he could…could what?

He pounded his fist onto the mattress. It was so perfect. How could a lion do that to him? Still, there was the spear point. They had to find that. And the scarf he'd left in the path. Once they did their autopsy thing and saw he'd been stabbed, they'd figure it out. He didn't need the glove. Just a matter of time.

But suppose the lion, like, ate Leo. They wouldn't be able to see the stab wound, would they? He needed a back-up plan. Somehow he had to make them think murder with a capital M.

Killing Leo had been the hardest thing he'd ever done. Harder than leaving the accident where that kid got himself killed two years ago. They were still looking for the car, his car, his BMW. But he didn't have it anymore. Stolen and stripped, chopped into a million pieces. But that was then, this is now. He'd need to get his plan moving again. People thought he was stupid. He'd show them stupid. He hadn't gotten this far just to see the whole thing go down the drain in flames.

Bobby's existence, his life as an adult, you could say, consisted of an endless string of mixed metaphors.

He went to the door where he'd dropped her shoes and purse. The shoes he left, but he carried the purse back to the bed. Who to call? Desiree. Brenda always told her everything. And Desiree was never far from her phone. Unless she was unconscious or seducing a pole at the club, Desiree was on line. He found her address and hit text.

HEY BFF...I DID IT, WE'RE IN THE $$...B.

He waited and sure enough the phone's ringtone sounded. He switched to vibrate and answered.

DID WAT?...D2

He thought a minute and then responded.

DID LEO N HE SED HD TELL BBY SO I TK HM OUT!

WTF!!!

HAD 2...2 MCH $ DOWN THE CRAPPER IF I DNT— OOPS GOT A GO...B

He closed the phone. He was about to turn it off but thought it would be better if it looked like she had lost it while it was on. More messages behind this one would make it seem more authentic. Later he'd slip out and drop it where the cops could find it. It buzzed madly in his hand. He stepped out on the deck and slid the phone under the step where he'd hidden the spear and scarf the night before. He had just closed and locked the slider when Brenda began rapping on the door.

Left her key in her purse. Dingbat.

THE GRAY MONKEY had positioned himself in the trees watching and waiting. He knew that sooner or later one of the doors would be left ajar and he could affect a raid. There was almost always fruit, and lately he'd solved the problem of opening the cold box. It had food, too. And he'd grown partial to the taste of lipstick. He watched the man put something shiny under the step. He waited, then swung from branch to branch to the ground, scuttled across the lawn, retrieved the phone, romped back to the tree, and climbed back to his perch. This was something new.

THIRTY-NINE

LEO'S HEADACHE HAD not improved with coffee, and his stomach was acting like it had joined the Teamsters and was on strike. He liked to think of himself as a plain speaker, blunt. When his body refused to accede to his will, he became noticeably rude. His acquaintances would say rud*er*, that Leo was characteristically rude. That was not true. On occasion he could be positively charming. That's when he was most dangerous. The pounding on the door seemed almost in sync with that in his head. It stopped all conversation between the men. Modise had shifted their focus. What else would push in to screw up his day?

"Get that, will you, Travis?" Leo felt annoyed. He had things to do, and he couldn't get a minute's peace without some jackass beating on his door. Travis opened it. The hotel manager stood on the threshold once again.

"I am sorry to bother you again, but we have found Mr. Farrah."

"Swell, now we can all celebrate. Where did he turn up?" Leo was past politeness.

"I am sorry, but you see, he has met with an accident." The manager had that look. The one you see on the face of someone who's afraid there will be trouble, yelling, or maybe a lawsuit.

"Is he hurt?" Leo mentally calculated the cost to the company of flying Farrah back to the States and then on to the Mayo Clinic. He winced at the number that popped up.

"I am afraid it is worse than that. Your friend is dead." The poor man reflexively took a step backward as if he expected a blow. Leo relaxed a bit.

"Dead? What do you mean, he's dead. What happened? Did he fall? Heart attack? What?"

"It appears the lion about which we were speaking before, the one we warned you about, often if you remember, has taken him."

"Holy shit. Did you hear that, Yuri? There really is a lion, and he ate Farrah. Farrah was toxic. Probably killed the beast, too."

The manager did not share the joke. "Indeed, the lion is dead also, but I do not think your Mr. Farrah had anything to do with that."

"This is awkward. Is he in pieces or what?"

"No, he is quite whole. As I said, the lion was dead beside him. We have removed Mr. Farrah's body to the police station for examination and will release it to you in a day or two. It is routine, the police say."

"No rush. Farrah isn't in one, why should they be?"

Inspector Modise stepped into the room behind the manager, who turned and left, shocked at the American's callousness.

"Your friend is dead, and we don't know what happened."

Travis had remained silent until now, but this was something new, even exciting. "I thought that guy said the lion got him somehow."

Modise ignored him and spoke to Leo. "Do you know anyone who would like to have seen him dead?"

"His ex-wife certainly, in a New York minute, but

she's in Winnetka at the moment, and I don't see her slipping over here forming an alliance with your local beasts to knock him off, and leaving without someone knowing, so you can rule her out. She probably gets the life insurance, though. I wonder, does double indemnity cover a lion attack?"

"The lion was only a peripheral player in his death, we think. The game ranger believes he must have been stabbed somehow, and the lion found him later."

"Could he have fallen on something sharp and then...I don't know, run into the lion, which finished him off?"

"Anything is possible. Mr. Farrah may have encountered the lion, become so frightened that he ran into a broken tree limb and then fell and the lion carried him a ways and—"

"And then dropped dead?"

"It would seem so."

"Sounds very odd to me. I mean, what are the chances? Anyway, I can't help you inspector. He left here at about ten o'clock last night and was on his way to the bar. I told them that. Henry was not a likeable man but not one you'd hate either. It has to be an accident."

"Yes. Well, we shall see what the autopsy shows."

"We should go see this," Travis said.

The men stood and single-filed out the door. Modise turned toward the hotel; the three others headed to the Sedudu bar. They passed Brenda on her way back. She chose to ignore them. She could be rude, too.

At the edge of the campground, a clot of people watched as a group of men supervised by a woman who, they were told, was the gamekeeper, lifted the carcass of the lion onto a tarpaulin and then into a truck bed.

By the expressions on their faces, the lion must have been very heavy.

"Ow." Travis hopped on one foot, and stared at the ground. "What the hell was that?"

"What was what?" the two men pivoted back to see what had caused Travis to yell out. He pointed at the ground, then reached down and held up the spear point, now covered with grit from the dozens of feet that had walked by or on it in the last hour.

Greshenko held out his hand and took the point from Travis. "It is a replica of an *assagai,* a Zulu warrior weapon. It would be on the end of a spear shaft. They sell these in the gift shops. They are made in South Africa by the thousands. Tourists buy them for souvenirs. Some camper must have lost this one."

"It's not authentic?"

"Not hardly. Listen, if all the *diassagai* in circulation today had been once on spear shafts in 1879, the Brits would have lost the Zulu War. He stepped to a green-painted oil drum marked *waste,* and dropped the point in. It hit the bottom with a series of clangs. That drew the attention of the woman gamekeeper. She left the men and the lion and approached them.

"Excuse me, sirs, but could you tell me what that was that you disposed of in the dust bin?"

"A spear point they sell at the gift shop," Travis said. "I nearly bought one, but until Greshenko's little speech I'd forgotten all about that. Brenda Griswold purchased one, though."

"I am Sanderson. I work for the park, you see. There are questions about this death I cannot answer. I think I should have that, if you don't mind."

"Help yourself. Do you think Henry stabbed the lion,

or did the lion stab Henry?" Leo had not mellowed much since he'd left the room. Sanderson retrieved the point from the bottom of the barrel and wrapped it in her neckerchief.

"I do not think either of those interesting possibilities are the case, sir. I do not know if this *lerumo* has anything to do with this killing. But the man you called Henry had a wound in his stomach that could have been made by such a thing. I will hold it for the police."

"Then you think Henry was murdered? I know there is a feeling among the populace in my country that the only good lawyer is a dead lawyer. I didn't know it was true here as well."

"I do not know the ways of America. In my country we respect the men and women who devote their lives to justice. It is a noble calling, I think."

"Wait another sixty years, and then you'll see it differently."

Sanderson's puzzled look suggested she did not understand or appreciate this man's cynicism. She scowled at them as if to say those Americans, they have so much and they value so little.

FORTY

BRENDA'S FEET HURT. She hadn't realized that the concrete walkway turned into gravel before she would reach the scene of the late Henry Farrah's demise. She limped back to her room, making a point to snub Leo, Travis, and the Russian guy. And she was in no mood to put up with any more of Bobby's evasion. He'd been into something and she needed to know what it was. Like the time he ran from the accident. The jerk was drunk, the paper said so, so it wasn't really Bobby's fault. She wasn't about to lose her regular paycheck, so Frankie had fixed it with a garage and the car disappeared and the new one showed up. She didn't see any problem there, and it did give her a hammer to bonk him with when he started to stray.

She hurried along the path and stewed over his behavior, past and present. First he screws them both over by selling out to Leo and now something else was on his pea brain. He knew about Travis, for sure, but he musta let it go. No surprise there. She had a way, things she could do, like, in bed and stuff, which would keep anyone except a eunuch in place. So what?

Since she'd dropped her purse with her key, she had to knock to get in the room. She thought she heard the slider slam, but she couldn't be sure. Bobby let her in. Why was he grinning? She saw the series of beer cans lined up on the dresser and thought she had her answer.

"You shoulda seen it. Cops and animal people and everything."

"Did you see Leo?"

"Just for a second when he went by. Travis and the Russian guy were there, but I didn't say anything to them either, you know."

"What did he look like?"

"Okay, I guess. I don't know, Leo's Leo. The lion was, like, huge. I mean it was like a half a ton or something."

"Not a half of a ton. Lions don't weigh a thousand pounds. Maybe five hundred, though."

"Yeah, well, this dude was humongous. They had him on this tarp and were getting ready to put him in the back of this truck when I left. Where's my purse? I want to call Desiree and tell her. She'll flip." She found the bag and began rooting around in it. "What happened to my cell? I always keep it in here."

Bobby busied himself with reading the label on his beer can. "Hey, did you know they brew this stuff right here? It's called, like, Saint Louis beer and has a steamboat on the label, but they make it here."

"What did you expect, they call Mr. Budweiser to ship them their beer? You seen my phone? I'm sure I had it this morning."

"There isn't a Mr. Budweiser, you're thinking about that Coors guy, and you were yakking with your slutty friend Desiree at breakfast. Maybe you left your phone on the table."

"Desiree is not a slut. On the table? I don't think so. Shit, where is it? Give me your phone. I'll call my number and follow the ring if it's, like, in the room. If it isn't and someone found it, maybe they'll answer."

Bobby passed her the phone. "So the lion didn't, like eat Leo?"

"Leo? Why would he eat Leo? Leo wasn't the dead guy."

"What? I thought they said Leo was killed. That fat police guy said he was killed. Then he said the lion got him."

"No, dummy, *you* said it was Leo. The police said 'one of our party' and you said Leo. Why did you jump on Leo being the dead guy, anyway?"

"It wasn't Leo? Who was it?"

"That stuffed shirt, Henry Farrah. What's the difference? And again, why'd you go for Leo."

"It couldn't be Farrah. I saw…"

"Saw what, Bobby. You saw what?"

"Nothing. I just remembered something, like…maybe I thought I saw him at breakfast or something."

Brenda knew men, and Brenda knew Bobby. He was lying like a rug. She'd need to press this. Maybe after a matinee or in the shower later, she'd get him to talk. She punched in her cell phone number and listened for it to ring. Nothing. No ring, no answer.

"This is definitely not a Kodak moment. This is a WTF moment."

She tossed the phone back to Bobby. It hit him on the forehead. He didn't even see it coming. He was in, like, a daze. Weird.

THE GRAY MONKEY had managed to flip the phone open. Someone once suggested that if you put an infinite number of monkeys working at typewriters and waited long enough, eventually they'd recreate all of the world's classics. Whether that would include advertising copy and genre fiction was not specified. This monkey acted alone. The beeping sound the buttons made when he pushed them delighted him so that he kept up a steady stream of notes. Would the same infinite number of monkeys playing keyboards recreate all of the world's great music?

A single monkey with a cell phone?

Unlikely.

He spent the better part of an hour admiring his reflection in the phone's shiny surface. He poked and scratched and managed to initiate the phone's picture memory. Brenda had saved stills and some short videos. The latter were not the sharpest pictures possible, but they did move. A sequence of images showing a family of lions popped up on the phone's tiny screen. They were moving but he didn't hear any sound. When they stopped he poked at the screen again hoping to prod them back into action. They didn't move. He had yet to acquire the concept of replay.

He was busy chittering his low opinion of predators in general and lions in particular when the phone vibrated. Startled, he leaped back on the branch and the phone slipped from his grasp. It fell, bounced off a tree limb, hit the riverbank, and plopped into the Chobe. A nearby crocodile who'd been watching the monkey, in hopes he would soon be thirsty and visit the river, watched disinterestedly as the bright silver object splashed into the river and settled into mud.

It would remain visible for less than five minutes.

FORTY-ONE

THE SUN HAD already set when Sanderson dropped Rra Kaleke off at his home and she pulled up in front of hers. Exhausted, all she wanted for was a bite of dinner and a bed. She would not be so lucky. The lights were on and music poured through the windows and doors.

She opened the door. "What is this noise?" David Mmusi, had his MP3 player attached to speakers and he and Mpitle were dancing in the main room. Michael sat slightly askew and propped up in a chair in the corner, smiling, and nodding his head to the music's beat.

"Mpitle, David Mmusi, how is this?" The young couple jumped apart as if they'd been prodded with a sharp stick like the men use to move their cattle.

"Mma, I have dinner for you," the young girl said and hurried to the stove.

"Good evening, Mrs. Sanderson." This from David.

"How was your day?" She could hardly hear Michael over the din.

"Turn that music off, please. It is harming my ears. So, you are here again, David? Does your mother know you are here?"

"I was just going, Missus."

"Sit down, sit down, David. You can stay. I am only worrying about your parents. If they are okay with this situation, then I am also."

She flopped down in the best chair and kicked off her

shoes. "What a day. We have a dead man, a dead lion, and a very thick policeman."

Mpitle carried a bowl of stew to her. She placed it on the small table and returned to the cooking area for utensils and tea. When she returned, Sanderson noticed her scarf.

"Where did you come by that scarf? I am thinking it cost some pula."

Mpitle's complexion darkened. "It is a gift from David."

"David, have you a rich uncle, perhaps, that has died and left you a fortune? Does the Safari Lodge pay you so much you can afford..." She turned the edge of the scarf over to read the maker's label, "a Dolce and Gabbana scarf? I do not know about these things but I am pretty sure this one cost more pula than I can earn in a month."

"I did not buy it, Mrs. Sanderson, I found it. I wish I could have bought it. Someday I will buy many wonderful things for Mpitle."

"Of course you will. Where did you find it?"

"On my way to the bar this morning when I went to work. Just on the path near where there are tree limbs that hang over. I think one of those limbs must have pulled it free."

"If it was at the lodge, you must return it. Some guest there will be looking for it. It is expensive, not a thing they will dismiss."

Mpitle looked distressed. The beautiful leopard pattern showed off her dark skin. Sanderson's heart went out to her. She had so few beautiful things. She remembered the Americans at the scene earlier and their careless, dismissive attitude. She sighed.

"David, tomorrow, you must go to the manager and

ask if anyone has inquired about a missing scarf. Mpitle, you take that thing off and fold it away very carefully. We will say that if no one has asked for it in the next week, you can keep it."

Mpitle's smile lit up the room brighter than the dim bulb suspended from the ceiling.

"And you, Mr. David Mmusi, what do you mean by showering such expensive things on my daughter? What are your intentions, young man?"

David looked apprehensively at Sanderson, saw her smile and returned it, relieved.

"One hundred percent honorable, Mma Michael."

"Hah," said Michael. They all laughed.

"You can resume that music, but softer please."

The strains of American pop music again filled the room but at a significantly lower volume. Sanderson spooned her stew and wondered about the scarf. If David found it at dawn, it must have been dropped very late at night, or else whoever lost it would have returned to find it. Or…or what? Or it might have been lost during the struggle that happened when that man was stabbed. Sanderson insisted, in spite of Superintendent Mwambe's refusal to listen, that the man did not fall on a stick. She fingered the spear point in her patch pocket, the weapon she'd retrieved from the dust bin. What if…? Sanderson grimaced and spooned another bite. She was a game ranger, not a detective. It did not fall to her to think about these things.

"What of your lion and dead man, Mma?" Michael had not forgotten even if the young people had. They, like their generation, she thought, were focused almost exclusively on themselves and in the moment. Michael had developed a more philosophical attitude since…

"Was the lion the same one you have been hunting with Rra Kaleke and Mr. Naledi?"

"Ah, that is a puzzle. This man from the lodge met with Sekoa. Do you remember me telling you of the pride that has a range out near Natanga?" Michael nodded. "Well, this lion was pushed out by another, younger male and he found himself near the lodge. I do not know why; that is a mystery. He must have been running from something or been very hungry to come so close."

"Then it was not the lion you and Rra Kaleke were hunting?"

"No, no, that one is far away by now. No, this is another lion, much bigger. That first lion was young. Anyway he is lying there with his big head on the man's chest, like he is taking a nap, you know, asleep, only both he and the man are dead."

"This lion killed the man then?"

The two dancers stopped to hear the story. "No, that was the part that Mwambe refused to hear. The man was dead when the lion found him. The only wound he had were teeth marks in the shoulder where he was picked up and carried."

"Perhaps the shoulder biting was enough to kill him. It could be. I think I would just die if a lion grabbed me by the shoulder." Mpitle's eyes were as large as saucers.

"No, I do not think that is the case. There was almost no blood in that wound. That man's heart had stopped beating before Sekoa picked him up, I am thinking."

"So what do you believe happened?"

"Someone wearing a scarf and having a spear point stabbed that man and left him for dead. He…or she—I think the scarf makes us say it is a she—did not know about the lion, or they would not have been out there looking to murder somebody. No person with a working brain would do that."

The idea of a lady murderer brought the music and dancing to a dead stop. Murder is not unknown in Botswana, just rare, and this close to home, unique.

FORTY-TWO

As it happened, Brenda spent the afternoon alone. Her efforts to seduce her husband and wheedle information from him fizzled. Her invitation to a couple's shower failed. She stripped and stood under the hot water for fifteen minutes. He never showed up. She dried off, wrapped a towel around her waist and stepped back in the room. No Bobby. No note, no goodbye, nothing. The draperies to the deck were not drawn and she looked out toward the trees and the river beyond. A gray monkey sat on the deck staring at her.

"See anything you like?" she asked, dropped the towel, and gave it a very professional grind and bump. The monkey put a finger in his nose. Brenda knew nothing at all about monkey communication but she was pretty sure it did not intend the gesture as a compliment. She gave him a one-fingered salute. The monkey returned it.

She spent the remainder of the afternoon shifting through her clothes and packing some of them. Rose Hayward messaged they would be flying out in two days. Brenda sorted and packed things she knew she'd not be wearing again. She held up a simple black dress, her jacquard Dina Bar-el with a scoop neckline. She couldn't remember why she packed it. It had been on sale for five hundred dollars, and she thought she heard they might meet the President? Something like that.

The missing items still rankled. What happened to her cell phone? She used the land line and tried to call it again. The local phone system could not connect to her cell. And what happened to her other glove? Then she realized her Dolce and Gabbana scarf had gone missing as well. The thing cost over three hundred dollars. Bobby had flipped when he'd seen the bill. The clothing, she guessed, might have been left in Travis' room, but the cell phone?

Then she got it. Bobby, the master dolt. He'd taken it so she couldn't call anybody. He did that once before when he got angry about something she did. What now? Travis probably, but with Bobby, you could never tell. She'd get even when he came back. She'd freaking lay into him like the time when he'd skipped the hit and run.

The sun set and still no Bobby. Probably drinking in the bar. Too bad the lion died. She'd like to feed him to it.

LEO, TRAVIS, AND Greshenko spent the afternoon looking at properties. They stopped for lunch at the Old House Restaurant. Travis thought it was a mess, although the food tasted good and the size of the steak seemed gargantuan.

"This country produces some of the finest beef in the world," Greshenko said. "They ship most of it to Europe, where it is sold as Scotch beef. Apparently the French and Germans think only Scotland or the British Isles can breed cattle up to their standards, and certainly nothing this good could possibly come from Africa. That attitude is the sad residue of colonial bigotry, by the way. They came to this continent, exploited its people, its natural resources, obliterated its history, and practiced genocide in places. Yet, even now, they think of this part of the world as backward and benighted."

"Does anybody have it right?"

"America, a little, Russia, maybe more so, and the Chinese, Japanese, absolutely. Asians understand how it feels to be discounted by white people. Europeans and Americans have always missed the Asian genius. And now they, we, will pay for our stupidity. China and Japan will own this continent if they want to."

"Little strong there, Yuri." Leo had heard all this before. His contacts with the State Department prior to their visit had included a thorough briefing, at which the poobahs had admitted some of their past errors but still maintained the US had not been tarred with the same brush as the former colonial powers. He hoped they were correct. He, for one, wanted to invest in the country in a modest way.

"It's just that I have such wonderful memories of this country. You should have seen it. Gaborone was barely a village. What you see of the capital has all been built since the early sixties. Sir Seretse Khama, who would become the country's first president, was knighted by the British, and independence was brand-new. It used to be called Bechuanaland before, and Lobatse was no more than a collection of rondevals, lots of them." Greshenko's focus shifted to long distance, back in time. "The changes that have occurred in the years since the Brits left are nothing short of phenomenal. You Americans think you define the cutting edge of nearly everything, but you are beginning to look and act more and more like tired Europeans. You want to see the future? Look no farther than this country."

"Perhaps you'd like to immigrate?"

"If I could, I would." Greshenko looked wistful.

"Greshenko, how did you come to your present...ah, occupation?"

"When the USSR, as you called us then, became just R and F, Russia and friends, so to speak, it created an economic cataclysm. You cannot go from state socialism to capitalism in a period of months or even years. The whole infrastructure my generation had come to accept and rely on collapsed before our eyes. Before, we had employment, housing, all of the necessities. Not in abundance or necessarily in the manner we might have wished, but all preordained and certain for most of us. Party loyalty produced security. Then, nothing. As a... government functionary..."

"You mean out-of-work spy."

"That would be an oversimplification, but yes, I suppose that would be one way to put it. I had no, how do you say, marketable skills. I tried many things, and one day I came to a fork in the road. I chose one way. Perhaps I should have gone the other. Who knows? Sometimes the choices we make have consequences we cannot predict until it is too late."

Greshenko shrugged and changed the subject. "So, Travis, tell me about the gas reserves and mineral possibilities here. You understand, I hope, that if your company were to come into Botswana to exploit the minerals or gas, the government would be a major stakeholder in the enterprise?"

"What? Why?"

"They believe that the minerals, the diamonds, this country's wealth, you could say, belong to the country and to its people. The profits from the exploitation or sale must benefit the owners, not the exploiters."

"That's crazy."

"As I said, if you want to see the future? Look no farther than this country."

They spent the rest of the afternoon discussing extraction of minerals and the outside possibility of franchising the Old House in both Botswana and in the States.

Toward evening they parted, each to his own room. Leo let himself in and reached for his pills. His indigestion had not improved; his headache had started up again, and he had cold sweats to go with the belly ache and angina. Great. His supply of nitroglycerine tablets down to three. He'd have the pilot bring some from the States when he flew in to pick them up in two days. He popped several pain killers and antacids. Getting as bad as Farrah...no, not Farrah, Farrah had had a blind date with a lion. Poor Henry.

He stretched out on the bed and closed his eyes. When he was a child, his grandmother would put a damp washcloth on his forehead. That would have been nice, but he hadn't the energy or inclination to fetch one for himself.

As he relaxed, he had his epiphany. Not a near-death experience, although that's what he thought at first. To have a near-death experience, the logic goes, you have to be near death. And he was not going there. Not yet. Not today. But he did realize that he'd made the correct move setting Travis in place. He needed to step back. Lucille had been after him to slow down since his last coronary. He guessed he should. He could function as the chairman of the board and use what time he had left to travel and play at his real estate speculation. Maybe he should join Greshenko and move here. That assumed the Russian could separate himself from his masters.

He wondered if Lucille would like to live in Botswana. Probably not.

Before he slipped into unconsciousness, in that no-man's-land between waking and sleeping, an image flitted through his mind. He, not the lion, lay flat on the grass, his head resting on Henry's chest. The image cased him to groan. Then he drifted off to sleep. A sleep so complete that he did not hear someone knocking at his door or an attempt to open the slider to the deck. He had double-locked it after the monkey nonsense.

FORTY-THREE

MMA SANTOS HEARD about the dead American from her neighbor. She made a determined nod of her head at this most satisfactory news. The man who murdered Sesi with his big automobile had been punished. That was as it should be. She had visited the *moloi* and bought a talisman. The old man's eyes had lighted up like *ditshikanokana,* like fireflies, in the gloom of his hut, at the sight of the strange currency she'd pulled from the front of her stained *mosese.*

It had taken her several days to locate the automobile. She'd slipped the bit of *boloi* behind the back seat. Still, it came as a surprise that the magic had been so strong. She assumed it would affect the vehicle, which she believed had done the actual killing, and it would crash, so it came as a great shock when she learned the man's death had been the result of a lion attack. She supposed that since she had paid the witch with one of the bad man's bills with all the zeros on it, she'd purchased more power than she might otherwise have if she had bartered some cheese and milk for the charm.

She beamed. Justice.

INSPECTOR MODISE SPENT a fruitless day asking area headmen and subchiefs about witches, diviners, and purveyors of magic. They all claimed to know nothing. They were either stupid, liars, or reluctant to tempt fate. People crossed one of those at the risk of life and limb, or all of the above. He decided the only thing left for him do was take the bit of skin to Gaborone and have tests run. Tracking down a ritual killing presented a two-fold problem. First, the difficulties presented by a superstitious populace, to risk magical retribution if they revealed a local practitioner, and secondly, how to assure the report had any substance in the first place. This same populace would as likely ascribe magical intervention as not, particularly when anything untoward befell them. Who better to blame than a neighbor with whom they'd had a falling out?

His next task required speaking to Superintendent Mwambe. The man had been in the force for a long time. Perhaps, too long. He represented old thinking. Modise did not wish to aggravate him. This was Mwambe's district, after all, but to insist that a thing was black when it was clearly white, and only because he did not want to acquiesce to a woman…well, he could not let that pass. That Sanderson woman, she had a head on her shoulders. She knew something of animals and she should be listened to. If she said the lion did not kill the man, it was so. And, well, she was a handsome woman, and that was the truth.

"Mwambe, there must be an investigation. The examining physician says that the man had a deep puncture wound to the stomach area and this puncture went into his heart. He is bleeding to death before the lion goes to him."

"But he has a great wound on his shoulder. You saw it, Modise."

"I saw the wound being made by the lion that is picking the man up to take him into the bush. I also see that it does not bleed very much. You know what that means? It means the heart is not beating and so no blood is being moved about. You see?"

Mwambe did see. He also saw he would have to work with Sanderson on the investigation. That did not please him. But he was a policeman and his personal displeasure at the effects of modernity could not interfere with that. He clenched his jaw in a small effort to dissipate his annoyance at this turn of events and nodded his agreement.

"Also, I am required to return to Gabz this afternoon. I will take the sample of *boloi* with me for testing. If you can please keep your ears open for any hint of a *ngaka*. The government is concerned about even the possibility of ritual killing, even of the monkeys. Also, keep your man on Greshenko. I cannot determine what he and the party of Americans is about, but until they leave I want to know everywhere they go and who they meet. I do not think it is just a coincidence that the dead man traveled with them. And finally, there will be an attaché from the American Embassy here this afternoon to enquire into the death as well."

Mwambe had shifted from nodding to making entries on a note pad. The words *American Embassy* required double underlining.

If Mma Santos was pleased, Bobby Griswold was anything but. He faced a huge dilemma. He could dummy up and let the whole scenario play out, and Farrah's death would remain an accident. That would put him back where he started, no better but no worse off than before. Alternatively, he could proceed with his plans. Make sure Brenda took the rap for a murder, apparently accidental murder, of Henry Farrah. If he could mistake Henry for Leo in the dark, so could she. That would get rid of her without the bother of divorce. Botswana was a country with capital punishment. She'd be a swinger alright, only this time at the end of a noose. He smiled at his pun. He'd use it when he returned home. *Brenda was a swinger right up to the end!*

But suppose they just put her in jail?

He could also try for Leo again, but that would be pushing it. Why didn't Leo just go on and have a heart attack? Could there be a way to get that done? Well, why not? What happened when you had one of those? With his bad heart, how much longer could he last? Bobby had looked up coronary infarction and heart attack on Wikipedia once. If he could catch Leo unawares, say, and wrestle him around, he could, maybe, make him have a coronary. Maybe just get him on the bed and put a pillow over his face. Heart attacks caused something called cerebral ischemia. He'd looked that up too. Not enough blood to the brain. He sat in the Sedudu Bar and turned his options over in his mind. He hadn't seen the scarf on the path where he'd left it. That must mean the cops had it. That and the spear point. So if they were to put two and two together, Brenda could be in big trouble.

He walked back to the rooms and knocked on Leo's door. No answer. Leo must still be out with Travis and the Russian. He'd wait.

An hour later, Leo came down the walkway. Bobby ducked behind a pillar and watched. He heard the door slam. Should he or shouldn't he? Even though he had avoided a murder conviction, assuming Brenda didn't swing. At best, a maybe, and even though he was positioned to remain in *status quo* as a result of his earlier errors, Bobby seemed ready to step over the line again.

He hesitated and then knocked on Leo's door. No response. He knocked more loudly. He jogged around the building to the back and peered through the glass door. There was enough space between the curtain's edge and the catch for him to make out Leo on the bed. Asleep? Better yet. He tried, without success to force the slider open.

Maybe Leo was already dead. Maybe this would be his lucky day.

FORTY-FOUR

SANDERSON TOOK THE call sitting in an empty office. Mr. Pako now lorded over a different staff several kilometers away. The rest of the game rangers and assistants were busy elsewhere. Since she'd finished her assignment regarding the killer lion, so to speak, she had nothing pressing to do, and had there been a situation requiring her attention, no one would tell her to do it. She wondered who would replace Pako. What he would be like? Until he arrived, she would be at loose ends. She assumed her new boss would be male. It is always so.

The voice on the other end of the line belonged to the last person in the world she would expect to wish to speak to her. This week seemed full of surprises. First the lion attack, and now Superintendent Mwambe wished to consult with her.

"Sanderson, will you come, please, to police headquarters? I need to have a conversation with you about the dead man that the lion took."

"Yes, certainly. I do not think the lion took the man, if you mean it is the cause of the man's death."

"That is what I must determine, and you will give to me the reasons why I should agree with that notion."

Before she could respond, the line went dead. Mwambe had rung off.

The drive into Kasane took no more than fifteen minutes. Sanderson worried about how Mwambe would react

to her insistence that the white man's death could not
be attributed to the lion. She had picked up a rucksack
containing the spear point on her way out the door. Superintendent Mwambe waited for her, seated behind his
desk. A scowl bisected his face.

"So, Sanderson, tell me why and what."

"Sir?"

"Why should I not dismiss this man's killing as an
accident? Why should I put this department on the task
of investigating the murder of a tourist? It would be a
thing that will not please the tourist board, you know.
It is bad enough you could not capture the lion before
it struck again, but these accidents happen from time
to time. They are understandable. A murder is another
thing completely."

"Yes, but—" Sanderson could feel the heat on her
neck when she realized he wished to place the blame on
her and her failed hunt.

"The what," Mwambe continued, ignoring her, "is
what happened to that man that makes you think he was
such a victim? I do not wish to have that sort of report
to send to Gaborone. The American Embassy is sending someone to look into this. I would prefer to report
an accident."

Sanderson collected her thoughts and simultaneously
bit her tongue. Since her childhood she had become accustomed to men's superior way of talking to her. It was
just the way, but this Mwambe must certainly be a fool.

"First, sir, with respect to the lion. This animal is not
the same as the one that took the boy weeks ago. That
lion is either already dead or on the Makgadikgadi Pans
by now. We have tracked him enough to know that. He

might double back and become a problem in the future but not at this time."

"How can you be so sure of this? A lion is a lion, after all. Are you telling me you can separate them without even seeing them?"

"The lion that you say killed the boy was young and still not so big. You can see that in the spoor. He is lighter and smaller. The lion that killed the American is big and heavy. His tracks are different. Also, this lion was the one we named Sekoa. He used to be the ruler of a pride in the park. All the guides and gamekeepers knew him. He seemed very sick. He is being looked into now by the university scientists to test him for disease, you see."

"Two different lions, you say?"

"Yes."

"Then the first one, the one who kills the boy, is still loose? Should I tell the lodges of this?"

"There are always animals, and there will always be a threat to humans in certain areas and times. People come to the Chobe to see them, and they know if they come this close to them, they run a risk. Everyone understands that. But the animals are not so foolish to come into Kasane. Well, except for the elephants when the morula fruit is on the ground. In the Okavango, it is different, of course."

Mwambe squinted and puffed. He did not look happy. "I will accept that for now, but how was this murder accomplished? I saw the wound, and that is all. It could have been made all sorts of ways. What caused this one, I want to know."

"The wound came from this." Sanderson removed the spear point from her rucksack, unwrapped it, and placed it on the desk.

"And what is that?"

"It is a spear point, one of the 'made for the tourists' *diassagai* that they sell in the gift shop at the lodge."

"Who would want such a thing?"

Sanderson shrugged. The tastes of tourists were a mystery to her as well as to most of the population in the country. A few entrepreneurs, sensing a market, came up with these things. That was all she knew.

"I must make a call." Mwambe lifted the receiver from the phone and dialed. While he waited, he poked at the spear with the eraser end of a pencil. "It is too dirty to be much use to us for fingerprinting. Where did you come by this?"

"Some Americans, the friends of the dead man, I think, came to see their friend and stumbled on it in the brush. They tossed it in the big dust bin. I went and pulled it out. I thought maybe this is the thing that made the wound and I should keep it for you to investigate."

Mwambe swiveled in his chair, turned his back on her, and made his call. "I have for you an item. I require you to look at and tell me if it could have caused the wound in the dead American." He listened and swiveled back toward Sanderson. "Sanderson says she found it at the scene. It is a spear point like they sell at the lodge. You know of these things? You do?...I see."

He hung up and studied the weapon for a moment. "The examiner says that he knows of this item. He has seen wounds made by such a thing lately. Some of the boys at the lodge had a fight and one was hurt, not too badly, it seems, but...He has asked the lodge not to sell them anymore. They said they will not stock them after this supply is exhausted. He is sure you are right about the wound. He almost said so in his report but, in the absence of the actual weapon, could not. So you have brought us a murder weapon, Sanderson. Can you offer anything else?"

Sanderson considered mentioning the Mpitle's scarf and decided to wait. "How much strength must a person have to stab a grown man with this *assagai*?"

Mwambe shook his head. "You must ask the examiner. I am thinking it would require some force."

"Could a woman have done it?"

"Oh, I do not think so. It is a very deep wound, I believe."

Of course the superintendent would say that. She would have to ask the examiner herself. However, this time she hoped Mwambe had it right. She did not like the idea of a woman, any woman, becoming a killer.

Female lions, yes. Female humans, no.

FORTY-FIVE

BRENDA HEARD BOBBY fumbling at the lock. She stepped over to the bed and stretched out letting her skirt ride up a few more inches than necessary. The lights were off and the room dim. Only the late evening glow provided any illumination. She'd get him. He pushed his way in.

"Where you been at?"

"What?" Bobby jumped and reached for the light switch. "I've been around. Like, what's it to you? Mr. Gorgeous Travis Parizzi not paying you any attention anymore?"

"Screw you. Listen, hot shot, I figured it all out."

"What? You figured what out, Brenda? You finally remember what you had for dinner? Not hippo, right?"

"Very funny, coming from you, genius. I know about the phone, Bobby. I know why you took it, and I know—"

"You don't know jack, Brenda."

"Like when I couldn't figure out the hit-and-run? Hello, you mean like that? I know you, Bobby, and I know you're into something and it isn't good. Tell me I'm wrong." Brenda noted the sudden pallor on Bobby's face. She must be hitting pretty GD close, she thought. What had he done, besides take her phone to mess with her mind?

"Look, Bren…" Bobby only called her Bren when he wanted something kinky or was in trouble, or had a load on, or any and all of the above. "Take it easy. You can't know, because…"

She waited for him to finish his thought. He didn't. Push, her instincts told her. He's been into something really heavy, and it could be, like, worth money.

"You're in deep kaka, Bobby, and unless you square it with me, this is a promise, either you tell me what you did, or there'll be hell to pay." Bobby looked stricken. "The phone, Bobby, gimme my phone, or I spill it to the guys at the top." She wasn't sure what *at the top* meant but it seemed to have a serious effect on her husband. He collapsed into a chair as though his knees gave out and stared at her and then out the glass doors. "Bobby—the phone."

"Bren, you have to cover me, okay?"

"Sure, why not? We're a team, right. We stick together, right? Like, forever, right?" The last was not so much a question as a threat. "Forever," she repeated, this time louder, and stared him in the face. She watched as what must have been a kaleidoscope of really scary images flew across Bobby's eyeballs.

"Right, a team. We…yeah, a team."

"So, the cell phone is…where?"

"I hid it outside under the steps. You might want to erase the messages on it, just to be safe and all."

"Messages? What messages? Did I get a call? Why should I erase them? Desiree called, didn't she? What'd she say that you don't want me to see? Go find my phone, Bobby."

He stood and walked to the door, paused, looked back at her and, when she waved him on, opened the slider and went out. She watched as he reached under the step, frowned, and knelt to reach deeper.

"It's gone."

"What's gone? You mean my phone's not there? Look some more. How can it be gone?"

Bobby lay flat on the ground and scrabbled in the dirt under the steps. "Get that flashlight. I can't see anything out here."

Brenda dug through the pile of clothing and paper bags on the bench and found the flashlight. She walked to him and handed it down. "Anything?"

Bobby swung the light around, inspecting the length of the step. He pointed it toward the building. "Not here."

"Jesus, Bobby, what did you do now? Where's it at?"

"I swear to God, Bren, I put it right here, right under this step. It's not there anymore. Somebody musta took it."

"Like who? Who crawls around under porch steps looking for cell phones?"

"I don't know. The cleaners could have found it, or the guys that, like, mow the grass. I don't know. The cops maybe."

"Cops? Why the hell would cops look under our steps? It's not going good for you, Bobby. You need to talk to momma."

"I'm thinking about Leo, I mean Farrah, getting killed is all. They might want to know how and are looking for clues. You know what I mean."

Farrah, Leo, clues? Bobby wasn't making any sense, not that not making sense was anything new. Brenda decided to let it slide. It would all come out in the wash, or in the shower, or in the bed. She'd know soon enough what he'd been up to, and it didn't hurt for him to think she already did.

"Get in here. We're going to be late for dinner, you need to clean up, and I need your Blackberry until I can replace my phone. You jerk, that phone, counting the silver case it was in, cost me over two hundred dollars. You're gonna replace that."

Brenda wheeled and went into the room while Bobby struggled to his feet. He looked desperate.

THE MEDICAL EXAMINER inspected the spear point and shook his head. "Besides the fact that it has been dragged through the dirt and spent time in the dustbin, too many people have handled this thing. Even if we could lift prints, they wouldn't tell us anything, Sanderson."

"I suppose not. But I would like to know this thing. Could the wound that killed the man have been made by a woman?" Sanderson tried to ignore the pervading odor of disinfectant and bleach in the room which didn't quite conceal the scent of death.

"A big woman, for certain, but in this case, I do not think so. The man was tall and heavy. You know, he was fat around his belly. Whoever struck the spear into him did it by taking a step or two forward toward him, to build momentum, you see, and then he stabs him. You could not just push it in. It is not very sharp either, so..." He shrugged and turned the point over in his hand.

"When did this happen, do you expect?"

"Ah, that I can answer. We have two deaths close together, the lion and the man. So what one can't tell us the other can. We can call the time of death much closer, because of the size of these two. The lion is so much bigger and will cool at a different rate than the man. So we calculate the rate of cooling for both and then see if they agree. If they do, then we can guess more accurately. You see?"

Sanderson nodded, even though she didn't see, not

exactly. It's enough that the examiner thought so. Something about body temperature?

"So with these two numbers in mind, the temperature of the lion when we find him and the temperature of the man, and then correcting for their initial core temperatures and size…" Sanderson shook her head in mild frustration. All she wanted was the time, not the science. "I can tell you that these two old fellahs died between nine at night and two in the morning."

"But that's five hours. That is a wide range, yes? It will not be easy to pin anyone down. Not at the lodge where people move about at all hours."

"Well, nine at night will include many, but two in the morning? It's the best I can do." The examiner looked chagrined. "What of Mwambe. Isn't he the investigator?"

"Oh, yes, but…" She left the thought unfinished. The examiner nodded. He understood.

Tomorrow, Sanderson thought, I will check the gift shop and discover who bought spear points. If I am lucky, they won't have sold that to a man. She picked up her rucksack and headed home. Would David Mmusi be there again this night? That was another problem she needed to address.

FORTY-SIX

BRENDA AND BOBBY made their way to the dining area. The sun had dropped below the treetops, and the shadows stretched across the path. The birds were in their final round of singing before signing off for the night. Brenda glanced off at the river.

"Look, there's a hippo down there. That's the first one I've seen this close to the hotel. I wonder if it's a sign." Bobby did not respond. "You listening to me, or what?"

"What?"

"I said there's a…never mind. What's on your mind? You're, like, spaced out."

"I'm thinking about something is all."

"Well, don't sprain your brain, genius. You better let me do the thinking. When you get yourself in that mode, it's always trouble and costs us money."

"Yeah, well, whatever."

They entered the dining area and chose a table. Brenda sat and waved to the waiter. Bobby remained standing.

"I forgot something. I gotta go back." He turned and started toward the main walkway. "Order me something with meat and all."

"Forgot what? It's a buffet, Bobby. You don't order; you go get. What's the matter with you?"

"Okay, then order me a beer. I'll be right back. Fix me up with a plate, why don't you. Be sure to get the good desserts before they're all gone." He began walking away.

"The room is the other way. That leads to the front desk."

"Oh…right. I know. I'm going to ask about your phone. Maybe someone turned it in."

"Yeah, well good luck with that. Ask about my scarf, too, while you're at it."

"Scarf? Oh, yeah, your leopard scarf." Brenda frowned when he said that. Why?

He hurried along toward the front of the lodge. At the desk, he stopped and inquired about Brenda's phone. He hoped they had it. He'd be able to erase the messages if they did. No, sorry, they didn't have any phones. He forgot about the scarf. He stepped through the front doors and made his way to the gift shop. He needed to replace her spear. The clerk looked up when he entered.

"I need one of those spear things you had before. I don't see any more." This was not good.

"I am sorry, sir. We took them off the shelf. The authorities asked us not to sell them."

"You don't have any?"

"Well…" She looked doubtful. "There is one more under the counter. It is not for sale, officially. If I sell it to you, you won't tell anyone, will you?"

"No, sure, I mean no way. How much?" He pulled out his wallet and rifled through the bills. He didn't have any pula, only American bills. "Here, keep the change." He tossed a twenty on the counter.

The clerk pulled an *assagai* from a box under the counter and placed it next to the bill. "I will need your room number."

Bobby snatched the spear from the counter top and headed toward the door. He gave her his room number and rushed away.

THE CLERK FILLED in the room number on the sales slip and was about to enter the date, then thought better of it. The previous day she'd been told not to sell the item. No sense getting into trouble over that. She wrote the date for two days earlier. She tore off the customer copy and crumpled it up. She tossed it into the dust bin and added the store copy to the pile of similar receipts under the cash box. She paid for the spear with her own pula. The twenty dollar bill she folded and put in her purse. She would not steal, but the American bill she could exchange with Rra Botlhokwa. He gave a better rate than the bank or the exchange. He'd told all the workers in the lodges to bring the big bills, the euros, pound notes, and dollars, to him for exchanging. He said he ran an importing and exporting business. No one believed him. Surely the foreign money traveled across the border into Zimbabwe for certain people to pay for the sorts of things for which Zim dollars would not be accepted.

But that did not concern her. She would profit from this night.

BOBBY MADE A circle around the front of the lodge, dashed across the parking lot, and back to his room. Once inside, he switched on the lights and looked for a place to hide the spear point. Not hide exactly. He needed to put it somewhere so that it looked like it might have fallen out of sight, so that Brenda could find it. He dropped it on the floor and kicked it under the bench at the foot of the bed, like it had fallen back there. He shoved a pair of his dirty socks on top. When they packed in the morning, Brenda, or maybe he, would find it. Surprise, it was there all the time. He rushed back to the dining area and sat.

"So, did you get it?" Brenda had a habit of talking

with her mouth full. She'd acquired the shopping habits
of the rich and famous but none of their table manners.
It sounded more like, "Zochew geddit?"

"Get what? Where's my beer? What's this crap on my
plate?"

"I didn't know what beer you wanted. I was afraid it
would be warm by the time you got here, and anyway,
you should drink wine, not beer. Beer makes you burp
and the stuff on your plate? That's your dinner. There
are brown lumpy things that are some kind of game.
You're the expert on dead animals, you tell me. And
there are some yellow stringy things. No clue what they
are. There was this sign that said what they were, but I
forgot to read it. And I think they told me those things
that look like brown Cheetos are called *phane*, they're,
like, fried caterpillars."

Brenda lowered her eyes and sipped her wine. She
was enjoying herself. He scowled and stood, took his
plate to the clearing counter and picked up another, clean
one. Fried caterpillars. How dumb did she think he was?
He piled food on his new plate and sat down again. The
waiter loitered near the kitchen door. He waved him over
and ordered his beer.

"So, did you get it?" she asked again.

"Get what, the beer? Soon, I guess."

"No, you moron, not the beer, you said you had to go
back to the room because you forgot something. What
did you forget, and did you finally get it?"

Bobby looked confused. Then he had a brief moment
of enlightenment. "They didn't have your phone at the
desk. I asked." He remembered he should have asked
about the scarf, too. "They didn't have your scarf, either." Well, they probably didn't, and it was just a scarf.

"I asked if you found what you forgot."

"Yeah I got it." Oh yeah. He pulled out his wallet and flipped it open. "I forgot this, and I don't like walking around without some cash."

"You had that when you left. I saw you put it in your pocket. You went all the way back for nothing?"

"Yeah, I guess so."

Not for nothing, sweetheart.

FORTY-SEVEN

GRESHENKO AND TRAVIS met for dinner. They expected Leo to join them, and so waited for a few minutes while they'd watched, bemused, as the Griswolds entered, Bobby rushed away, returned, and then traded his plate, which they'd seen Brenda pile high with *phane,* for a clean one.

"What do you suppose all that was about?" Greshenko said.

"With that pair, there is no telling. I'd wager a small sum it could spell trouble for someone, sometime, however."

"You would know, I suppose. Tell me, what's she like?"

"How would I know that?"

"Come, come, Travis, everyone except the husband knows about you and Brenda Griswold. And I'm not sure he isn't on to you, as well."

Travis squirmed in his chair. Had it been that obvious? Leo knew, but if Bobby also knew, why hadn't Brenda said anything? That thought lingered for only a second. He knew why. Brenda toyed with men and relationships the way a child played with her Barbie dolls. More than likely, she simply didn't care if her husband knew or not. She could control him. Ergo, she must know something that kept him in tow. It seemed unlikely she could keep him corralled with sex alone, although given her talent in that department, and if Bobby were relatively inexperienced, it might be possible.

"Past history, Yuri. A moment of passion born of necessity…hers not mine. It's over. They seem to be together again, at least to the degree they were ever a couple."

"If you say so, but if I were you, my friend, I would, how do you say…cover your six?"

"Watch my back. Yes, I suppose so, and maybe wear a cup while I'm at it."

"Excuse me? A cup?"

"Figure of speech. On to business. I don't know what has happened to Leo. We should start, and he'll pick up when he gets here."

"He did not look so good this afternoon. You know, gray and tired. He has a bad heart, yes?"

"He does. And the constitution of one of these water buffalos, I think. He'll be okay. He probably just fell asleep."

"If that is so, we should leave him at peace."

"Right. Can I ask you a personal question?"

"Of course, if you understand I may not wish to answer it."

"Why are you here, really? I know Leo thinks you can help connect with certain parties because he thinks he may have to work with the shadier edge of the business community. But you can't be here just for that."

"I told Leo I was also sent by my associates to scout the territory, so to speak."

"Are you?"

"No, not really. That is what I told them in Chicago, and that is what I said to Leo, but it's only a…um, shell play."

"Shell game. What then? Pardon me if I don't believe you if you say altruism and world peace."

"Travis, you are too young to be a cynic. You should spend some time in the army first."

"I did, and that's where I learned it. So, why are you here?"

"A hope for a change. Truly there is nothing here that would attract my associates. Not yet, anyway. Once the country becomes more highly urbanized and the government more complex, they may be interested. They, the Tongs, the Yakuza, the Sicilian Mafia, and us, all eventually, but not just yet. This country is very careful about crime and criminals. If any society can resist the organized variety, they can. But that will be the decision of a history not yet acted out."

"Not even the diamonds?"

"That is between the two governments. Russia is a major producer of diamonds and the largest not affiliated with DeBeers. This country, on the other hand, is a major stakeholder in DeBeers. There could be some stress and strain there, but it will not involve criminals. That group will find it easier to deal with surrounding countries and their so-called blood diamonds."

"So your hope? What is it?"

"I listened to Leo explain his intention to build a casino and high-end resort here. I do not know where he came up with the idea, but I think it is a good one. At least worth pursuing. So I came along to see."

"The authorities, whoever they are, would permit it, you think?"

"With qualifications, yes, I think so. It will not be easy or sure, but I think maybe it could work."

They sipped their wine in silence for a moment.

The Griswolds no longer entertained them. In fact they seemed on the verge of leaving. Travis noted that Brenda had eaten very lightly. No action today, apparently.

"And you, Yuri, where would you fit in?"

"I hope to convince Leo to keep me on as the, what would you say…liaison person."

"Would your associates, that's what you called them, the men in Chicago, would they be okay if you didn't return?"

Greshenko shrugged. "It would not be worth their while to come and get me, as long as they were sure I was not working against them. They will check and make sure I have no outstanding debts, so to speak, and then they will forget me."

"Have you any 'debts'?"

"None that I can't take care of. Also, I know things. They will not bother me, I do not think." Greshenko's doubtful expression did not match the confidence of his words. Travis cocked an eyebrow. Maybe he could and maybe he couldn't.

"This casino/hotel/spa. Will it pay?"

"Oh yes. If you construct a high-end spa and casino and promote it in the States and Europe? Oh yes."

"But this is the end of never. Who'd come?"

"You are wrong. It may seem that way to you. Botswana does not share the panache of Kenya. No *Snows of Kilimanjaro*, no Hollywood hype, television specials. Only McCall-Smith and his quaint mysteries. But some know and have made their way here. This is where Richard Burton and Elizabeth Taylor came for their second honeymoon. Prince Charles is alleged to have met Camilla Parker-Bowles here on the sly, and the Clintons have visited. The country is promoting low-quantity, high-quality tourism, high-end, if you see. This would fit right in to that strategy."

"There has to be a down side."

"There are the hoops through which one must jump. Ministers to persuade, tribes to deal with, world opinion about a deluxe resort on this river. There are people in Europe who believe this is still the nineteenth century when it comes to thinking about Africa. They expect to see hunter-gatherers, lines of bearers carrying the white man's goods into the interior. Your President Roosevelt shooting lion and gazelle. They will make a fuss about brash Americans exploiting the pristine wilderness with crass commercialism. That sort of thing."

"That's all?"

"No, there is the really important part. You must also include local investors. I told you about the minerals and gas, yes?"

"You said the government would be a major partner in any venture in that arena. The government would have to be part of this, too?"

"Not the government, I don't believe. But local. You see, the colonial powers spent nearly two centuries raping this continent. The people do not want to see that happen again. If it is on their land and if it is profitable, it must profit the owners of the land, the government for all the people, the local tribes and groupings. You see?"

"It will be complicated?"

"Very. And time-consuming. You cannot do this from a desk in Chicago."

"No, I suppose not. You would stay and see to it?"

"As I said, that is my hope."

"How do you know so much about this country? I know you lived here, but years ago."

"A friend of mine from the old days is in the news service business, you could say. He knew of my interest, so he forwards the government news letter, the *Tautona Times*, to me when he can."

"Ah, that would explain it. We'll have to run the notion of a local presence by Leo. For what it's worth, I'd back you."

Greshenko smiled his thanks and stood.

"It would be best, if we let him sleep. We can talk again tomorrow and find out then what he thinks."

It was late and Greshenko would need to find a cab. He still hadn't heard from the car rental people. They were probably having difficulties finding a replacement tire.

FORTY-EIGHT

THE HYENAS HAD ranged far to the west, almost to the Okavango Delta. They had some modest successes hunting and scavenging. They felt no urgent need of feed again beyond the instinct all predators have that there is never enough. So, they would not cease pursuing game. To kill and feed was instinctual and neverending. The matriarch stopped and turned. The pack waited. What would she do? If one were to shoot a film of them, using night vision technology, perhaps, their eyes would seem to glow a terrible, but fitting, phosphorescent green. But that would be a phenomenon created by reflected light. Animals with powerful night vision all share that characteristic. At night, when caught in a beam of light, their eyes glitter. Only fantasy figures have eyes that truly glow evilly; evidence of emitted light.

So, the dozen hyenas, young and old, watched and waited in the darkened savannah for their leader to give them direction. One of the younger females growled— not quite a challenge, she did not yet possess either the courage or the experience to attempt a takeover of pack. Not yet. The matriarch lifted her head and yakked. It is not clear how much her next step relied on intuition and instinct, how much on experience, or if there might be some sort of animal clairvoyance at play. With animals, who can tell? But she yipped again and set out in an easy lope back east, back toward the fence, back toward their

old enemy. But it was not Sekoa they sought now. Something new was on the move.

SANDERSON SAT ON the wall of the small courtyard outside
her door and contemplated the waning moon, her bright
red truck a shade of dark gray in the night. She smiled
at the HiLux, Michael's success. Michael had drifted off
to sleep after dinner, a very little of which he ate, and
Mpitle soldiered on with her homework until ten.

Sanderson thought about Mwambe and Pako. She
would not miss Pako, but compared to Mwambe, he
seemed, in retrospect, almost enlightened. She crossed
her ankles and inhaled the smell of roasting meat. Mrs.
Maholo, the woman in the village who had the honor of
possessing a washing apparatus, had meat on the spit.
It seemed late to be about cooking, but Mrs. Maholo
worked long hours at the clinic, and that would explain it.

What to do about this murder business? It seemed
very clear to her that Mwambe wished the whole matter
to disappear like the smoke from Mrs. Maholo's kitchen.
He worried so much about the attaché from the American embassy due to arrive the next day. A lion accident
could be handled. Everyone knew there were certain
risks in visiting a game park, especially when warned
by the hotel of a new threat, a recent death, in the neighborhood. A murder, on the other hand, could cause difficulties, could create an investigation by higher-ups, a
visit, perhaps, by the head of the Department of Intelligence and Security himself. The examiner told her the
man was part of an American delegation in the country
at the invitation of the president. She, and all of her con-
temporaries, held the president in the highest esteem. It
would not do to have him embarrassed by this murder.

What if a Motswana had done it, or a robbery by some poor drifter from Zimbabwe had gone wrong? It could be, and what did that say about safety in the district? She shuddered at the thought. She would not like to be that person if he were caught. Mwambe had a serious problem to deal with.

Should she also let the problem go? What purpose would be served by finding a killer, when ascribing the event to a lion would do so nicely? But there remained the matter of truth. Botswana, her Botswana, did not lie, not to its people and certainly not to other governments.

"We do not do that," she murmured. "If a thing is so, it is so. It would be wrong to say otherwise."

But she knew in her heart that Inspector Mwambe would not—perhaps, she conceded, he could not—see it that way. What to do? These were weighty matters and would keep her awake late that night.

"What is troubling your *mowa,* Mma Michael?" Sanderson jumped. Rra Kaleke had slipped up beside her without a sound.

"My spirit is troubled, Rra. It is a problem that has presented itself to me, and I do not know what to do."

Kaleke sat next to her and focused on the moon as well.

"You are a good woman, Mma Michael. You are too modern for this village, I think, but we are all admiring you anyway. Can you tell me this problem that keeps you from your sleep?"

"It is this man who we found with Sekoa and who is dead. Sekoa did not kill him. This you know."

Kaleke nodded and lit the stub of a cigarette. He'd smoked half after breakfast and had saved the other half for the night, before sleeping.

"That man had a wound that only a *motsu* could have made."

"It was a spear point, Rra. You saw it. I took it from the dust bin that day. The examiner said there were traces of blood on it, the man's blood. Someone stabbed him, and he must have awakened Sekoa when this thing happened. That old lion went to him, but the man must be dead when he finds him, and so he took him in the bush. Inspector Mwambe wants the investigation to go away."

"Why would the Baboon want that? Solving a murder would be a great thing for him. He would be admired and possibly receive a medal."

"I do not think he would get a medal. He has reasons for wishing the thing away that are not altogether wrong, Rra."

She explained Mwambe's dilemma and her own. Kaleke listened and nodded from time to time. When she finished the two sat in silence once again. Night birds twittered in the distance, and she thought she heard a hyena laughing—at her? At humans who strained their brains thinking of ideas like justice and loyalty and patriotism? In the park, life and death played out simply. You were predator or you were prey, and violence defined your existence. Life was for the strong, the fleet, and the cunning. That lion, Sekoa, he broke the rules of the bush. He died of old age.

We should all be so lucky.

"I will pray for you, Mma. It is not a situation that I envy you. I will pray that you will be led to right decisions. I will ask this of *Modimo* for you."

"Thank you, Rra. I will pray for direction, too. But it would be very much easier to pray if I knew what right decisions were in this case. Then I would only need to pray for the courage to do it."

"You are not a fearful person, Mma Michael. You are strong. We all know that. Maybe you are too strong for a woman. I do not know about that anymore, but courage is not a thing you are missing. You will do the right thing. Now, go to your house and sleep. Tomorrow you will know."

He stood and strode away into the night. Sanderson watched as his figure was swallowed by shadows. Would she know? Must it be left to her? She did not believe sleep would come soon, nor would there be any rest for her if it did.

FORTY-NINE

SANDERSON AWOKE EARLY. In fact, she had not slept well after her conversation with Rra Kaleke. She hoped his prayers were more satisfactory than hers had been. She set out food and left a note for Mpitle to take care of the house and her brother until she had to leave for school. Sanderson drove off to the Safari Lodge. She would find a coffee there and see about the business of the spears. The engine of the HiLux coughed a bit more this morning than usual, and she thought she could smell steam, the sort hot engines make. She worried about that. She would be careful. Then, on impulse she turned toward her office. Mr. Pako no longer ruled that roost. She would check out the Land Rover. Since there was no one else in charge yet, she decided she would be the one, at least for this day, until the new man arrived.

She pulled up in front of the lodge in the Land Rover and cut the engine. This vehicle ran no better than her *bakkie* and coughed several times before it chugged to a stop. As she stepped out onto the gravel, she noticed the police vehicle parked further down the circle. Was Mwambe going to ask the questions after all? She hoped so. As she considered whether she should climb back into the Land Rover, Derek Kgasa exited the police car. Derek she knew from school. They had shared textbooks and sometimes traded lunches. Derek was Mwambe's nephew, which explained how he came to be a policeman. Sanderson knew enough about his brain power to know influence had more to do with his appointment than skill. But she liked Derek; everyone did.

"So, Sanderson, you are here to help me with this?"

"Why do you think that, Derek? Did your uncle suggest it?"

"No, he said you would probably not let this mystery lie quietly, and if I could, I should try to talk you into a sensible way of presenting these events to the Americans."

"Sensible? You mean your uncle wishes it, and me, to go far away and for some time."

"He called your boss, Mr. Pako, in Maun, but he could not convince him to call you off. His words were 'That woman is not my responsibility anymore,' and he hung up. I am assigned to do this investigation, you see?"

"You, Derek? Your uncle, with all the importance this investigation has for him, will turn it over to you instead?"

Derek smiled and scraped at the gravel with the toe of his boot. "You know, Sanderson, I am rubbish as a policeman. I try, but except for answering the phone and directing traffic, I have no talent for this work."

Sanderson knew this. Everyone knew this, but she was mildly surprised to hear such a confession from him.

"Why do you keep at it, then?"

Derek shrugged and smiled some more. He had always been a cheerful follower, and she supposed he became a policeman because someone told him he could.

"So, what will you do, Derek?" He shrugged again and looked uncomfortable. "Maybe we can help each other, then. Do you know what you would like to do next?"

"I should interview people, and soon. The manager says the party of Americans will be leaving tomorrow. If there is anything they can tell us, I must find it out now."

"Do you know how the man came to die? Did you have a conversation with the medical examiner?"

"No, my uncle told me the man was attacked by a lion, but there were suspicious wounds to the body and I should inquire. I do not know what that means."

"Derek, the man was stabbed with a spear point. They sell these things here in the gift shop. I think we should visit the shop and ask if anyone bought one lately. And if they did, were they connected to the Americans, don't you think?"

Derek's eyes lit up. He stood straighter and nodded. "You are correct. We will ask about that." He started toward the gift shop and paused. "What shall we ask?"

Sanderson sighed and led the policeman into the store. The clerk had just opened for business. When she saw the policeman's uniform she stopped what she was doing and raised her eyebrows. "Yes," she said. "Can I be of help?"

Sanderson waited for Derek to begin. He stood like an old baobab tree, which pretty much described him, very thick and hollow inside. When she realized he would not ask the woman the questions, she spoke up instead.

"Can you help us, yes. You sell *diassagai* here, don't you? I don't see any now, but we were told you did."

The clerk looked first at Sanderson and then back to Derek. When he nodded his head quickly, she turned back to Sanderson. "We do not sell them anymore. We had a request from the authorities to stop. Some men were fighting with them and there were injuries."

"When did you stop the sales?"

"It was two days ago, I think. I can check for you."

"It is not that important. What we would like to know is if you sold any of them before the ban and if so to whom did you make these sales."

She pulled the sales slips from the drawer under the cash box and shuffled through them. She put four slips to one side.

"These are the sales for that item in the last two weeks. You will see they are identified by date and the room number of the guest. Some also have names. This one, which has no name, must have been bought after five. You see this is Alice's initials on it. She runs the store from five 'til closing." She handed the slips to Derek who, in turn, handed them to Sanderson.

She glanced at each. "We must take these to the manager for identification." The sales clerk looked doubtful. "It is official police business, Missus, we will return them as soon as we can. Let's go, Derek. We have some more queries to make." And Sanderson led the policeman out of the store and off to the manager's office.

"You are very good at this," Derek said. The admiration was evident on his broad smiling face. "You should become a detective like the woman in the books."

"I don't think that is a realistic thing to do. That woman is from another day and age. Can you see me acting like that?"

Derek shook his head. No, there was no way this Sanderson would ever be mistaken for that old *mosadi*. But he still seemed stuck on the possibility of Sanderson having such a glamorous position. She was a handsome woman, for sure.

"Forget it, Derek. It will not be. I am only hoping to retain my current employment. I do not know what the new man who comes to replace Mr. Pako will say to me after he has heard from that man."

As they walked to the manager's office, Sanderson sorted the slips and arranged them by date.

"This is very curious, there are *diassagai* being sold to people with the same room number a day apart. Why would they buy two?"

"Tourists are strange people, Sanderson. Perhaps they wished to have a pair for an arrangement. Maybe they buy them for a friend. Who can say. They are very curious people."

"Or one of them wished to cover up the fact that the first went missing and maybe found its way into that man's belly."

FIFTY

THE AMERICAN ATTACHÉ arrived in Kasane early, accompanied by Kgabo Modise. The director at DIS thought it would be a good idea if they had presence at the interview. And, in that case and because he'd been on the scene at the time the body was found, Modise should be the one to go on the trip. Modise wished he'd selected someone else. He never felt comfortable in the presence of officialdom in general and this particular official in particular. The president, briefed on the potential diplomatic difficulties Henry Farrah's death might create, insisted they fly to Kasane in OK1, the president's plane.

Modise's rise in the ranks of the police service had not been meteoric, but swift nonetheless. When the new Directorate of Intelligence and Security had been formed and subsumed the Criminal Investigation Department, he'd been absorbed into the new configuration. They were acutely interested in the Greshenko-Botlhokwa connection, which was why he'd drawn the assignment in the first place. He knew he should be pleased that the director thought to send him, but this lion caper was one add-on he could do without.

Inspector Mwambe, overwhelmed by the government's reaction to his *little problem*, nearly fainted when he saw the plane touch down. The inclusion of Kgabo Modise did not increase his ease, either. In the police car, he asked if the attaché had been briefed sufficiently.

As he did not know what Modise might have said, he knew he must tread lightly until he could determine what would be an appropriate thing to say. He'd practiced his response in front of the mirror the night before. *It is most serious and a full investigation by my best man is now under way,* he'd recited it a dozen times, altering his expression until he found one that he thought combined both competence and sympathy. But now? What to say? Modise knew of Derek's capabilities or lack thereof. *My best man* was not going to wash.

"Inspector Modise has filled me in, but I would like to have your take on the occurrence. You are, after all, local and familiar with this sort of thing far more completely than the folks in Gaborone—no offense, Inspector Modise."

Modise smiled. "None taken, Excellency."

"Call me Harry."

Mwambe heard but could not see himself calling the American official by his first name. These Americans, they have no sense of propriety, so familiar. He tried to concentrate. He began his speech for the attaché, stuttered, and began again.

"It is most a serious situation, and I have launched a full investigation by my best…by my team…we have begun our investigation into it. There were…there are, certain complexities with this situation that must be resolved and—"

"Tell him about the wound," Modise interrupted.

Trust Modise to root around like a warthog and make a mess of this. "There was a most puzzling wound found on the body."

"It looked like he'd been stabbed." Mwambe wished Modise would shut up.

"Perhaps when we arrive at Headquarters we can have the medical examiner fill you in. We also have the photographs of the scene and so on."

"Yes, let's do that."

For the moment, Mwambe was off the hook. Perhaps he'd have a moment after they arrived to send someone else over to the lodge to help Derek and make a real show of investigating. Any hope he harbored to minimize the situation until the Americans left later in the day had flown out the window with the inclusion of Inspector Modise in the mix. He would need a miracle to get out of this one. Divine intercession did not seem a likely outcome.

Annoyance did not do justice to the way he felt.

THE HOTEL MANAGER seemed eager to help the policeman, less eager to speak to Sanderson. Her presence confused him. She understood why. There was no way he could know, or should know, that at that moment Derek stood as helpless as a gazelle caught between a pride of lions and a river full of crocodiles.

The manager said he would identify the guests if he could. He hemmed and hawed, eyebrows dancing up and down, as he flipped through the bits of paper they'd handed them. Sanderson caught a whiff of coffee and remembered she'd planned to have a cup here and that she had not eaten yet.

One purchase, the manager finally reported, had been made by the English couple who had come to Kasane to add to their bird-watching totals, a pastime that seemed peculiarly British. Another belonged to an important man from Francistown who spent many weekends at the lodge with a woman the manager did not think was his wife, and the remaining two belonged to the young couple who were with the American party.

"You cannot miss them," he said. "Their name is Griswold, Robert and Brenda Griswold. The woman is always dressed in a…a flashy manner, talks very loudly, and entertains the game drivers with her appearance and remarks. The husband will usually be found in the bar. The English couple left yesterday, and the man from Francistown on Monday. It would appear that you will only be able to interview the Americans."

Derek thanked the manager, and he followed Sanderson back outside. "So, we have our murderers."

"No, Derek, no murderers, not yet. These spear points are sold everywhere. It is not necessary that the one that killed the man came from this lodge or this gift shop."

Derek's face collapsed into a frown. "What then? How will I ever be able to know the killer?"

"It is not so easy being the detective, you see. We must ask some questions of these two people. But you must appreciate that they may not be involved at all."

"But how will we know? They will have stories, alibis. They are married, they will not point the finger at one another."

"We shall see. If they can produce two spears, it will not be them. If they cannot, well then, we will ask some more questions. We will suggest the presence of fingerprints. I don't know, Derek. I am a game ranger, you are the policeman. Let's see if we can find a coffee and something to eat. We can discuss what you should do then."

BRENDA SURVEYED THE heap of clothing and paper bags at the end of the bed. She poked her husband in the ribs.

"Wake up. We have to go to breakfast, and then I want to go to the pool and get some sun. I'm beginning to fade. Too bad they don't have a tanning salon here. I need to get back home. Maybe we can fly to Miami Beach when we do."

Bobby grunted and rolled over.

"No, I mean it. We have to get moving. Listen, before we go to breakfast, at least let's get these dirty clothes in one bag so we can pack up quick tonight."

She rolled out of bed, pulled on the tee-shirt she'd discarded the night before, and yanked one roll-along from the closet. She tossed it on the bed, unzipped the main compartment and tackled the mess on the bench. She gathered armfuls of clothing and dumped them into the bag, mashing them down so that she could zip the bag closed. When she finished with the bench, she reached under it to retrieve Bobby's dirty socks and underwear.

"Wow, look at that."

Bobby opened one eye. "What?"

"My *assagai*. It was here all the time, under your smelly socks." She held it up for him to see and then pulled the paper bag with its sales slip in it from the trash can and put in the spear. She slipped that in a desk drawer.

"There, that's that. I wonder what happened to my other glove? Maybe it's under the bed. Get up, Bobby, I need to lift this mattress. And you could use a shower."

Bobby said something that sounded like mumph and swung his feet to the floor. Brenda peeled off the tee and headed to the shower.

"Me first."

FIFTY-ONE

AT LEAST THE coffee was hot. Sanderson preferred the way she brewed coffee to the hotel's version. However, as the staff had not charged her for it, she could not complain.

"What now, Sanderson?" Before she could make a suggestion, Derek's hand-held squawked. "Yes, hello? Who? Yes, of course." His face took on a look of near panic. "He's coming here."

"Who's coming here?"

"My uncle, the American attaché from Gaborone, and another policeman. What do I do?"

"Well, you can sit here and look afraid of your shadow or, you can hide somewhere, or you can carry on your investigation."

"My investigation? What investigation? I haven't done anything yet."

"You questioned the manager. You have some suspects. You have a plan."

"I did nothing. It was you, Sanderson. You asked the questions. What now?"

"Derek, the questions I asked were answered by the hotel manager and the saleswoman because you were there. They didn't respect my game ranger's uniform; they respected yours, you see. Now, what we must do is find this young couple the manager tells us about, and ask them about the spears. If it comes to nothing, well, you are investigating, and your uncle will be happy."

"You really think so?"

"Do you have a better plan, Derek?"

Derek did not. They gulped down their coffee and headed toward the room assigned to the Griswolds.

BRENDA HAD PUT on her very skimpy bikini and rummaged through the bag she'd packed with laundry earlier for a cover-up when Bobby exited the shower.

"Put on your trunks, Bobby, and a shirt. We can go straight to the pool after we eat. Maybe they have poolside and we can have lunch there, too."

"Always it's food with you. As much as you eat, I wonder why you don't weigh, like, a ton or something."

"It's not always about food, and besides I have this high metabolic rate. A doctor told me that one time, and that's why I don't have a weight problem like Desiree and some of the other girls. If they ever stopped dancing they'd, like, be huge or something." She gathered her tote, stuffed a towel, sunblock, and three magazines in it. "Come on, we gotta go."

"Hold on to your hair for a minute. I can't find my flip-flops. They must have been shoved under the bed."

"I packed them, wear your Nikes. They're better on the boards anyway. Come on, come on."

"Slow down, Bren, you'll bust a gut." There was a tentative knock at the door. "See who's at the door while I put on my shoes. Why'd you have to pack my flips anyway?"

"Bitch, bitch, bitch. I got it."

Brenda dropped her cover-up on the bed and went to the door. A policeman and the animal person stood outside. The policeman's jaw dropped when she opened the door. It must be a new thing to see a bikini, or something.

"What's the problem, officer?" Brenda leaned forward and gave the cop a peek. It always worked. She hadn't had a traffic ticket in years. What the heck, there was a time when that peek would have cost some serious money. The animal person answered. The cop seemed tongue-tied.

"We wish to ask you some questions about the death of Mr. Henry Farrah."

"Sure, come in." She stepped back and ushered them in the room. "Bobby, it's that cute animal person...what do they call you, Hon?"

"Game ranger."

"No. I mean your name."

"Sanderson."

"Just Sanderson? Not, like, with a first name?"

"Just Sanderson."

"Oh. So, you want to ask us about the death of Henry. We don't know anything about that, do we, Bobby?"

He finished tying his shoes and stood. "No, nothing. We were together all that night."

"No, that's not right. I was with...a friend and you were...where were you, exactly? I never asked."

Bobby looked stricken. "With you, Bren. You have to remember."

An inkling, a suspicion, a niggling doubt, crept into Brenda's consciousness. Bobby's secret did have something to do with Farrah. But what? He was going to owe big-time for this one. "Oh, yeah, he was with me. We were, like, playing cards—strip poker."

The policeman started to cough and excused himself. The woman squinted her eyes and glared at her.

She wasn't fooled, and Brenda realized, she hoped not too late, that this woman was no backwoods bimbo and she'd better be careful.

"Just kidding, officer."

Bobby edged toward the sliding glass doors and glanced out. The gray monkey stared back at him.

"We are interested in the purchase of a souvenir at the gift shop. A spear point. Did you make such a purchase?"

"Oh yeah. I got it right here." She leaned sideways, reached into the desk drawer, and pulled out the bag containing the *assagai*. "See, here's the sales slip and everything. I also got an outfit the same time, only I lost one of the gloves. Say, speaking of lost, did anybody turn in a cell phone? It cost a bundle. I could, you know, offer a big reward if you find it. Bobby thinks maybe one of the groundskeepers took it. Could you, like, interrogate them? You're a cop, right?"

Derek finally got himself under control. He kept his eyes on the decidedly uncomfortable husband. "Yes, I am a police officer. There were two spear points bought by you, it seems."

"Two? No, just this one. Bobby said maybe he would get another one but what would we do with two? You didn't go back and buy one, did you?"

"Me? No. Why would I do that? I didn't buy one, no, of course not."

"We have a sales slip that indicates someone from this room bought one the day after yours was purchased."

"Well, it wasn't us. The clerk must have misunderstood."

"That is always a possibility, of course, but you see the room number is written right here."

"Bren…?"

"It's a mistake. We only have one of them."

"As you say. Of course we can always ask the clerk to come and see if you are the one."

"Bring her on. Hell, I got nothing to hide," a remark which had to be counted as a huge understatement, considering her costume.

"Listen, why don't you get her and bring her back? No, wait a minute, we'll be at breakfast. You can meet us up there."

"I am not so sure that we can do that."

"Well, we are done here, unless you have something else to ask. Come on, Bobby, I'm starving."

The woman named Sanderson reasserted herself. "We are asking because a spear point like the one you hold has been determined to have been used to kill Mr. Farrah."

"No shit, I thought the lion, like, ate him or something."

"The lion held him in his jaws, but it did not kill him. The man was stabbed first."

"Holy cow. What do you think about that, Bobby? Good thing we can account for our *assagai,* right?"

Now she had it. Almost had it. But not quite. Bobby must have pulled another hit-and-run somehow. Why, no, who? She'd find out as soon as these two uniforms left.

She had the door handle in hand and was attempting to usher Sanderson and Derek out the door when another group pushed in.

FIFTY-TWO

WHEN SHE'D ENTERED the room, Sanderson had scanned
its contents. It was a thing a woman would do, but probably not a man, making a quick inventory of the expensive
clothes in the closet, the luggage, the bottles of perfume,
and the skin products on the dresser. Signs of indulgence,
of indiscriminate spending, of money. Sanderson did
not like this nearly naked white woman, standing there
without a thought in the world of how she must appear
to others. This spoiled woman could not have been more
than two or three years older than her Mpitle, except in
the eyes. The eyes were different. This woman had a
child's body but old eyes, eyes that had seen too much
in a very short time. This woman could lie, and cheat,
and steal. But she was not a killer. Sanderson knew that
as a woman knows about another woman. She could not
say the same thing about the boy.

She reached across the bed and handed the woman her
cover-up. The woman took it and hesitated. Sanderson
jerked her chin up, as she would to her daughter, indicating the woman should put it on. She did.

"Uncle...Inspector Mwambe," Derek said. "We are
investigating this couple over the purchase of—"

"I know what you are doing, Derek. You must not ha-
rass the guests of the hotel. The manager tells me you
and Sanderson were asking about the purchase of souvenirs. That is not something that should be concern-

ing you. I will take over now. And we will not require Sanderson's assistance either."

Sanderson heard Mwambe with half an ear, but focused her attention on the boy. He looked pleadingly at his wife.

"Brenda, help me out here."

Sanderson held up the receipt from the gift shop. "There was another *assagai?* Mr. Griswold, did you buy this one?" Sanderson said, ignoring Mwambe's scowl.

"No, not me…it's a mistake, no way."

"Sanderson, that will be all."

She continued to disregard the inspector. "The sales slip reveals a purchase by someone in this room, bought at night…the same night Mr. Henry Farrah was stabbed to death on the path to the Sedudu Bar."

"It wasn't…That's all wrong. I didn't buy it then…it wasn't me." He looked around at the police, at her, and pointed at his wife. "It was her. That's my spear in the bag. Hers is the one that's missing. See I thought she might have done it, and so I bought that one to take the place of the one she used to…She did it."

"What?" the wife screeched. She hugged her coverup around her. "Me? You weasel, what are you trying to do? If you think you can dump this on me, you are so not going to! What did you do, Bobby?"

"Sanderson!" Mwambe seemed ready to have a fit.

The third man in the party stepped forward. "Mrs. Sanderson, please continue."

"I think this slip indicates that a second spear point, the murder weapon, was bought the night the man was killed. I do not know why he was stabbed. Perhaps this man is angry at him. Who can say? They meet on the path to the Sedudu Bar and…You know," she faced the boy and continued, almost conversationally, "Botswana is a country that does not encourage crime. It is a capital-punishment state, a fact that brings much criticism from nations that, as we know, have very much higher rates of violent crime than we do."

She gazed at Bobby as if inviting a response. She did not have long to wait. Griswold took one more look at the monkey guarding the slider, pushed past the men, and bolted out the front door.

LEO PAINTER WOKE, weak and groggy. He lay very still, gathering his thoughts. He'd slept for a long time, he knew. Since when? Yesterday. His day came back to him, the meetings and the awful feeling he had later, chest pain, nausea, sweating…My God, I must have had a heart attack! I could have jumped ship right then and there and nobody would have known. A sobering thought, but not the first time he'd had it. Something of the sort had been on his mind when he'd slipped off into unconsciousness the previous day. Something about Travis. What about Travis? And Lucille, too, he'd have to find a way to convince her to come with him to the Chobe. For a visit, anyway. Life could be good here. A slower pace, a place to build.

He sat up. A sliver of sunlight bisected the room where the draperies were not quite drawn across the doors to the deck. He wondered if his monkey friend had tried to pry his way in again. He had a vague recol-lection of someone or something rattling the door last night. He should get up and dress. Travis and Greshenko would be looking for him. He was hungry. Breakfast. He donned a pair of slacks, golf shirt, and loafers and headed to the door. He'd clean up later. He needed coffee, now.

He opened the door just in time to see a panicked Bobby Griswold careening toward him.

"Bobby? What's the matter?"

Griswold skidded to a halt.

"It's all your fault, Leo. You're supposed to be dead."

"I very nearly was, Robert, but how is that your problem?"

"Why didn't you go to the bar that night? Why did you send Farrah instead? You did it on purpose. You always screw with me."

Griswold turned back, saw the men tumbling out the door of his room and pivoted again.

"It's your fault, Leo, you've ruined everything."

"What do you mean? What's that about Henry?"

Leo stared after the boy, who charged away, down the path and toward the Sedudu Bar. Inspector Modise and a policeman, hot on Bobby's heels, nearly bowled him over next.

"What the hell is going on here?"

"We need to stop him. He knows something about the death of your colleague."

"What? Robert? I don't think that's likely. He has the courage of a frog. His wife, maybe. He's the frog, she's the snake, but Bobby wouldn't...you really think so?"

"We will not catch him now. But, there is nowhere he can go. Eventually that young man will reappear. We will assemble a search team and find him. And you are correct, Mr. Painter. We should have a long conversation with Mrs. Griswold as well. One or the other, possibly both, of them, is responsible for the immediate death of Henry Farrah. Who else may be contributory to that sad fact is another matter."

Leo flinched as if slapped. The man had a point if,

as he'd indicated earlier, Farrah bought it on the way to the bar. Leo had sent him on that journey, his last, as it turned out.

Bobby had asked him to do something that night and he'd forgotten. He'd met with Farrah, and then he'd dismissed him. He remembered what Bobby had asked.

"I may be able to help you, Inspector. There was something Bobby wanted me to do that night and I forgot. I may have sent Henry to his death—a death, by the way, I believe was intended for me."

FIFTY-THREE

BOBBY NEARLY LOST his footing when Leo stepped out from his room and into his path. He heard men chasing him. Leo! It should have been Leo. Everything would be fine if he'd just done what he'd been asked to do. Leo made some noise, excuses. Always excuses. Gotta get away, have to hide somewhere. Where? There were trees ahead; he'd hide there. He had his phone. He'd call Brenda. She would know what to do.

While he was growing up, his mother had always taken care of things. His father objected. Said the boy... *boy!* Said he needed to face the consequences of his actions. What a crock. But his mother didn't care. Then his father disappeared. No loss there. Crap, Brenda didn't have a phone anymore. The police must have found it. They would read the text messages. No, that wouldn't work now. They didn't have it. If they did, she'd be out here running her ass off with him.

He kept pounding on. It was the one thing he could do without thinking. Thinking got you in trouble. What had Leo said? *Botswana is a capital-punishment country, and its courts would not be reluctant to hang you, particularly if it deems the crime to have been premeditated.* Christ, help me...Brenda would fix it. She had to. Where else would she get the deal she had with me? Hell, she didn't have to love him or anything. Just be there and get him out of this mess. She did it before. She could do it again.

He listened to his heart beat, adjusted his stride to match it. A track coach told him that was how you ran marathons. Run to the rhythm of your heart. He slowed a bit and felt better, stronger. He could run all day. Nobody was going to catch him. Not today. Not ever.

Brenda. She would be mad at what he'd said. She'd get over it. He'd make it up to her; take her to Miami Beach like she wanted. Maybe Cancún. She could lie in the sun and get brown. Tan lines were sexy. Can't think about that now. He needed her. She'd fix it. She always did.

He plodded past the Sedudu Bar. He tried not to look at the place. Why had Farrah come? Why didn't Leo? He must have suspected something and sent Farrah to scout out the ground. Leo was sharp. You had to get up plenty early in the morning to beat him. He always hated me and Brenda. He was the one who talked me into the divorce. Wait 'til Brenda found out about that. She'd fix him all right. Damn straight. Brenda was smarter than people thought.

Beautiful, too. Tan lines…Jesus!

"You don't think I did it, do you?" Brenda sounded desperate. Leo had never seen her that way. She always stayed on top. She knew how to market her sexuality. But nobody was buying today. Well, almost nobody. The young policeman with the round face looked like a puppy in a pet store window. Brenda's cover-up kept flying open. That was probably the young man's problem. Sanderson, the game ranger, looked like she'd like to put Brenda over her knee. So would he, as a matter of fact.

Not going to happen.

"No, Brenda, I do not. I certainly think you are capable enough to do it, and for all I know, you may, in fact, have had a hand in it, but at this juncture I don't think you did it."

The fat, older policeman frowned. "It is not appropriate to speak yet of murder."

The game ranger let out an exasperated sigh. "Inspector Mwambe, you must listen to what has been said. That boy, or this woman, purchased a spear point the night the man was killed. It is no longer in their possession."

"I didn't buy that one. You can ask what's her name, the girl at the gift store who works at night. She knows me. She'll tell you."

The game ranger rounded on Brenda. "I do not think you killed the man, Mrs. Griswold. I think you are a shameless woman and you have much to answer for, but I think your husband did the killing."

"Why the hell would he do something that stupid? Answer me that."

Leo took her elbow and led her away from the angry game ranger. "That afternoon he asked me to write a codicil to my will so that he would inherit the stock he'd just sold me, should I die before he could redeem it, that is."

"He what? You mean if it was you that had been murdered, he'd have…Christ, enough stock to…what? Take over the company."

"He'd have nothing of the sort. The will that codicil referenced was to the one Farrah drew up years ago. There is a later will I made with my new lawyer. It leaves Robert nothing."

"But Farrah said…you dirty son of a—"

"Gently, Brenda, will or no will, your fate, and perhaps Robert's, is still in my hands."

"But why did he kill Mr. Farrah?" Mwambe asked. He was having difficulties following the direction the conversation had taken.

"A mistake. Robert called me just before Farrah arrived. He asked me to meet him at the Sedudu Bar. I forgot. Farrah left my room angry and thirsty for more booze. In the dark, Bobby stabbed him by mistake. I must assume some responsibility for that. I'm sorry."

BOBBY CLEARED THE area around the bar at an easy lope but ran into a fence. He jogged in place considering his options, then turned and started up hill, running parallel to the wire. He thought he heard a car approaching behind him. He turned. It must be still around the corner. He needed to hide. Ten meters further on, he saw a gap in the fence. Bits of what appeared to be fur clung to its edges. Beyond it were bushes. He could hide there. He sprinted to the gap and squeezed through and headed back down hill. The car rounded the corner. He crouched behind a large clump of shrubbery. The car passed. He couldn't see if it was a police car or not. When he felt sure it was gone, he stood and resumed his run. He would follow the fence the other way. It would take him to the river. He could hide there and think. Maybe when it got dark, he could slip back and talk to Brenda. She would know what to do. They just needed a plan.

The Chobe Game Park is a broad, relatively flat plain down near the water, but the ground rises to the south, and there it is covered with a thick stand of trees. The high branches provide food for elephants and giraffe. Ungulates feed on the underbrush beneath the canopy. If you are a predator, it is a good place to hunt. Prey have few choices. They must follow the food, knowing predators will be waiting for them. In the dry season, all animals move to the river and to water. Bobby's primitive instincts were leading him north, to the river.

Close to the Chobe it is rare to see a stone outcropping, and large tree roots are also nearly nonexistent. So it must have been bad karma that brought these two rarities directly in the path Bobby selected. His eyes were focused on the river glittering in the distance. He should have been looking down. His foot caught on the root. He pitched forward. His head encountered the rock with serious consequences. He rolled, unconscious, into a large bramble that effectively screened him from the road and, later, from the search parties sent to find him. He lay prone in the dirt, unmoving, his left arm doubled up beneath him, fist pressed against his solar plexus, his head turned at an unnatural angle, and bleeding from his ear.

He was still there six hours later when the hyenas found him.

FIFTY-FOUR

SANDERSON RECEIVED THE call from a game drive guide. He'd noticed some activity near the road. That rarely happened, as game generally stayed clear of human habitation and especially the main roads. When he'd worked his truck with its gaggle of tourists to the center of what he took to be a stand-off between competing packs of hyenas, he saw the body. His passengers were in a panic, and the best he could do was reverse the truck, shout, and sound his horn. The hyenas scampered away a few meters but seemed ready to return. One of his passengers got sick. He couldn't stay.

Sanderson left the men at the police station bickering over the likelihood of Robert Griswold's guilt and his wife's probable implication in the murder of Henry Farrah. Inspector Mwambe had finally let go of his hope to sweep the affair under a diplomatic rug. Enough was enough.

She managed to arrive at the scene before the safari truck drove away. She fired a few rounds into the air to scare off the hyenas and called for help. An hour later, the mangled remains of Robert Scott Griswold were removed, and she returned to her desk. She had paperwork to do. Three bodies related to animal encounters in nearly as many weeks.

There was a pink call sheet on the desk. She would deal with it later and only then discover she'd been promoted to the district superintendent's position. A position she'd accept only after giving careful consideration and then refusing an offer from Kgabo Modise to join him in the DIS. He'd received the results of the DNA test on the *boloi,* and they indicated the scrap of skin left in Greshenko's SUV was, in fact, human. He wished her to help in this and, who knew, other things?

Michael would be pleased. Rra Kaleke would express his doubts, but she would see the smile he tried to hide.

THE EARTH GLOBAL GULFSTREAM V left Kasane later than planned. It made one stop in Gaborone to clear Botswana customs, and another in Cape Town to top off its tanks. The plane flew north along the coast of Africa on its way home. The passengers were fewer in number on the return trip. And two urns containing the ashes of Henry Farrah and Robert Griswold rode in the baggage compartment.

Leo had been chagrined to learn that had he simply approached the Ministry of Environment, Wildlife and Tourism and perhaps the Tourism Board, all the machinations with Botlhokwa might not have been necessary. Whether Greshenko knew this or not, he did not know. The two of them would have to have a discussion about that later. After a lengthy meeting with both the DIS and officials from the Russian Embassy, Greshenko had been granted a residence permit to remain in Botswana. It had been part of the deal Leo negotiated in return for dropping any recriminations and forestalling more investigations into the two deaths. But for now, Greshenko had been given a second chance to select the better fork in the road. He and Greshenko, he thought, just a pair of old lions—lions in winter maybe.

The recently widowed Brenda Griswold was not with them. Leo could not manage a deal for her. Given her relationship to Bobby, who obviously could not testify for or against her, it seemed to the police unlikely she knew nothing or had nothing to do with Farrah's death. There was enough evidence, however circumstantial, to at least hold her for further questioning. Leo had left her, looking frightened and alone, staring out at him through the Plexiglas that separated prisoners from family. Leo had arranged for her legal representation. It was the best he could do. With her make-up applied minimally, she'd looked the part of grieving widow. Whether she grieved or not was another matter. The Botswana legal system would deal with her for now.

Leo felt as though he'd aged ten years in the last seventy-two hours. "I'm thinking about Brenda. I don't know why, the girl showed nothing but ill will toward me. But, you know she has next to nothing to return to. You are probably aware of Robert's debt picture. Assuming she can wriggle her way out of this mess, and after she pays them off, she'll be out on her rear and on the street."

"She'll manage, Leo. She has marketable skills. She'll land on her feet, or back—whatever."

"Tut, tut, don't be so hard on her. Not now. Anyway, Travis, I had a come-to-Jesus moment on this trip. I had as close to a near-death experience as I ever care to have, and I learned something. Would you like to know what that is?"

"Certainly."

"I built this company up from Harry Reilly's dream of wildcatting for oil to what it is today. To do that, I had to apply some very sharp elbows to a fair number of people to move them out of my way. Married three times, sold out my principles on occasion, make that often, and probably suborned more politicians in my time than Botswana has produced—certainly more than is healthy for any government. I would not last a New York minute in a country like the one we just left, by the way. I had a great and exhilarating ride. I wouldn't change a thing about the past, but you know what gives me the greatest pleasure now?"

Travis shook his head, Leo thought, indulgently.

"What I remember most, and best, are the times, too few I'm afraid, that I behaved decently and did something because it was the right thing to do. Travis, take the advice of one who is on the downhill side of life, fill your days with those moments as often as you can." Leo thought Travis looked skeptical.

"Any immediate recommendations for me?"

"Yes, as I said before, I know a good deal about Brenda. Spent money to find out when Bobby ran off with her. Her life has not been an easy one…Don't look at me that way. I know a tramp and a conniver when I see one. Nevertheless, I'll ask for a favor. She will have some money I promised Bobby in exchange for the rights to his shares. I don't have to, but I intend to keep that promise. She may blow it or she may not. I would like to think if given the chance, she could change."

"Leo, she is like the leopard we never saw in the game park. She won't change her spots. Assuming she beats this rap and is deported, she'll be back to pole dancing and looking for another sucker and another soft berth."

"Very probably, but you owe her something."

"Owe? Me? She tried to—"

"I know what she tried, and don't forget, I know your

part in it. The least you can do is take care of her stuff. I want you to clear out her apartment, put the contents into storage or whatever. I happen to know she'd accumulated a few very expensive pieces, a Mondrian for one, and Bobby's car, which probably cost more than one of our miners make in a year. Secure it all, get an appraisal, put it in storage, whatever. Then, if she does get off, she'll have something to start over with. You can do that for her."

"She'll think I'm doing it because I feel guilty."

"Don't you? You should, a little at least. You set her up. That's why I said, you owe."

Travis looked ruefully at Leo. "I'm not sure about the feeling guilty bit, Leo. You think I should, I gather."

"As a general rule, it's a bad thing to let that particular emotion interfere with what you have to do in business…at least at this level. But in Brenda's case, a little guilt won't hurt you, and it might do you some good."

"Do me some good? Is guilt something that works for you?"

"Once in a while. Not often enough, I'm afraid. Just do it, Travis."

"I'd be wasting my time and the company's money."

"You are probably right, but I'd like you to try."

Travis nodded his agreement. "Can I order you something to drink?"

"Some orange juice would be good. I would say a martini, but I'm not up to that at the moment. My doctor would shoot me if I did."

The two men sat in silence sipping at their drinks. Travis appreciative of his scotch and soda, Leo, resigned to the juice.

"Have you thought about how you'll spend your time, Leo, now that you have some to spare?"

"I told you I'd like to start a few little projects inside the real estate division."

"I remember. You know, I've been thinking about what you said to me with respect to the mines and drilling for water, developing the land."

"And?"

"With respect, I still think you're off-base. Finding water and developing the land would be a high-risk, low-return undertaking."

"We've been over this. But, perhaps you have something better in mind?"

"I do. For example, we have options on nearly a thousand acres in southern Arizona and California. Is that correct?" Leo nodded. "Why drill for water and tap an already attenuated Arizona aquifer? Does the world really need more suburbs, more houses? Let's drill deeper, let's build something better."

"Go on."

"Geothermal energy, Leo. There are places in the world where the earth's natural heat is close enough to the surface so that we could tap it, produce superheated steam, recycle the water vapor, and power steam generators. Electricity."

"You know this?"

"Some of it. The rest needs research, but near fault lines and volcanoes the magma is close enough for us to experiment. And then there is the land."

"The land?"

"Instead of a thousand acres of tract houses, why not a thousand acres of solar panels? We are at a point where, with government subsidies and increased cost for kilowatt hours, it will not only be feasible, but profitable. And wind generators. There are parts of the desert that could support both on the same piece of land. Think of acres of solar panels with windmills spinning overhead. Alternative energy, Leo, that's Earth Global's future."

Leo looked at Travis as if seeing him for the first time.

"I knew there had to be a reason I wanted to let this company go and turn it over to you. I'm obsolete, aren't I? Don't answer that." Leo shifted in his seat and sipped his juice. "I guess I'm like that old lion. Without the government's protection he and his kind would be long gone. People like me are an endangered species."

Travis kept his face neutral, but Leo realized he had it right.

"There is no room for us anymore. We've ravaged the land and now there's almost nothing left. We will die off. The day of the corporate predator is done, I guess. Funny, I never thought of it that way. For me and my generation, it was a matter of reaping the earth's bounty— almost Biblical, you see? Reaping and sowing. Only we didn't sow very much and reaped to excess. Lots of bare earth and…So, no more predators. What are you, Travis, if not that? I can't think of a benign predator."

"Maybe we're honey bees. Bees take the nectar and pollen that's there, that will dry up and be blown away with the wind anyway, and chew it up and spit it out as honey, pure energy."

"Honey bees? Sorry, doesn't work for me. You remind me more of a wasp, Travis. Do wasps make honey?"

Travis smiled. "Africanized bees, then."

"Yes, that might work. Mean sons-of-bitches. Take over other's hives, kick out the old queen, and spread their version of beedom around the world. Yes that might work."

Leo sat back and finished his juice and made a face.

He didn't like orange juice all that much. Maybe with a splash of gin…He let his mind shift into neutral. He envisioned his son dying somewhere out there in San Francisco. Young Leo had been barely in his teens when the divorce occurred. There had been a great deal of anger. Leo had a company to run. His wife, ex-wife, Reilly's daughter, had a score to settle. Contact with his namesake had been difficult at best. Then, as the poison spooned out by the boy's mother took hold, cut off entirely. Divorce is a miserable institution that hurts children far more than the correspondents.

"Did you know my son is dying from AIDS?"

"No, sir, I didn't. I'm sorry to hear that."

"He's gay, Travis, can you imagine that? Gay, and with another man holding his power of attorney and claiming spousal rights."

Travis said nothing. Leo studied the mahogany finish on the built-in side table, ran his palm across its glassy surface and sighed. Had he started sounding like an old man? He surely felt old. Maybe he'd had enough.

"You don't have children."

"No, sir, I don't."

"Sorry, I knew that, of course you don't. You're lucky."

"Yes, sir, I guess. I'd like to, someday though."

Leo nodded absently. "When we return to Chicago, after we sort out the board and your place in the company, I'm going to fly to San Francisco to see him and that man. Check him out…Children are not supposed to die before their parents, are they?"

"No, sir, I guess not."

Leo stared out the window through wispy clouds at the South Atlantic. Somewhere over to the west would be South America, another market, another opportunity, another challenge, but not for him. Not anymore.

So, this is how power passes from one generation to the next. Not like that poor lion. The game drive guide said he'd been forced out by a younger male. If Travis had had his way, the same would have happened to me. This way is better.

"One last thing, Travis. If I ever find you've strayed off the reservation again, I will send you and your career off to the equivalent of the elephant's graveyard—where old MBA's go to die."

Leo smiled and signaled to the flight attendant.

"I'll have that martini now."

* * * * *

GLOSSARY

Setswana is a dialect of Bantu, as is Zulu, and many other languages spoken in sub-Saharan Africa. The stem is Tswana.

+ Ba . . . people of the . . . *Ba*tswana
+ Bo . . . the country of the . . . *Bo*tswana
+ Mo . . . a person of . . . *Mo*tswana
+ Se . . . language of . . . *Se*tswana

a re tsamaye!. Let's go!

assigai. Zulu word for spear, + *di*, *diassagai*, spears

bakkie. Afrikaans' word for pickup truck

bolihokwa. important

boloi. witchcraft

cattle post. ranch

combie. small bus or van

ditshikanokana. fireflies

dumela. hello + *Mma, Rra*. ma'am, sir

gabz. a contraction for Gaborone

ke itumetse. thank you

ke teng. I am well

kgokgotsho. wind-pipe

kgopa. snail

kgosi. Chief

kgotla. court yard, meeting place

kraal. Afrikaans' word for corral

lerumo. spear

manong. vultures

MK. see *Umkonto we Sizwe*

mma (pronounced ma). Mrs. as a title of respect

modimo. God

moloi. witch, diviner

monontsha. fertilizer

mosadi. woman (*Kgosi Mosadi.* woman chief)

motsu. sharp point, arrow

mowa. soul, breath (of life)

nagaka. witch

no mathata. no problem, no worries

ntate. father

o tsogile jang. how are you?

panel beaters. auto body shop

phane. fried or cooked caterpillars, considered a delicacy

pula, (literally rain). the currency of Botswana and *Thebe* (Drops), coins

pheri. hyena, + di, *dupheri.* hyenas

roko. dress

rondeval. a circular hut fashioned from mud and woven branches, with a thatch roof, traditional dwelling of the Tswana

rra (pronounced rah). Mr. or sir (with respect)

rre (pronounced ray). Father, and designates a superior type of Mr. usually a clergyman, something of that sort.

rremogolo. grandfather

sala sentle. Stay well, goodbye

sekoa. invalid, sick one

sesi. sister

tau. lion, +*di.* lions

Umkonto we Sizwe (MK). "Spear of the Nation": a

guerilla organization, the active military wing of the African National Congress.

wulu. Wool

See also: *http://en.wikipedia.org/wiki/Tswana_language*

NOTES

- Whereas Gaborone is pronounced with the G as a guttural ch (as in *loch),* the contraction, Gabz, has a hard G.

- People are often called by the names of their first-born with the appropriate title; i.e. Mma Barbara or Rra Robert.

- Botswana's religious configuration is predominantly Christian (62 percent Protestant, 5 percent Roman Catholic). Indigenous religions constitute 23 percent, Islam, 0.3 percent and Hindu, 0.15 percent

The following appears at Botswana's official web site:

> *The Republic of Botswana is situated in Southern Africa, nestled between South Africa, Namibia, Zimbabwe, and Zambia.*

> *The country is democratically ruled, boasts a growing economy and a stable political environment. Botswana has some of Africa's last great wildernesses, including the famous Okavango Swamps and the Kalahari Desert.*

Botswana is the largest exporter of gemstone dia-monds in the world as well as a large beef exporter to the European Union.

For more information about this fascinating country, go to *http://www.gov.bw*.

REQUEST YOUR FREE BOOKS!
2 FREE NOVELS PLUS 2 FREE GIFTS!

H HARLEQUIN®

INTRIGUE

BREATHTAKING ROMANTIC SUSPENSE

YES! Please send me 2 FREE Harlequin® Intrigue novels and my 2 FREE gifts (gifts are worth about $10). After receiving them, if I don't wish to receive any more books, I can return the shipping statement marked "cancel." If I don't cancel, I will receive 6 brand-new novels every month and be billed just $4.74 per book in the U.S. or $5.49 per book in Canada. That's a savings of at least 12% off the cover price! It's quite a bargain! Shipping and handling is just 50¢ per book in the U.S. and 75¢ per book in Canada.* I understand that accepting the 2 free books and gifts places me under no obligation to buy anything. I can always return a shipment and cancel at any time. Even if I never buy another book, the two free books and gifts are mine to keep forever.

182/382 HDN GH3D

Name	(PLEASE PRINT)

Address	Apt. #

City	State/Prov.	Zip/Postal Code

Signature (if under 18, a parent or guardian must sign)

Mail to the **Reader Service:**
IN U.S.A.: P.O. Box 1867, Buffalo, NY 14240-1867
IN CANADA: P.O. Box 609, Fort Erie, Ontario L2A 5X3

**Are you a subscriber to Harlequin® Intrigue books
and want to receive the larger-print edition?
Call 1-800-873-8635 or visit www.ReaderService.com.**

* Terms and prices subject to change without notice. Prices do not include applicable taxes. Sales tax applicable in N.Y. Canadian residents will be charged applicable taxes. Offer not valid in Quebec. This offer is limited to one order per household. Not valid for current subscribers to Harlequin Intrigue books. All orders subject to credit approval. Credit or debit balances in a customer's account(s) may be offset by any other outstanding balance owed by or to the customer. Please allow 4 to 6 weeks for delivery. Offer available while quantities last.

Your Privacy—The Reader Service is committed to protecting your privacy. Our Privacy Policy is available online at www.ReaderService.com or upon request from the Reader Service.

We make a portion of our mailing list available to reputable third parties that offer products we believe may interest you. If you prefer that we not exchange your name with third parties, or if you wish to clarify or modify your communication preferences, please visit us at www.ReaderService.com/consumerschoice or write to us at Reader Service Preference Service, P.O. Box 9062, Buffalo, NY 14240-9062. Include your complete name and address.

HI15

REQUEST YOUR FREE BOOKS!
2 FREE NOVELS PLUS 2 FREE GIFTS!

ROMANTIC suspense

Sparked by danger, fueled by passion

YES! Please send me 2 FREE Harlequin® Romantic Suspense novels and my 2 FREE gifts (gifts are worth about $10). After receiving them, if I don't wish to receive any more books, I can return the shipping statement marked "cancel." If I don't cancel, I will receive 4 brand-new novels every month and be billed just $4.74 per book in the U.S. or $5.49 per book in Canada. That's a savings of at least 12% off the cover price! It's quite a bargain! Shipping and handling is just 50¢ per book in the U.S. and 75¢ per book in Canada.* I understand that accepting the 2 free books and gifts places me under no obligation to buy anything. I can always return a shipment and cancel at any time. Even if I never buy another book, the two free books and gifts are mine to keep forever.

240/340 HDN GH3P

Name	(PLEASE PRINT)	
Address		Apt. #
City	State/Prov.	Zip/Postal Code

Signature (if under 18, a parent or guardian must sign)

Mail to the **Reader Service:**
IN U.S.A.: P.O. Box 1867, Buffalo, NY 14240-1867
IN CANADA: P.O. Box 609, Fort Erie, Ontario L2A 5X3

Want to try two free books from another line?
Call 1-800-873-8635 or visit www.ReaderService.com.

* Terms and prices subject to change without notice. Prices do not include applicable taxes. Sales tax applicable in N.Y. Canadian residents will be charged applicable taxes. Offer not valid in Quebec. This offer is limited to one order per household. Not valid for current subscribers to Harlequin Romantic Suspense books. All orders subject to credit approval. Credit or debit balances in a customer's account(s) may be offset by any other outstanding balance owed by or to the customer. Please allow 4 to 6 weeks for delivery. Offer available while quantities last.

Your Privacy—The Reader Service is committed to protecting your privacy. Our Privacy Policy is available online at www.ReaderService.com or upon request from the Reader Service.

We make a portion of our mailing list available to reputable third parties that offer products we believe may interest you. If you prefer that we not exchange your name with third parties, or if you wish to clarify or modify your communication preferences, please visit us at www.ReaderService.com/consumerschoice or write to us at Reader Service Preference Service, P.O. Box 9062, Buffalo, NY 14240-9062. Include your complete name and address.

HRS15

REQUEST YOUR FREE BOOKS!

2 FREE NOVELS
FROM THE SUSPENSE COLLECTION
PLUS 2 FREE GIFTS!

YES! Please send me 2 FREE novels from the Suspense Collection and my 2 FREE gifts (gifts are worth about $10). After receiving them, if I don't wish to receive any more books, I can return the shipping statement marked "cancel." If I don't cancel, I will receive 4 brand-new novels every month and be billed just $6.49 per book in the U.S. or $6.99 per book in Canada. That's a savings of at least 19% off the cover price. It's quite a bargain! Shipping and handling is just 50¢ per book in the U.S. and 75¢ per book in Canada.* I understand that accepting the 2 free books and gifts places me under no obligation to buy anything. I can always return a shipment and cancel at any time. Even if I never buy another book, the two free books and gifts are mine to keep forever.

191/391 MDN GH4Z

Name _____ (PLEASE PRINT) _____

Address _____ Apt. # _____

City _____ State/Prov. _____ Zip/Postal Code _____

Signature (if under 18, a parent or guardian must sign)

Mail to the Reader Service:
IN U.S.A.: P.O. Box 1867, Buffalo, NY 14240-1867
IN CANADA: P.O. Box 609, Fort Erie, Ontario L2A 5X3

Want to try two free books from another line?
Call 1-800-873-8635 or visit www.ReaderService.com.

* Terms and prices subject to change without notice. Prices do not include applicable taxes. Sales tax applicable in N.Y. Canadian residents will be charged applicable taxes. Offer not valid in Quebec. This offer is limited to one order per household. Not valid for current subscribers to the Suspense Collection or the Romance/Suspense Collection. All orders subject to credit approval. Credit or debit balances in a customer's account(s) may be offset by any other outstanding balance owed by or to the customer. Please allow 4 to 6 weeks for delivery. Offer available while quantities last.

Your Privacy—The Reader Service is committed to protecting your privacy. Our Privacy Policy is available online at www.ReaderService.com or upon request from the Reader Service.

We make a portion of our mailing list available to reputable third parties that offer products we believe may interest you. If you prefer that we not exchange your name with third parties, or if you wish to clarify or modify your communication preferences, please visit us at www.ReaderService.com/consumerschoice or write to us at Reader Service Preference Service, P.O. Box 9062, Buffalo, NY 14240-9062. Include your complete name and address.